Lineberger Memorial

Library

Lutheran Theological Southern Seminary   Columbia, S. C.

Carolina Moon

Also by Jill McCorkle

NOVELS
The Cheer Leader
July 7th
Tending to Virginia
Ferris Beach

STORIES
Crash Diet

Carolina Moon

a novel by

Jill McCorkle

ALGONQUIN BOOKS OF CHAPEL HILL 1996

Published by
ALGONQUIN BOOKS OF CHAPEL HILL
Post Office Box 2225
Chapel Hill, North Carolina 27515-2225

a division of
WORKMAN PUBLISHING
708 Broadway
New York, New York 10003

LIBRARY OF CONGRESS CATALOGING-IN-PUBLICATION DATA
McCorkle, Jill, 1958–
    Carolina moon: a novel / by Jill McCorkle.
    p. cm.
    ISBN 1-56512-136-8
    1. City and town life—North Carolina—Fiction. 2. Women in
business—North Carolina—Fiction. I. Title.
PS3563.C3444C37 1996
813'.54—dc20   96-16115
                                                            CIP

10 9 8 7 6 5 4 3 2 1
First Edition

For my Dad

Thanks to close friends and family members who read this in earlier forms. To students and colleagues at Bennington, Harvard, and the New England Writers' Workshop who have heard me read the same parts aloud for over three years. Thanks to Lee, Louis, Shannon, and Liz. And as always to Dan, Claudia, and Rob.

A very special thanks to the Carr family for wonderful times spent at the Lone Eagle Nest—Holden Beach, North Carolina.

Carolina Moon keep shining,
Shining on the one who waits for me.

—*from "Carolina Moon" by Benny Davis and Joe Burke*

Carolina Moon

Part One

*I*t is still dark when Wallace Johnson drives through town to the post office. He's worked this Sunday morning shift for years and he's gotten used to it, gotten used to the absolute quiet, the seasonal rush of summer folks from all over creation. It dwindles in September to the couple of hundred locals and the weekenders whose real lives are elsewhere. Mountains of postcards, *wish you were here!*, also dwindle, to property tax notices and missing-children flyers. He has watched this coming and going his whole life and has rarely felt a longing to pick up and leave, himself.

The doors of the small cinder block building stay locked while he sorts the mail left in the box last night. He is to where he can count down the Sundays he'll spend this way. In just two months, early November, he'll be retiring, and his Sunday mornings will be spent sleeping or reading or fishing. To some it might seem like life doesn't offer Wallace much, but it does, every day, every meal, every good cup of coffee he pours from the metal thermos he brings in with him.

He has just settled in when he recognizes the handwriting on an envelope in the box. For twenty-five years now the letters have arrived every month or so, no pattern, except that they're always dropped in on Saturday nights. They are all addressed in the same loopy script, all addressed simply to Wayward One; Wallace is supposed to file and bag them with all the other "dead" letters that are dropped into the box without stamps or real addresses, children's letters with play tattoos in the corners, letters to Santa Claus and to God. He was forty years old when the first Wayward One letter came; it was late fall, and other than a wadded up tissue and an empty Coke can, the letter was all that was there that morning.

It seems a lifetime since the first one. Wallace's children were still in high school, his oldest son just accepted into the state university, the youngest running track. When he looks back he sees years filled with worries, first over the mortgage, then the expense of college. Now the tuition days are over, and his sons are off with families of their own, little children who call him and Judy long-distance to sing songs and say snatches of things that don't make much sense. And he feels accomplished, responsible for something good.

That first letter he found was in red ink and doused with cologne. That's what got his attention, the cologne, a scent he almost recognized. It had been a slow morning, a hard morning; he'd have loved nothing better when that alarm sounded but to turn it off and roll into Judy's warm back. Judy smelled of Wind Song and had for years. Every holiday when the boys were little that's what they gave her. Sometimes Wallace had wanted to put out his hands and make the world stop and let him breathe it all in. Sometimes he found himself waking and wondering what it was all about anyway. Why does everybody follow the pattern, follow the schedule? Why couldn't he wake up one Sunday morning and just not show up at work, wake only to roll back into the deep warm comfort of his own world. *He could be wayward.* Without thinking past that moment he had torn into the envelope and held the smudged yellow papers in his hand, the script so looped and sprawling that it was difficult to read:

10/29/69 11:30 PM

Oh Dear, how could you? WHY did you? I've heard all the accounts, all the stories. I felt that people studied my face for reactions every time your name was mentioned. Of course, I'd felt that way since the first time I ever laid my eyes on you in that ramshackle club down at Ocean Drive. I was too old to be hanging out at such a place so you sure as hell were. There were pinball machines beeping and ringing and that song "What Kind of Fool" kept playing over and over. There was talk that they might tear down the Ocean Forest Hotel and I remember thinking what a different world it had become since I was a child and staying there. I knew who you were, everybody did. You waved to people you had never met and acted like you were friends.

You were wearing a wrinkled, white cotton shirt, the cuffs pushed up to your elbows and the tail hanging out. If only I had had the sense to stay away from you. I hate you for what you've done and yet I feel that it's not all over. I don't know what I mean to say exactly; it's kind of like a feeling I have about things. Did I ever tell you that I sometimes feel too powerful for words? It's not something you really go around spouting.

I remember the first time I ever felt that way I was a child and sitting way up under our house. It had been torn down long before you moved to town, but you can picture it. It was a house much like that one across from the old A&P, the one with the wraparound porch and dark green awnings on the upper windows. It looked bigger than it was, so much of the space given to high ceilings and the way it was built—way up off the ground. That's what I liked about it. I could stand on my knees as an eight-year-old and still not hit my head on the rough boards of the foundation and plumbing. It was my world and it made me feel powerful.

I drew it all out, the whole world in the dry black dirt. I'd hear my mama walking around above my head. I'd hear doors creak and furniture absorbing the weight of somebody or another. "Sugar, where are you?" she'd sometimes yell out, and I'd sit quietly, the late afternoon light coming through the lattice work that surrounded the underneath part of the house. There was something magical, almost mystical about the way that light hit my legs and the world I'd drawn there in the dirt, the fancy houses and the shops, the places where people wore long dresses and drank tea.

I felt so strong in those moments, made stronger by my silence, my absence from the world above my head. I knew when my mother ran some water in the kitchen sink or flushed the toilet. I heard her ring the phone on the kitchen wall, short cranks, nobody in town had more than three digits to the number. I remember thinking that this is what it felt like to be dead and in another place; this is what God must feel as he sits back and does nothing while sirens sound and cars honk, people scream, and Mamas spend more time on their hair than on their children. I still feel that way, have off and on my whole life. There are times when I feel as powerful as God, when I play God, for that matter.

That would scare a lot of people to hear me say such a thing but not you, never you. Nothing scares you. Not even death. When I heard about it, I said, "What a hateful selfish bastard." My husband heard me and he questioned me, looked hard at me. He knew. I asked why you didn't get a prescription, take some sleeping pills? Why didn't you throw yourself in the river? I felt sorry for your wife and I told people so. I said, that poor child, to have to live with his daddy doing such a selfish thing, to feel like his daddy didn't love him enough to live.

No, in my world I would've killed you a different way, a stronger way. I would have leaned my head up against the lattice work of my childhood home and peered out at the bed of hollyhocks in my neighbors' yard. I'd have kept myself there in the cool darkness out of the bright hateful world. I'd have lulled you in like a spider into a web, and spun and spun my cottony threads until you were bound in a cocoon and unable to breathe. Or maybe I would have pulled you into the Ocean Forest, that huge brick building, ocean front like a castle, and I would have pulled you into the big old elevator and led you down deserted hallways to a room facing the sea, heavy silk drapes whistling with the wind and we would have hidden in a tangle of white cotton sheets.

If I had had the power, I would simply have loved you to death, but who had the chance? Who really had the chance to love you. I was there for God's sake! I was there just minutes before it happened. Did you ever even think how this was going to make ME feel? Your bed still smelled of ME, like this letter, like the red scarf I had draped over your lamp and forgot to take. I wonder what happened to my scarf. I wonder why you didn't do as you had promised you would and just go back to sleep. But no. I imagine the door clicking behind me and with that click your eyes opening. You were just waiting weren't you, waiting to get up and kill yourself without any thoughts about anybody else. Truth be told you never wanted to be loved. Well, you screwed up didn't you? For somebody so unworthy of love, you had yourself some folks who did. You had me.

After he'd read the letter, Wallace had put it in a plastic baggie and sealed it up, just as he would do to a letter on its way somewhere and damaged in the process, but instead of the standard drawer, he had made himself a new file, a weathered gray cardboard folder there at the back of the cabinet. Someday someone might come looking for that letter.

He knew that it was likely connected to a suicide that took place down at the far end of Ferris Beach. The owners of the house had rented to the same man for years and they were angry that he killed himself there. It was bad for business. Children made up ghost stories. All Wallace had ever heard was that the man was a writer of some sort. Then here came the other side of the story—her side—not the wife, but *her*, this woman with the red scarf and cologne, this woman he might someday meet, and somehow touch the very cog of a story that would continue to spin forever. Over time, the beach house had given in, as if to the pressures of the suicide and all the ghost stories, and slowly let itself be taken over by the shifting shoreline. To Wallace, it seemed fitting in a sad way to let nature finish what she'd started. He fishes down at that point often and watches the two shores of the inland waterway fight for control. Sandbags, slick white walls of plastic, are lined up on both sides to prevent erosion but the water keeps coming, keeps washing; it takes what it wants to take. Sometimes, when the blues are running, Wallace stops baiting his hook because the fishing starts to interfere with his pipe smoking and his scanning of the horizon. At the right time of day, you can see the tip of a sunken barge. The water pulls and spirals into the wreck. You can see a school of sleek silver dolphins arching in the distance. Sometimes the fishing interrupts his thoughts of the woman; how she might come to search the strand for lost traces of the life she used to have.

Now here he sits again, breathing the familiar cologne. This may be the last letter of hers he ever gets. This could be the final piece to a puzzle. He reaches for a letter opener and slits the envelope open carefully; his pulse quickens as usual and in his mind there comes a woman's voice, a voice from one of the neighboring towns in this rambling county. He is on her side, and he doesn't have the chance to tell her. He hasn't told Judy about the letters. In all of the years of their life, this is his only secret. Somehow it seems right that every person *needs* a secret.

Dear Wayward One,

I find myself thinking of the old days lately, I find myself thinking of your hands now nothing but bone, your ring hanging loosely, a tiny flash of light there in your padded darkness, like the fillings of your teeth, the cufflinks I heard you wore—her cufflinks, her present to you. I've always meant to write you about that and always forget.

It seems so silly now to think of how mad I got when I heard what you wore, like you could have really done something differently! I was mad that you didn't wear the cufflinks I gave you, those funny little mice with rhinestone eyes. They were the cheapest gift I could find that Christmas because I was so mad at you. I wanted to give you something as cheap and ugly as I thought you were because I loved the hell out of you and couldn't stand the thought that right there across town you were trying to make your life work, trying to make the son you'd run out on love you. On behalf of somebody who was run out on, I can honestly tell you that it doesn't work that way. Buy him a dog, fill his stocking with candy, it just isn't that easy and it was foolish of you to think so. I was hoping that he'd still smell the dishonesty on you; that he'd smell me on your neck and face and so would she. I imagined her perking up her ears like that stupid little dog you bought, her eyes glassy with hate. I was there, you know. I never told you but I was there for the big reunion. I was in a borrowed car, just parked and waiting, the boy extending his hand to you like you might have been a complete stranger, the wife turning her sharp little face away from your kiss. I couldn't picture you in bed with her, not then, not now, not ever, though I don't know why I can't.

I mean didn't I go straight home to my own husband and pull him under the mistletoe? I pulled him around his whole life. I pulled him by his manhood and by the heart, and he loved me every day of his life. He knew about you and loved me just the same. Then you were gone and now he's gone. And it's your hands I keep thinking of now. I think of your blunt square nails, nicotine stained and warm, rough on the sides of your thumbs from your habit of weeding out the grass from between the bricks of your old rented walkway. How many nights did you squat there and pull and pull, obsessed with getting every new little sprig that had taken root in the night while we whispered and kissed, risking hurt and humiliation. The hands.

What a small part of the body and yet a whole life is there, every trace of the fingertip, skin and cells. I remember the time you sunburnt your back on an overcast day, the blues were running too good to stop you said, it didn't feel hot, it was barely May. Ten days later you lay face down while I loosened the dead skin and pulled it off in strips. I held a piece up to the light and I could see the marks and texture, like dried glue or gummy paste. You said, "Peel me, it feels good" and I continued the whole afternoon while you dozed under my touch. I peeled you like a plum, a grape, your skin glazed in salt. I would love to feel your hands right now, cupping my face, pulling me to you. Sometimes I wish you had burned to ash, that you were somehow scattered to the wind, rather than confined there in your dark satin box, empty sockets and protruding jaw, hip blades protecting and housing absolutely nothing. You are nothing in my life, and everything.

All these years have passed and I am still haunted, still longing. I see you now in a younger form, a thinner, sweeter form. You appear at my door, your toolbox in hand, and I lead you in, watch your back as you walk away. Through this image, this apparition of what might have been you, I have found some bit of forgiveness. Could it be I'm getting soft in these later years? Remember that joke about when you get old everything that's supposed to be soft gets hard and what's supposed to be hard gets soft?? Well, maybe that applies to my heart. Maybe what I can do is help others find love and peace and security.

These things are not easy to come by, but that's old news and I don't feel like dealing in old news today. I'm feeling tired, you know? I'm real goddamned tired. I'm so tired that every now and then I start thinking that I understand *what you did and then I really get mad because I've never been weak a day in my life and you, my love, were nothing but. I truly wish I could hate you for it.*

Wallace pours another cup of coffee and looks at himself in the chipped brown mirror over the small lavatory. A lifetime has just about come and gone. How easy it is to respond to bells and rings and calls and cries. How easy it was for this poor woman to devote a whole life to a dream, to spend all of her time looking to what life was or is going to be. The best part of going fishing is the getting ready; buy your cut bait or bloodworms, get some beer and a bag of ice, cooler, snacks, sandchair, then spread it all out, set it all up like a little world, like that woman did as a child up under her house. Wallace Johnson would much rather read about a place far off from home than go there. He has always known that if he went, it wouldn't live up to what he'd thought. He has been this way his whole life, and now with retirement in view, he's starting to feel good about the way life has gone. There's a need for the anchors and the cogs, a need for those who stay in place and mind the shop. How else is there such a thing as history? How else can a child come home if he should need to?

*T*om Lowe parks his truck off to the side where the asphalt road buckles and disappears in a slope of slick sandbags and warning signs. The old cottages on this stretch of the beach are condemned, their doors and windows boarded up, porch wood rotten and sagging. When the tide comes in, the waves will lap the steps of the last house, leaving a ring of brown foam; the water will rise up to what's left of the road like one of those mirages you think you could drive on through.

Tom unlaces his workboots and tosses them onto the seat of the truck, slaps his leg, and calls to the old black-and-white collie riding shotgun. It is still low tide, and once they maneuver their way over broken concrete and splintered boards, they are on the strand and walking out to where there used to be still more houses. The sand is hot and squeaks with every step. The only other person in sight is a fisherman way down at the point.

Even though Tom's hometown is only fifteen miles inland, there are children there who have never seen the ocean. They don't know the origin of the sharp briny odor they accept as home, have never heard the constant rushing of the surf. Their summers are spent in the flat, sandy blueberry patches and dusty tobacco fields of the area. Many of their families have no cars.

Tommy Lowe had led such a childhood. His father loved the ocean, and his mother rejected everything of importance to his father. If his father had spent all their money on air, talked only of air, then his mother would have bound their heads in plastic dry-cleaning bags.

But Cecil Lowe's passion had been the ocean—his ultimate dream an oceanfront lot, where high-tide waves would slap and spray creosote-pitched pilings. He bought such a house in 1953, and Tommy's mother never forgave him. She was pregnant and wanted a house in town. At the time he had sold one short story to the *Saturday Evening Post*, and he believed that first publication foretold a career of literary honors and money pouring in. The Lowes divorced a year later, not long after Hurricane Hazel hit the Carolina coast with a roar and persistent force that left his father's dream property submerged. Ten points for the ocean, zero for Cecil, he was heard to have said out at the Waffle King Diner, the one spot in the dry county where there was liquor for the regulars. I surrendered when I saw the front porch cave in, he laughed, his eyes already glassy. For years he regaled folks around town with his tales of observing the hurricane, how, minutes before Hazel struck in full force, he fled to a friend's house on the inland waterway, how they proceeded to drink through the storm, how fortunate they had remained in one of two rooms left standing.

Tommy himself saw the ocean for the first time when he was six. A couple in town, Mr. and Mrs. Lonnie Purdy, loaded up the whole first-grade class in a big yellow school bus and took them on a field trip. Though he didn't know it at the time, the Purdys had chosen to park the bus on the very piece of property that belonged to Tommy. They and the children had stood at the back of his lot at low tide, the very spot where thirty years later he dreams of a hot tub and permanent keg. That is, if the ocean ever coughs up what rightfully belongs to him, this pitiful birthright, submerged land and a stack of yellowed copies of the *Saturday Evening Post*, all with the same date, all with the same words in the table of contents: "'A Dream of Lost Lovers,' by Cecil Lowe," a rather hot title to be found under the Norman Rockwell cover painting of a happily freckled, peachy-keen family, like Tommy Lowe never knew.

But at six, he'd known nothing of his property. All he knew was he was thrilled to be there, thrilled to be in the presence of the Purdys, a couple so weird that children automatically assumed they were rich—Mr. Purdy drove an old Cadillac and wore driving gloves, and Mrs. Purdy wore long flowing dresses and a snake bracelet on her plump upper arm.

What Mrs. Purdy told each new first-grade class was that she had grown up in Fulton and not seen the ocean until she was in high school. She told the children that the first time she ever saw the ocean, the first time she ever smelled the salt air, she felt she had seen the whole creation; she said she couldn't put it into words, not then and not now, but the sight of the water, the swells and spray, gave her life "perspective." Tommy remembers her saying that word, *perspective*, her shiny pink lips sounding it slowly, her painted-on eyebrows going up in a way that said, *Do you get what I'm saying?* She told the children that she had something to give back, a debt to pay, which is how she got the principal to hand over the school bus keys every September. The first-graders had never seen a grown-up who wore such strange-looking clothes. They had never known an adult who listened to them so hard, eyes wide and never blinking as she twisted her long dark hair around and around her hand. She had hair longer than any of the girls in the class, and it was exciting to be with her, to stand close enough to catch a whiff of her perfume. Even after Mr. Purdy died, she made this yearly pilgrimage so every first-grader in the town of Fulton, regardless of the last name or street address or money available, spent at least one September afternoon rolling in the sand and wading in the surf. Come that perfect fall day (and she invariably picked a good one), the children would all be there, lined up in front of the school waiting for a seat on Mrs. (now she uses Ms.) Purdy's bus.

THESE DAYS, TOMMY does a lot of work for Ms. Purdy (she has recently changed the pronunciation to Pur DAY). She dresses the same way exactly and her hair, though gray, is still yanked back in a bushy ponytail that reaches the middle of her back. Tommy does carpentry and brick work, furniture refinishing and repair. He recently finished building a huge deck to surround the hot tub he installed for her new business (a quit-smoking clinic), and now he's building a closet in the small apartment she has over her garage. He once tried to tell Mrs. Purdy (she insists he call her Quee, though it doesn't come off his tongue easily) what an impact she made on him with that trip, but she wouldn't allow it. He was hoping to work his way up to thanking her for the other time she had helped him as well, that time when he was in high school with nowhere else to turn.

Now he kneels in the firm, damp sand that belongs to him. He pays forty-one cents a year in county taxes and eleven cents to the city. Every day he takes a break from his work and comes here, sometimes just to sit, sometimes to wade in and pace off the lot, seventy feet deep and fifty feet wide. He sits back, jeans and sneakers wet and sandy, and scoops his hands into the sand. One of the few times he actually talked to his father, they were here, at the beach. Tom was ten and interested in the stories his father had to tell about the pirates who once inhabited these very waters. Cecil told him that their name, Lowe, was derived from George Lowther's, a pirate from England who killed himself. "It makes sense that he would," Tom's father had said that day, the hem of his khakis damp, the sleeves of his white dress shirt rolled up to just below the elbow. Then they drove back into town where his father took him to the new bank building to ride the elevator up to the third floor. It was the highest building in town.

Tom tried that day to absorb all he could about his father. It had been six years since he had seen him and might be another six before he saw him again. He realized he had his father's coloring, the straight, almost black hair and hazel eyes; he had the sharp facial bones and full lips. But his father was a lanky six feet and two inches, and Tommy was one of the shorter boys in his class.

In the car, his father talked about Atlantis, how maybe somewhere out in the depths of the ocean there existed a whole world that had been swallowed, bottled. Tommy had tried to imagine it, his own town submerged, wavy and dark in the deepest depths. He imagined their house, a small brick ranch washed through: windows black, drapes undulating like sea anemones, sparse furniture held in place by the weight of the water. Cecil talked about how easily the world could come to an end—it could happen in numerous ways, to the world at large or to the world of an individual. "For instance, the world your mother and I created," he said and paused, the car idling at the intersection. "It ended." He stared straight ahead, jaw clenched, and in that moment Tommy understood why his mother hadn't wanted to let him go on this outing. This was what she was scared about. This is what she must have meant all of those times she told Tommy that his father was a dark-hearted man. "It was sad that it ended," he continued. "I love your mother. That wasn't what it was all about." Tommy wanted to ask then—as he has many many times since—what *was* it all about, then? Was it him? Had his being born ruined that world, because his father had certainly never said anything to take that burden away from him.

His mother, on the other hand, told him many things, maybe too many things. She told him how she waited to hear from his father during Hazel, how Tommy was just an infant but Cecil had thought nothing of heading down to the beach with his buddies. He sat there, shit-faced (Tommy's mother had used the word *inebriated*), and watched the storm, which he later described to Tommy's mother with such clarity—the slate gray of the sky darkening still, while ferocious winds swept porches and piers into the sea like so many matchsticks. The rush of the blinding rain and the crazy kick of adrenaline as he braced himself for death.

Tom's mother had told him that when his father returned home two days later, it was like she was seeing a ghost. He hadn't shaved, and he stood all hunch-shouldered out on the stoop where the rain still dripped from the aluminum awning that had fallen to one side. She told Tommy that she greeted him with a shush and pointed to the corner of the room where Tommy was sleeping in the playpen. Cecil went straight to the corner and knelt there, addressed his child as if he were an adult, informed him that it was a great shame but due to forces of nature beyond his control he had just lost Tommy's inheritance, a lovely piece of oceanfront property that should have been worth thousands. Whenever Tommy's mother told that story, he tried to imagine his father out on the stoop, looking like a ghost. He wanted to believe that his father was like Gray Man, the famous apparition who arrives as a warning, a safety sign to those lucky enough to glimpse his shadowed form. It was in a book Tommy had read at school along with other ghost stories like "The Maco Light," in which a headless man wanders the train tracks in search of his head, and the one where a Confederate general appears at dusk on the very spot he died at Fort Fisher.

THIS SUNKEN PIECE of property haunted his childhood as he tried to imagine the house that had once stood. That house was his father's world, a pirate's cove, a treasure chest, golden words and a .38 revolver, while fifteen miles away his mother paced the small hallway from her dark bedroom to the front window. His parents' romance was a story everybody in town knew because it was one Cecil Lowe told so often, his wooing and loving of one Betty Jean Kirkland, a shy sweet girl who was known all over town as the girl whose mother sewed wedding gowns in a fancy shop downtown. Her mother's mannequin, Betty Jean often stood on a stool up in the window of the store, all dressed up in white shiny cloth while her mother knelt and tucked and pinned the fabric. She was pretty and slight, *like a lovely silver moth*, Cecil once wrote in a poem. The day he arrived in Fulton on his way from the bus station to the only hotel in town, he spotted her there in the window. He walked straight into the store and in perfect tune and pitch, asked the woman at the desk, "How much is that girlie in the window?"

Tom's mother's stories were either good or bad. There was no gray area at all. His father was *first* handsome and brilliant and courtly and devoted and *then* despicable and hateful, selfish and cruel. He had been courtly and devoted on that October afternoon he and Tommy kicked through the leaves and entered the brand-new bank building. Everything still smelled of paint and plaster and the rubber backing of the new tan carpet in the offices. They rode the elevator in silence as Tom's father talked about *real* skyscrapers and the way they are built to sway, built to give in to nature just enough that they can survive. "Not a bad code to adopt," he said as the doors slid open and they stepped into the empty, glassed-in space. From here Tom could see the steeples of all the area churches, and he could see the Confederate statue in front of the courthouse. He stared at the cuffs of his father's pants, still damp from their walk on the beach.

"I'm taking you to all of my favorite spots today," his father said. "Good view, huh?" His hands were deep in his pockets, and he jingled keys and change as he paced from one end of the room to the other. "Right over there is where I first saw your mother"; he leaned his forehead onto the glass and it was difficult for Tom to discern if he was staring down at Main Street or back into his own eyes. "She was quite the belle of the ball." He pulled a lighter from his pants and then reached into his shirt pocket for the pack of Lucky Strikes there. "But all did not go as planned." He walked to the other end of the room and lit his cigarette, his hand cupping the flame as if he were standing in a windstorm. "I come up here and I see before and after. I look at where I first met your mother—the beginning—and I come over here and I see how it all turned"—he breathed in and blew a thin stream of smoke into the glass—"or rather *didn't* turn out." Tom walked over and followed his father's pointed finger, looking through the glass, beyond the parking lot of the First Baptist Church, and right into the side corner of his own house, just one window visible, the rest safely concealed by the privet hedge and the large oak tree.

"You just can't get away," he whispered. "You see?"

Now he leaned against the glass, his hands cupped like blinders while the cigarette in his right hand burned dangerously low.

"I've been up here at night before and watched your mother sitting there in the window. It's where she always sat at night and where she still does. I planted that privet hedge. I dug a trench and filled it with water."

Without turning away, he crushed the cigarette into the window-sill and pointed his finger, squinted his eye as if lining up a scope.

"No sir, Tommy. You will always be accountable for every second of your life. Do something good, and you can use it forever. Do something bad, and it'll haunt the hell out of you. Your mother can act like I'm not a part of her life, but every night when she sits in that chair and looks out on that privet hedge, every night when I may or may not be watching her, every night when she's watching *you*, then I'm there."

It was this memory, the view from the bank building, that is Tom's last of his father. The only other memory he had was from when he was four, and now he isn't sure if the memory was real or created. It is true that he was in the grocery store with his mother, and it is true that he saw his father. What he remembers is a tall man stepping from behind a pyramid of apples, green and red and yellow, the old checkered floor littered with pasteboard boxes and crates. He remembers several pieces of fruit rolling and landing in a succession of thuds, as his mother grabbed him by the hand and pulled. "Stay away," she said through clenched teeth. "Haven't you done enough by now?"

"No, no I haven't," he followed them up and down the aisles, his dress shoes clicking with each step. "He's my son, too. I want to make it up to him."

"Good," she said. "Sell your underwater house for what you paid for it and send him to college some day. Buy him some school clothes and that Matt Dillon doll he talks about nonstop!" She stopped suddenly and pulled Tommy to her, smoothed his hair as if to apologize.

"He'll go to school."

"You're damned right about that." She froze and put a hand to her mouth and then let it drop to her chest, mouthed an apology to the woman in the checkout. Her mouth was quivering and her hands shook as she opened her billfold to pay for their food.

"Tommy," his father had whispered then and held out his hand. In the memory or what he believes to be memory, there is a sense of recognition, the hand reaching for him is safe, welcoming. "I love you," his father said. "I never meant to hurt you." Tommy doesn't remember if he reached back. What he remembers is all the times he tried to reconstruct the memory, tried to chisel an image of Cecil Lowe into his mind. Even after the day at the bank, Tom had clung to the earlier memory, the part where his father said, "I never meant to hurt you."

And his mother confirmed his memory. Yes, they *had* seen his father in the store, his father *had* told Tommy that he loved him, *had* reached out and tried to get him to move away from his mother's side. Tom's mother said, yes, it was true that his father never meant to hurt him at all, and that's why he chose to stick a gun in his mouth and blow himself away. And who was called to clean up that mess? Who? And all that was in the will was left to Tommy, that's true. How wonderful. A moth-eaten tuxedo, twenty copies of that godforsaken story, and an underwater lot.

Now his mother never even mentions Cecil Lowe unless Tom brings him up. Her life is church socials and the civic center, where she hands out programs for whatever ballet, school play, or band recital is held. Now the tide is coming in, the water up and foaming over the outline of the master suite.

His own home fifteen miles away is nothing more than a flatbed camper on an empty lot. The camper's two halves open like wings to form beds on either side, a canvas roof zippers down to the little half door. This is the property his mother gave to him, a lot on which she had dreamed of building the perfect house, but for whatever reason decided to stay where she was. It's right in the middle of what is becoming the very nicest neighborhood: curbed and guttered, BMWs and Volvos in every drive, antebellum and Williamsburg, Tudor and contemporary; new houses springing from the earth like plants, growing and spreading to fill in every square inch of space with three-car garages and satellite dishes, swimming pools and tennis courts. The earth is scooped to the side and the grass is trucked in and rolled out, watered like clockwork by the underground sprinklers at every house on the street, skipping, of course, Tom Lowe's yard and camper.

People want to say something to him. They try to, in what they think are subtle ways. They say things like, "You must be planning some house, Tom," and he just stares back and smiles. The truth is that he was here first. He was here when there were no streetlights and pavement. He was here when the pine trees were so thick that his camper and the narrow dirt road leading to it were completely hidden. His drive is still dirt, which turns to slick red mud in a hard rain.

His trees are still thick and overgrown, wild blackberries rambling out front where he has recently (in response to the inquisitive neighbors) placed a giant thermometer sign. The sign says: "A home will be built on this site when the necessary money is raised." He didn't paint in any figures; he's not building a house, at least not on this piece of land. His house will be on the beach with cross circulation of sea breeze, a view from every angle. In the meantime he has collected up to two thousand dollars in anonymous "love gifts" (as *charity* donations are called locally), some of which he uses over at Buddy Dog to adopt the biggest and oldest (and thus oftentimes most undesirable) canines to be had and the rest to care for them. He now has quite a collection: two labs and three beagles, several mixed breeds, a greyhound recently retired from a track down in South Carolina, a springer spaniel (Calico Jack), and a feisty, sometimes ferocious Pomeranian (Anne Bonny)—all named for pirates. All are fixed and all wear Invisible Fence collars, so that when unsuspecting neighbors come up close to peer through his pine trees, they are met by what looks like a band of wild dogs. The biggest dog, Blackbeard, is the same mutt he had when he moved into the camper, the same one who rides around in his truck all day, a collie with bad arthritis who has slept in Tom's bed without any other invited guests for quite a few years. People act like his lack of a love life is far stranger than that he spends his time walking the boundaries of his underwater property and adopting behavior problem dogs. And that's how he knows that people have about as much hindsight and insight as those big fake-brick pillars that mark the entrance to his neighborhood. If they did, they would not have to look back far in his life to understand his solitude and his desire to opt for nobody over just anybody. If they did, they might jump on his father's suicide as an explanation, but they would only have grazed the surface. That's why he likes doing work for Ms. Purdy, Quee; she knows another part of his life. She knew him when he stood waiting to either win or lose. She knew him when he was a senior in high school and known all over town as TomCat. TomCat Lowe, a name that has stuck and followed him all these years later.

$\mathcal{T}$esting . . . testing. . . . It is early in the morning on June, oh, what the hell, June something, and I am tooling right down Interstate 95 to my new life. I just bought this cheap little recorder at an all-night diner where they had a lot of crap at the checkout. I also bought a rape whistle and a mood ring like I once had when I was in the ninth grade. I could've bought some fruit-flavored condoms (if that tells you what kind of place I was in), but I passed. I have taken a vow of celibacy, so relieved as hell to be out of the life that is now four hours behind me in the D.C. area. I plan to tell all on these tapes, my life, my secrets. I mean why not? I'm driving along thinking that that big old meteor or whatever it was that hit Jupiter could just as easily slam into Earth and wipe us all out and wouldn't I be so sorry if I'd stayed in a miserable life? Wouldn't I be sorry if I'd spent my days fretting over this calorie or that. Just prior to entering the marriage I'm now leaving, I was driving down this same interstate, and what did I see but a big white horse racing down the side of the road. At first I thought I was hallucinating, and then I thought it was a sign like from Revelation, coming for to carry me home or some such. Of course then I saw this red-faced farmer hauling ass, with a harness clutched in his hand and a deserted plow out in the middle of a tobacco field. Still, I should've taken heed. If a friend had told me that story, I'd have said, *It's a sign, stay single.*

I've always been asked for advice by others. It comes to me naturally, whether I want the position or not. It's like all I have to do is walk into a room, and within five minutes everybody who's anybody with a problem has come up and affixed himself to me. I think of myself as a crazy magnet. I say, Step right up, step right up, put on your iron filings suit and get sucked my way. Give me your lost and crazed. Are you on drugs? Are you afraid to come out of the closet? Do you like to tell others every graphic detail of your sex life or intestinal functions? Well then, clearly, I'm the woman you've spent your life looking for. The trouble is that I'm so goddamned sick and tired of listening to all your crap that I have decided to set up shop and just talk to myself for a few months since all of you problem types out there just don't happen to ever have time to *listen.*

If you're listening to these tapes, then there's a very good chance that I'm dead. So fine, listen. Sit back and enjoy yourself. My name is Mary Denise Parks, but everybody calls me Denny just like the restaurant. I am thirty-five years old and on my way to Fulton, North Carolina, where I have a job waiting for me. I am going to put my crazy magnet properties to good use and become a therapist. I have never been a therapist; I only took introduction to psych in college, where I majored in recreation. Serious recreation of course. I have spent the past several years going into rest homes and tossing balls of yarn into hands too old to catch and helping the more virile types glue dried beans onto boards in shapes of chickens and sunrises and so on. People say I'm good at what I do. People were crazy about me in Virginia, where I lived as the wife of an academic, an English professor who spent his whole life researching writers who had allergies.

As a result, he spent an enormous amount of time studying the sneeze, what part of the brain controlled it, bright lights, and so on. He couldn't shut up about that French guy who liked to *watch* others, if you know what I mean, and otherwise stayed corked up in his room his entire life writing one really long book, and then that woman poet from Boston whose name I can't think of either. He referred to them as "the asthmatics," which I said sounded like a punk rock band that might be into leather and little face masks, like Dennis Hopper used in *Blue Velvet*. People said my husband must be such an interesting person. Yeah, right, that's why I felt inclined to take off all of my clothes while watching *Body Heat* in a public theater. William Hurt was so close I could have spit a Raisinet and hit him. I was almost shed of *everything* when the manager of the theater came and asked me to put my clothes back on, and then somebody called my husband to come and get me. He was so mad, his jaw clenched tightly. I faked several sneezes to distract him and went on about my business. I knew I was out of there.

So here I am; my godmother, who I have not seen since I was five years old, is waiting for me. She knows what happened in Virginia; my mother called to tell her. My husband said if I got some really intensive psychiatric help that he thought he might some day be able to forgive me. He said that if I would submit to his advice and suggestions that he could make everything work. This from a man who couldn't even operate the VCR. This from a man who liked his sex like he liked his martinis, dry and neat. This from a man who couldn't stand NOT knowing an answer to a question, even at the risk of making a fool of himself, which I now understand is why he picked such a subject as "the sneeze" to occupy his pitiful little life. I was out of there. I had known within a month of marrying the old bore that I had made a mistake; I knew when one of the young residents who regularly came to Sunrise Rest Home asked me on a date and I had to stop sorting out kernels of colored popcorn and *think* about it. I never wore my wedding ring at work with the excuse of fear of losing it, since I had to wash my hands with industrial-strength soap a zillion times a day. Now that I've been brushing up on my psychology a bit, I know better. I had a subconscious desire to be asked out. I stared into that young doctor's big blue eyes, the dark circles underneath from all of his night hours tending the sick and the dying. I imagined myself in his arms, my mouth pressed against his. He said, "You know I don't get many nights off, but I happen to be free this Friday and a friend of mine is having a party . . ." I watched his mouth moving with the words and all I could feel deep inside of me was the seed of truth and reality like a bean soaked in water to soften and expand, burst forth with a vine of reckoning that squeezed the life out of me. How could I have been so stupid as to think that at the age of thirty my life had been over? I was just another one of those women who thought she heard that stupid proverbial clock ticking and jumped into the first relationship that seemed somewhat decent. What did I know? I never knew my father. He died when I was an infant. This is what I have in common with my godmother, Quee Purdy (she pronounces it Pur DAY, like she might be French or something). She ended her letter to me saying just that: "We are women who spent years missing our fathers and who cling to every story and bit of information we can collect about the men who gave us life. We are women who understand psychology. We are held together by our love for one person, your mother (as finicky and difficult a person as she is, don't say I said it). I am delighted to offer you a position in my newly founded and booming business: SMOKE-OUT SIGNALS, a place for addicts who want to quit." She told me that if I happened to be a smoker that she'd take two weeks to straighten me out before I began working.

She says that there are many nice folks in the town of Fulton, and she plans to introduce me to as many as she can. She says there are also numerous nuts to avoid, one of whom has just registered to come into Smoke-Out Signals. Quee calls her the Spandex Poet, says she is a birdlike, shriveled-up, whorish bimbo who specializes in haiku and penis imagery. Quee says that the two of us will have one hell of a wonderful time typing up notes on our clients and writing up the diagnostic papers.

The interstate is now flat as a board, and I'm within only a few miles of my destination. My mother grew up in this town, just two streets from where Quee lives. Whenever she talks about those growing-up years, she gets this far-off dreamy look like they might have been the best years she's ever known, but still, in spite of Quee's long-distance begging and my own questioning, she'd never ever move back. She would say something like: "Life goes on" or "On with the show!" Not long after I was born, Mom moved to New York thinking she had a chance of breaking into show business. We lived there just long enough for people in her hometown to refer to her as "the one who now lives in New York City," like that might make her suddenly sophisticated—forget that she was waitressing and we were living in Queens in an old building that overlooked that huge cemetery where you'd need a map and compass and three days of food and water to find your loved one. I was seven when she met my stepfather, who was in New York on business, and all it took was a marriage proposal and she kissed all that talk of Broadway and the northeastern experience good-bye, and there we were in Virginia in a two-story colonial house, with my mother sipping bourbon and churning out needlepoint pillows faster than most people can cough and spit. My mother's desires to make me into a child star disappeared as soon as she saw our new *veranda* and reappeared in dreams of debutante parties and what she called "little girl schools" where I might wear a little uniform and knee socks, ride a horse side-saddle, and meet somebody who would become a famous academic type. So? Consider it damn done.

Anyway, I'm signing off for right now. As I say, if you are listening to my secret tapes, then chances are I'm dead. I hope that it's something like the year 2050 instead of this year. I hope that I fell in love with a wonderful person and that I had a couple of perfect kids, a lucrative career, vegetable garden, rose arbor, good clothes, and leather accessories. I hope that people remember me fondly as a woman who had much insight into the lost and crazed who attached themselves to her. I hope people forget that I was stripping my clothes off in a public theater about the same time that poor Pee Wee Herman was doing things in another theater. Whoops! I shouldn't have reminded you about Pee Wee, in hopes that people will have forgotten all about his little episode and that his program will be back on the air. I think of myself as the Pee Wee Defense Commission. I hope that out there in the world somewhere *I* will have people who feel that way about me.

I will delete what I just said come to think of it. What I just now did reminds me of a card I once saw on an airplane when I was seated in that emergency exit seat. The card said: "If you cannot perform in the event of an emergency or you cannot read this card, please alert your attendant." Duh. Anyway, I hope that I'm remembered in a wonderful way. I hope that my funeral will be a happy, happy time. I would like to be cremated and thrown from the Empire State Building with a little bit left over for my remaining loved ones to put in little velvet bags and preserve like secret talismans. I want to be hurled to the wind on a bright clear sunny day. I want low humidity, so that my pieces will not stick like so much cheap cinder to the soot that already fills the city air. I want my pieces to blow. I would like for folks to tell stories and eat ice-cream sundaes. My funeral songs of choice are "Be Young, Be Foolish, Be Happy" by the Tams and "Already Gone" by the Eagles.

Speaking of which, my tapes are going to be labeled like they contain music. Quee has already told me that she doesn't care what I do in my garage apartment and she doesn't care who I entertain. She doesn't care what my sexual preference might be (hetero), and she doesn't care if I have fifty pets (fur allergy). She doesn't care what I eat, and she doesn't care what I wear (I had told her that I'm a vegetarian and prefer all-cotton anything to a blend). She doesn't care how I wear my hair (frizzy by nature, long by choice, auburn by henna), and she doesn't care what kind of music I play EXCEPT, and she repeated EXCEPT, none of that crooning that people thought was something when she was younger. She said she hated Bing Crosby and she hated Frank Sinatra and most of all she hates Perry Como. That's why this tape will read "Perry Como's Christmas." You have found this tape because my will instructed you to do so. If it turns out that I have died young, then I hope that the sky will darken and the rain will fall. I hope that people will stop what they are doing and feel my loss like a big empty hole, just for a second even, before they turn back to their televisions and telephones and video display terminals, because the truth is that if that has happened, then it is a damn shame. It is a big damn loss. It brings tears to my eyes just to think it.

SMOKE-OUT SIGNALS
Put your butt out and bring your butt in
Today's the day—you're guaranteed to win!

*Q*uee has run her ad in the local paper for two weeks now and she already has folks booked on a waiting list. The word is spreading around Fulton and in neighboring towns. "If smoking is an addiction like they say," she said on a local radio show, "then a smoker deserves to be treated like an addict. A smoker ought to be able to go somewhere like the Betty Ford Clinic and get loved and pampered right out of the addiction."

"And just how do you do this?" the interviewer asked. He was a round, red-faced fella, originally from Raleigh, who smoked like a locomotive. "I mean, I'm an addict. What can you do for me?"

That was the beginning. Quee promised to take him and reshape him. She promised him good food and long hot baths, foot rubs and back massages, scented oils and fine wine, endless videos on her brand-new wide-screen TV. He would have his own room for two weeks; he would have her undivided attention.

"My wife might not like it," he said and laughed a laugh that turned into a dry hack, a choking cough, a need to rush over to the water-cooler while Quee completed her wonderful free advertising.

"What? Your wife wouldn't like for you to stop choking and spitting all over creation? Your wife wouldn't like for you to have white teeth as opposed to brown?" Quee leaned in close to the mike and cooed to her waiting public. "You will have round-the-clock therapy, be it physical massage or talk therapy. Put your butt out and bring your butt in, honey. I can cure you."

NOW THE GUINEA pig DJ is in his last phase of the smoke-out. He's as lazy as a coonhound—oiled and loosened, with pores that are clean and clear. Quee has knocked herself out on him because this success could cinch the business. The final phase of his treatment will include a little talk therapy from Denny, who ought to be arriving any second now, if she didn't have to pull off the interstate to remove her clothing. The child temporarily lost her mind—totally, it sounds like—but at least she did have the good sense to get herself out of a bad situation.

Now Quee is seated on the big velvet ottoman with her client's plump foot in her lap. She has greased the foot with bag balm, and now she's massaging while he listens to his substitute newsperson on the radio. His arches melt under the firm pressure of her thumbs. "I may never go back to work," he tells her, his eyes closed, terry cloth robe (furnished by Smoke-Out Signals) pulled loosely around his body. "Marry me, Quee."

"Honey, you're not old enough for me," she says. "I like my men old enough to have gone around the block a couple of hundred times." She watches him jerk and then relax when she twists his ankle around with a loud pop. "I've buried so many men that they call me the Hospice Lover in these parts. Besides, you're married."

"Oh, yeah."

"Besides we got to get you back on the radio and get this guy that murders the Queen's English back selling ads where he ought to be."

"He's running overtime, too." He shifts, giving Quee a glimpse up his hairy thigh. No thrill there. Lord, Lord, you can't always be loving a man for his looks and parts. You gotta love the whole man, gotta find the heart and the soul. She preaches this very lecture all the time to her assistant, Alicia, who should already be here by now, steaming towels and getting ready for the future arrival of the Spandex Poet and several others chomping at the bit to get in. Quee's house is a ranch-style that has been added on to twice and will continue to be added on to if business is good. Her dream is to have a big extension out into the backyard, kind of like those barracks on *Gomer Pyle, USMC,* which was a show she hated but watched faithfully way back because Lonnie thought it was hilarious. Lonnie used to always tell Quee that she resembled Lou Ann Poovey, Gomer's girl, which of course was nowhere near true but was a sweet thought to be sure.

Alicia has kept a low profile with the radio man here, because her husband is also a DJ. Her husband, Jones Jameson, is known around the county as the local Howard Stern. He says horrible things on the radio, sex things, racist things. But he's real handsome, and comes from money (at least what might be *considered* money in this neck of the woods), so people try very hard to overlook him. Alicia is his complete opposite and certainly deserves better.

"The Big Man Jones isn't here yet," the substitute DJ is saying. "So we're going to go ahead and have the *Swap Shop* show. If you've got something you're itching to sell, something you mighta never woulda bought no way, then give us a call . . ."

"Turn it off, turn it off." Quee's client opens his eyes for the first time in an hour. "That idiot's going to cause me to have to smoke again."

"There, there, sweetie," Quee presses into his arch, rubs up and down with her knuckles until he relaxes again. She kneads his squatty calves. When he's almost asleep, she leads him back to his little room, which is kept dark and cool, turns on the ocean wave tape and the lava lamp and leaves him to the first of his several naps of the day. Sleep is very important to the person kicking a habit. Forget that he's now as fat as a little toad. The only mirror in this end of the house is a skinny mirror that she borrowed on time from a department store over in Clemmonsville; of course she had to go out with the manager a couple of times to get it, but that's what sacrifice is all about. She doesn't dare let the fat little DJ anywhere near his clothes, yet. She keeps him in her loose terry cloth robes that she bought in bulk from one of the local textile mills; she has now ironed SOS onto all the pockets. Fat. That will be her next project; move over, Duke University, with your old rice diet, here comes Quee Purdy, healer of man, fully licensed driver on the byways of life who knows a little medicine, psychiatry, chiropractic whatever, and therapeutic massage. If Elvis were alive he'd book himself at Quee's house.

"You are truly a genius, my love," Lonnie, her one and only legal husband, used to say. He said this on many occasions, but especially after he created Ceramic Meats. These are hand-painted, perfectly cast replicas of main dishes: turkeys, hams, and Quee's favorite, the crown pork roast. They are for the vegetarians of the world or those who just hate having all that leftover mess of critter parts to deal with. This centerpiece has tiny holes throughout so that you can light a candle (made to smell like the fat of whatever animal has been duplicated), and there in the center of your table you get the steamed-up smell of the meat you are not about to thank anybody for or eat. *Genius* is not even the word. "Who are you, really?" an old lover of hers once asked. They were still in the bed, the sheets damp and sandy. "Who do you want me to be?" she asked.

Now some jerk from a big department store has stolen her ceramic meat idea and made a killing in the Northeast. So be it. If one idea was all she had, she wouldn't be much now, would she? She is sprucing up the pink room for the Spandex Poet, also known as Ruthie Crow, who will arrive later today, when she hears a car door in the drive. She lifts up the mattress and places a golfball under it (Ruthie Crow is NO princess for sure) and then she goes and opens the door. It's Alicia, poor thing, she is a mess. Her hair hasn't been washed, and her eyes are all puffy. She is way too thin; the little two-year-old, Taylor, perched on her hip looks enormous in comparison. He has his daddy's handsome full face and big brown eyes.

"Jones never came home," Alicia says. "All night long I kept getting these calls, silence and breathing." She puts Taylor on the floor and eases down on the bench of Quee's prize oak hall tree that supposedly was once owned by the royal family, or so the man who runs and operates Fulton Antiques and Oddities said. Of course the old fool was lying, but who cares. She likes the furniture purely because it was a big solid hunk of oak, wood cut from a tree that must have been standing in the seventeen hundreds, if indeed it was as old as the man had said. Tommy Lowe refinished it for her and found a penny dated 1905 in one of the drawers.

"Was it that girlfriend?"

"I suppose so." Alicia bends forward and sobs, the heels of her little granny boots scratching up against the front of the hall tree. Taylor stands over by Quee's big fat cat, Pussy Galore, and strokes her fur while watching his mother. Lonnie named her. He loved those James Bond movies. They'd go to bed, and he'd say with an awfully bad accent, "The name is Purdy, Lonnie Purdy," and she would laugh and immediately pull down his baggy old pajama pants.

"So he's not with *her*."

"I don't know, Quee." Alicia looks up, the skin beneath her pale blue eyes so fragile-looking, tiny lines and capillaries like an insect's wing. "I mean could something have *really* happened? He usually at least calls." Taylor stares at her, scared like a little animal. "God," she whispers, her hand waving out to Taylor as a distraction of his attention. "I catch myself hoping . . ."

"I know baby, you've said that before." Quee goes and gets a little chewy treat for Taylor to give to Miss Pussy Galore. She tells him to see if he can get the kitty to do her trick of jumping on top of the wide-screen TV in the other room; that *Sesame Street* or some such must be on about now. When Taylor has disappeared around the corner, Quee turns back to Alicia. "Don't feel guilty for thinking it, either."

"Really?"

"Yes." Quee takes Alicia by the shoulders, and she feels as limp as a rag doll. Quee would like to shake the shit out of her, she'd like to say, WAKE UP! but she just waits for Alicia to stand a little taller and look her in the eyes. "I told you how he came around here one night last year, asking about you like you might have been his pet dog."

"You never told me exactly what happened."

"No, and I don't need to. He's trash."

"Why did I ever marry him?" Alicia shakes her head back and forth, limp blond hair falling forward. She needs to wipe her nose but sits there helpless and lost-looking.

"You were young," Quee says, ignoring the tinkling of the DJ's bell, which probably means he wants his goddamn back rubbed again. Yes, yes, it's what she has promised to the people who check in, but shit, has he no shame? "And Jones Jameson is a looker, no doubt about it."

"Who cares?"

"You did." Quee goes down the hall and in her sweet as a sugar plum tart voice says at the DJ's door that she is heating up the oil for his little rub right this sec. Turning back to Alicia, she says, "You cared. You probably couldn't believe that he was even interested in you." Quee waits for Alicia to look up, waits to catch the truth in those pale eyes before she goes to heat up the special massage oil (lard with sprinkles of Tabu—cheap as all get out), which she bottles in a fine china carafe that was owned by Napoleon's cousin-in-law or so the *junque* (he insists that if you ever have desire to use such a word that you spell it with a "q") man said.

"You grew up out there in the county where a double-wide trailer is considered high class, and here was this young, well-to-do, college-educated playboy who had screwed every little debutante and sorority girl in the state, and he was interested in you."

"My parents had a *house*. A nice clean house with a yard."

"Alicia, honey, a point. I was making a point. I'm saying that it's not unusual for people to fall in love with what they think others are falling in love with." Quee stirs the oil and glances down the other hall that leads to her private part of the house. It is a sanctuary, that part of the house. It is where she goes to fill herself up with the goodness that gets siphoned out of her over the course of a day. "I'm sure you were flattered when he asked you out. You were probably flattered when he wanted to sleep with you. You probably thought he was doing you some big favor."

"I don't know." She shakes her head, shrugs. Quee knows. She knows that's what happened. She saw that son of a bitch sowing his oats all through his high school years. Nice girls went out with him just because his daddy owned an oil company. She had dealt with many of the young women who had the pleasure of him pumping and slobbering on top of them.

Quee was at their wedding, and Alicia never even made the connection until Quee told her. At the time, Quee had quite a lucrative cake-designing business, and there she was setting up all the layers into what came to resemble a beautiful white swan, the little stand-up bride and groom riding on its back like when Thumbelina and the prince sail away into a happy life. She had come up with the idea herself, relying on a memory of the swan boats in Boston, a memory of breakfast at the Ritz, following a night of love-making in a Holiday Inn out on the turnpike. Lonnie had no idea why she was so interested in swans, and he kept asking why a swan instead of a dove. A dove, after all, was white and was a universal symbol of love, not to mention the role the cute little cooer played in Noah and the Ark: life, prosperity. Lonnie was quite the eclectic reader, and she adored him for it. She finally said she chose the swan because she had always felt like an ugly duckling herself and loved when it turned into a beautiful swan. She told Lonnie that if swans talked English, then that one had said, So fuck all you ducks who think you're something special.

"But you were never a duckling," he said. "Not that I ever saw at least."

"I was, honey. Once upon a time I sure was."

"You are the loveliest bird of all," he said at the reception, while she watched over her cake, making sure that no one tried to cut that perfectly curved, creamy white neck. She watched Jones Jameson with disgust as he leapt onto stage with the band he had brought in from Raleigh, a beer can in his hand, and began singing into the mike. He had already been hired over at WQTB and had told enough jokes to set the town on fire; he talked about somebody at the station who *niggerlipped* his smokes, and he said he knew this lucky old guy whose woman could suck a golfball through a garden hose. He asked the band to play that song "If You Want to Be Happy for the Rest of Your

Life." "Never make a pretty woman your wife," he sang while Alicia was in the bathroom changing into her little linen going-away suit that had probably set her back a couple of weeks' pay at the courthouse where she worked as a social worker. Quee hated him. As far as she was concerned, he was the type who gets entirely too far in this world. Alicia's poor old daddy spent the whole reception leaned against the wall with his hand in a loose fist. He looked like an old farmer come to town.

"Me poopooed," Taylor says now and runs into the room, reaches his arms out to his skeletal mother who shakes her head and sighs, as if she has no idea what to do next.

"I know," Quee says and takes Taylor by the hand. "Go tell Mr. Radio that I'm on my way. Ask *him* if he knows where your husband might have been all night. I'll change this diaper. I'll change this little stinky critter boy, oh yes I will, you know I will." She lifts Taylor, holding her breath as she hugs him close. "Let's go in the bathroom, lovey dovey, little ripe one, little love." She puts him down on her pink satin chaise over by the window. This is the business bathroom, designed for relaxation and the feel of somebody's living room rather than a john where somebody might feel inclined to have a quick smoke and flush. Tommy Lowe had planned the expansion himself, a lovely bay area of glass that surrounds the Jacuzzi. Tommy said he was building his dream bathroom, so she invited him to come in and use it anytime he took a notion; she said he needed to give up the cigs anyway. Now Taylor is pulling on her necklace, an amber heart that Lonnie gave her when they got married. He had just been reading all about it, about fossils preserved in amber, bones and wings and hair. He said he hoped that *they* were around long enough to be considered fossils. "Like what if some people thousands of years from now take a crowbar and pop off our bedroom door and find us spooned there."

He was following her through the house with this long saga of his. "Then they might take our bed with us in it and set it up in a museum and people will pass by and see us there all snuggled and think 'That could be me.' The sign would say: A Loving Marriage. Typical man and woman in a typical town in a typical year."

"Who's precious? Who's a precious boy?" she asks suddenly, needing to turn away from that image of Lonnie in her mind.

"Me am," Taylor says and slaps his plump hand up to Quee's cheek. "Me a kitty, rrrrrr."

"Me a cat," she says back in baby talk. "Me a cat with long claws and waving tail." She leans herself away from Taylor as she pulls down his tiny little jeans and reaches for the baby wipes that Alicia keeps beneath the sink. "Me love you little kitty," she purrs to him. She is feeling relief for this child, relief that maybe this time Alicia will get a clean start, that he has a chance of a decent happy life without the influence of somebody so full of hatred. She pulls up his pants and leads him back to the TV while she goes and tends to the diaper, carries it out back to where she has four cans lined up on a concrete block. All four cans are full, as they always are on Thursdays when the men come to haul it all off. Lonnie once told Quee that she heard the trash truck before the neighborhood dogs did.

"I've got a nose for trash all right," she had told him. She has said the same thing in so many words to Alicia about her husband. Quee stands out in the side yard and listens. Sure enough, she can hear the truck coming. It's probably a block away. She breathes in deeply, good clean autumn air, crisp blue sky. For some reason, it makes her think again of Lonnie and the early years with him. She thinks of the chicken pot pies they ate every day when he came in from the bank for lunch. She can almost smell those pot pies, the oilcloth on the kitchen table. Whatever happened to those dishes they had then?

Awful chipped-up dishes with roosters, matching salt and pepper
shakers, the salt one partly filled with rice to absorb the moisture. All
those years she craved wildness, so who would've thought she'd be
thinking of such things right now.

"Where are you, Lonnie?" she whispers in her head. "If you are
looking at me you must be thinking, Quee, you've flipped. You've
lost your lovely mind, my pet. Or did you always think that, Lonnie?
Sometimes I can't help but think you knew everything, even while
you were right here on earth."

A big gust of wind shakes the pecan tree, and there's the thud of a
nut on the garage roof. She can see Tommy Lowe's shadow there in
the window where he's working on the closet. He just comes and
goes on his own without ever disturbing her, that big old collie of his
seated politely on the front seat of his truck, a pack of cigarettes on
the dash. She'll get HIM in the clinic before it's all over; she'd love
nothing better than to work her hands over those lean limbs, the tight
ropey muscles of his smooth brown back. She once hinted to Alicia
that Tommy Lowe was the kind of man she *ought* to find—handsome
and good-hearted, forget that he lives like he's in a national park. As
if he has heard her thoughts, he pulls back the curtains and waves to
her. She blows him a kiss and begins hauling her trash cans down to
the curb. There was a time when the garbage men would come up
into your yard and empty the cans there, but now folks are required
to take the trash to them out on the street. No skin off of her nose.
She'd just as soon they not be snooping around her side yard, stepping
on her shrubs and seeing whatever lingerie she might have on her
clothesline, anyway.

"You better hold your breath on this one," she says and laughs.
"Take it and then drive as fast as you can."

"You bet," the old trash collector says, a wad of tobacco in his jaw, and heaves her cans up and into the back of that stinking truck. He reminds her of somebody, and she's not sure if it's of a real person or of somebody off of her special wall, a wall filled with faces of strangers, old family photos that she has purchased from the junque man, who tries to pass them off as royalty, or at least of big money from Raleigh or murderers who disappeared to Texas. Just last week Alicia confessed that the photographs gave her the creeps, that she feared their karma could leak right out and into the house. Quee, who had once dabbled in real estate, told her that she had a good sense of bad karma and had never felt a thing but benevolence from her acquired orphans.

"Even him?" Alicia asked and pointed to one of three portraits of the same gruff-looking man. Quee had said herself that he must've been some kind of son of a bitch for his family to sell off three of his portraits. She named him Oscar after the Grouch on *Sesame Street*; Taylor loved the Grouch, and Quee loves the idea of somebody making his home in a trash can. It has the same romantic appeal for her that little greasy-looking windows over gas stations always have, the notion that you could go in and have yourself a nice little apartment there, something that no one would ever suspect. You could have this beautiful life housed behind something grimy and cheap.

"He sure doesn't look so benevolent to me." Alicia kept glancing back at Oscar like she expected him to jump out and yell "Boo!" at any minute. Alicia has a pretty smile when it surfaces, timid and sweet, and Quee can only imagine that a man as awful as Jones Jameson must get some sexual kick from such a look. A sweet, smart woman reduced to ninety pounds of frayed nerve, a woman so jumpy that she won't even make eye contact with photographs if she can help it.

"Oh, honey, Oscar isn't bad at all." Quee started to say that compared to what's leaking into Alicia's own house from her own oozing husband, Oscar could be put up for sainthood. She started to say that Alicia should watch that movie where Farrah Fawcett burns up her husband's bed with him in it, but instead she told the story of Oscar as it had come to her, how Oscar was an immigrant, more or less, seeing as how he had no family in the area. Oscar loved the warm Southern weather, and he liked to stretch out like a cat in the sun and feel the heat on his face; he liked the squiggly red pictures that the bright sun etched into his closed eyelids. But most of all, Oscar loved a woman by the name of Emma, who had taken a neighborly interest in his welfare. He sensed a sadness in her, a loss they both knew. He loved the way she smelled like the pear preserves she was famous for making. He loved the way her hands moved gracefully over the banister of his porchrail. He loved her dark, thick hair that hung down her back like a young girl, even though she was a grown-up woman with a husband.

"Yes, poor, poor Oscar," Quee had said, surprised to see the solemn, totally believing look on Alicia's face. "He lived for the love he could never have, sustained on the crumbs she tossed his way, a loaf of bread, pear preserves, a muffler knitted at Christmas, the time they . . . Oh never mind," she said. "You don't care about Oscar."

"But I do," Alicia said. "I was wrong." And then she realized the absurdity of her affirmation, this faith and acceptance, sympathy and hope, for something created out of thin air.

"It's very easy to be wrong about a person's life," Quee whispered, wishing she could shake some sense into the girl so that she'd take her baby and get the hell out of her marriage. That seems like ages ago even though it was just last week.

NOW QUEE STANDS in the doorway and watches Alicia pacing and twisting the phone cord. "He said he was going to Raleigh," she says, and then is quiet, shakes her head as if the person on the other end can see her responding. "I have no idea, Officer. He said it was a radio reunion or something, that's all." She leans forward and picks up one of Taylor's little cars, runs it along the edge of the sink. "A gold Audi 5000. Yes." She pauses and her face turns red. "His vanity plate says IM2SEXY. Yes, yes." She hangs up the phone and feels her way into one of the kitchen chairs.

"They might think that means he's one of those bisexuals," Quee whispers and pats her on the shoulder. "Or they just think he's a jerk."

"Yeah."

"But that doesn't make *you* a jerk," Quee says. "There is no such thing as a jerk by marriage. You are not going to wake up one day and be like him. There is nothing in this world to stop you from walking out and starting over."

"It's that easy?"

"That easy." The bell rings down the hall, and Quee simply closes the kitchen door. "That's what Denny did. She'll be here any minute now."

"I thought you said Denny had a breakdown."

"I did, but it was just a little one." Quee takes Alicia's hands into her own and slaps them, massages, as if she's reviving some small animal. "I mean don't we all have little breakdowns all the time? It's just some people's are more noticeable than others."

"You think?"

"Damn right. Don't ever let anybody take away your right to have a little breakdown. Hell, foam at the mouth, check in somewhere. You have as much right as anybody to be left alone. And folks'll definitely leave you alone if they think there's been a little breakdown. My, yes."

"What about Taylor?"

"Oh, yeah." Quee runs out of steam with her lecture. Children change the whole operation regardless of what that operation might be.

"If not for Taylor, I'd have done all sorts of things, Quee." It is only now with the mention of her son that there is some life in that washed-out body. "He is all that I have, and I want him to have a good life."

"Yes, you're right."

Alicia leans forward and puts her face down against the table. She looks like there are no tears left in her, and it is one of those odd times when Quee has absolutely no idea what to say. She feels herself looming large and lifeless, clumsy and inadequate. It's not a feeling that comes to her often.

"You know I'll keep Taylor for you anytime," she says now. "I love that little booger, you know it."

"Yes."

"You can move in if you like, anything, you name it."

"I've got a lot to take care of," Alicia says, voice slow and eyes closed. Upstairs, Tommy's hammering is rhythmic and comforting, interrupted off and on by the thud and roll of a pecan on the metal awning over her kitchen window. Quee waits there until Alicia's breathing is regular with the exhaustion that has finally taken over. She can see into the next room where Taylor is all set up in front of the television set, that big yellow bird marching around. It's times like this she starts to hope there is no heaven and no afterlife. She hopes Lonnie is not looking down on her world right now.

ack McCallister's neighbors include a single mother of ethnic origin, who is into yard ornaments that reflect her Catholicism, and a bunch of twenty-year-olds who attend a small college in the next town and who, it seems, are majoring in beer drinking and peeing in the yard. The college kids are split up in two sides of a dilapidated duplex with peeling paint; they used to like to torture each other by blasting undesirable music back and forth. One night in the spring it was a war between Alan Sherman and Ray Stevens. When Mack heard "Hello, Muddah" for the third time and then "Guitarzan" for the eleventh, he went out on the lovely, lattice-trimmed porch of his perfectly renovated Queen Anne cottage and began shouting. "This isn't the goddamned trailer park!" he said. He was barefooted and in his pajama pants. The music stopped, but there was a price to pay. There were seven scrawny-looking guys peeping at him from their windows, seven guys who were seeing him as the authority, the *other side*, the *what's up your butt* breed. "Loosen up, dude," one guy had shouted before being shushed by his friends.

"Yeah, right, like you never acted that way." Sarah had been there, moving and talking; she stood in her thin cotton nightgown, half-hidden by the screen door. "I think the first time I ever met you, you were wearing a toga and singing 'Brick House' into a long-neck Budweiser." She slipped over and sat in the swing, her legs pulled up under her gown. They had only been in the house a month, the U-Haul boxes with his books still lining the wall. After ten years of criminal law in Raleigh, he had finally broken down and accepted her dad's offer to join his firm. "You're the son I never had," her father kept saying, but what he really meant was that he had one child; he had Sarah, and he wanted her back in his and Sarah's mother's lives full-time.

She said it was her dream. She never wanted anything else but to be with all of the people she loves, and this house! She wanted this pale purple house her whole life. "It wasn't always this color," she had said when the Realtor brought them to see it. "It was white for many years, but now"—she ran her fingers along the porch rail—"the trim shows up beautifully. It would look good yellow or gray for that matter, if you don't like it this color."

"What?" he asked, far more concerned with the asking price and the foundation than the cosmetics. "Don't like purple?"

"Mauve," she said, "it's mauve." Her period was ten days late that time, and she was absolutely sure that she was pregnant. They had been trying for the past four years. "Say mauve," she pinched his cheeks and kissed him, then fairly floated through the house. "Oh, it's just as I imagined," she said. "I always came here to trick-or-treat hoping that I'd get asked in, but a really old woman lived here and she rarely even came to the door."

"I thought a banker lived here. The banker whose wife is a potter," the Realtor said, seemingly upset that she didn't know the whole history of this house. Sarah waved her hand. "There was even another family before them; they are the ones who painted it mauve. The wife was from San Francisco and knew about these things, and then the husband got transferred back to Charlotte." Sarah knew far more about the town's real estate than their broker, who was not having to even try to sell the house. Clearly, as far as Sarah was concerned, it was sold.

"But think, now," Mack said. "Everybody always says *location, location, location*." He tilted his head in the direction of the duplex and then to the other little white house where the Virgin Mary stood smack between two mangy boxwoods.

"Well, but it's not like I don't know this town. I *know* this town!"

"But what about the neighborhood? What about the house in the new area?" He had liked the new houses they saw, the cathedral ceilings and Palladian windows, the big master baths with shower stalls and Jacuzzis.

"Up and coming," the Realtor said. "That neighborhood is more or less the threshold into the *other* neighborhood that abuts it." Sarah liked to imitate the Realtor, and whenever they were riding through town would refer to the *other* neighborhood. "In other words, *the* neighborhood."

But there was no changing her mind. That was months ago, and now here he is with the college boys on one side and the illuminated Holy Mother on the other. He keeps hoping that he'll turn and see Sarah there in the doorway, that there will be some act of grace, some voice saying that a mistake was made, rewind, start over. Somebody fucked up the instructions. The pretty little thirty-eight-year-old in Fulton, North Carolina, was not supposed to have an aneurism, but amnio, amniocentesis—she's supposed to be pregnant, you idiot, not in a coma.

Next door, the guys are playing their music at a reasonable level. They are coming and going with their dates. They wave or nod politely to him; they saw the ambulance that night, heard all of the commotion, saw him squat down and put his face against the stone steps and sob. They rarely have disco or Ray Stevens wars anymore. For all of their youth and wildness, they respect his sorrow. Mack watches them and feels like he's from another time altogether. If not for the occasional sound of Eric Clapton or Mick Jagger, he would be. If not for the calls and regular visits from June, Sarah's oldest friend, he might lose touch altogether.

They said it was something she had lived with since birth. Perhaps it was there *in utero*, waiting, ticking, feeding itself on her life. Maybe she had a sensation, a premonition, the kind that wakes you in the middle of the night, the kind you never breathe aloud. Every birthday balloon that popped, every firecracker on the Fourth of July, a foreshadowing of what she would one day suddenly feel there behind those pale blue eyes, a pressure that made her turn from the kitchen sink, her hands in yellow rubber gloves as she squeezed Spic & Span from a sponge. She was tackling the film of grease on the kitchen cabinets. She had the windows open and the lace curtain was moving back and forth, casting a filagreed shadow at her feet. "Mack," she called, barely audible, and he got there just in time to see her reaching, dripping gloves, wide eyes. He got to her just in time to keep her head from hitting the floor, and he sat there for several minutes just stroking her hair, wetting a cool cloth for her head. She had fainted before. He was actually sitting there feeling *happy*, thinking that maybe this time she really was pregnant. Later he had cursed those old movies that have it happen that way. The woman gets light-headed and faints when with child. But not the healthy woman. That woman scrubs her kitchen and eats an enormous lunch and at night straddles her husband's hips and laughs at the bulge of her body. The woman gets light-headed and faints when there's a bomb in her brain, when a vessel bursts open and fills her head with blood. He thinks of her there in the kitchen, and the sound that fills *his* mind is loud and rushing like the sound of a train, the sound of the surf, rushing, pounding. And yet it seems that it all happened without any sound at all.

DURING COLLEGE, MACK had once seen two men in a bus station. It was hard to tell what their relationship might be. They could have been brothers or lovers, even father and son. Their gestures were wild, furious. One, or maybe both, deaf, so that their anger came out of their fingertips, harsh angry signs in absolute silence. It happened long before he met Sarah, long before he glimpsed any sense of his future, and yet now, for some reason, it's a memory that haunts him. He thought of it a lot in the six weeks she was in the hospital, and now he thinks of it when he lies in his bed at night without her there beside him. The doctors insisted that a hospital bed be brought in; it would make the nurse's job possible—the turning and the tubes, the bathing—but he is still resentful.

Sometimes he can't help but wonder where his life would have gone if he had chosen another route, if he hadn't asked her to marry him. He would be in a house somewhere, wife, a couple of kids, and the news would eventually reach him through an old fraternity buddy or somebody who had been in one of his classes and seen him with her all the time. He and his wife would have been at a cocktail party or have driven up to the football game and there, while eating and drinking out of the trunk of somebody's Saab, somebody would have said, "Hey, Mack, remember that girl you dated for a while? That blond girl from the Kappa house?" And he would have put down his food and drink and sat there, stunned that something so horrible could happen to someone so young. Life would have continued in spite of the moment, his own life bright and lively, moving around and behind him. He would have sent a card or some flowers like that old boyfriend of hers, TomCat, she had called him, who appeared at the door late one afternoon a couple of weeks ago.

Mack feels guilty when he thinks that way. He smoothes his hands over his forehead. She is there beside him, breathing in silence. Maybe if he hadn't married her, if he hadn't been the one in her life, it wouldn't have happened. Maybe it was somehow related to their not being able to have a baby. Maybe she felt pressure from him, from her family, her mother who forever made reference to her grandchildren—future heirs of this small-town kingdom.

"That's absolutely insane," June said earlier today. She had come over with bags from Wendy's and they sat out on the porch to eat. She was wearing cutoffs and a big paint-splotched T-shirt, her dark hair yanked up on top of her head. She had spent the day painting her living room red to celebrate having discovered that the man she had been dating long-distance (she had been referring to "Ted" now for over a year) was not worthy of her time and had asked Mack if he felt like hearing the sordid details. The rest of her message was unspoken but loud and clear. She needed to talk to Sarah; she needed to tell *Sarah* all of these things, and he was the closest thing she could find.

"Mack," she said his name sternly. "They said it was inevitable. Think about it." She pushed her fries aside. "It could have happened when we were in high school. We could have been cheerleading in our little black and yellow skirts, yelling things like 'Sock it to 'em, Wildcats.'" She waited for him to smile. "Oh, Sarah was the *only* person who looked good in that horrible suit with those skinny little legs of hers!" She pushed off the floor of the porch, the swing rocking as she looked out into the yard. "I could have been the one who was there with her, Mack," she whispered. "It could have just as easily happened at a touchdown or when we were eleven and got up at six to

watch *Dracula* on Sunrise Theatre. It could have happened on the Girl
Scout campout or in the junior high cafeteria, or when we lay across
her bed eating M&Ms and potato chips, with her hair turned over
those huge pink rollers when she was getting ready for the prom!"
She stopped and took in a deep breath. "We're lucky we had her, you
know?" There was finality in her voice before she went back and cor-
rected herself. "Lucky we *have* her. It could have happened the day she
was born."

"That would have been a loss." He leaned forward and put his head
on his knees. By now June was used to seeing this. He could be himself with her. They took turns telling their stories about Sarah, when
they met her, things she had said and done. June's stories of whispered secrets and knowing looks were just as romantic and intimate
as his. They took turns talking; they took turns crying, the other
standing guard, and ready in case Sarah should suddenly call out.

Mack watched the woman next door herding her children from
the beat-up old Dodge into the house. Each one carried a big plastic
bag from Wal-Mart. For the first time he noticed the swell of the
woman's abdomen under her loose shirt. He had never seen a man,
any man, anywhere near the house. If Sarah were observing it, she
would suggest that it's the second coming, that they could rent out
rooms to the wise men and shepherd, park the camels in the backyard. June would probably be amused in the same way, but instead he
kept the conversation where it was; he wanted to stay way back there
with the Sarah he never knew, the Sarah who had a future with him,
an unknown guy growing up two hundred miles away; the Sarah who
had a future. "I never saw Sarah in hair rollers!"

"Oh, God." June waved her hand, her nubby nails torn and bitten
raw. "She was the roller queen! It was like the height of what to do. I
haven't even seen these rollers in years, big hard pink plastic and you

had to use mega bobby pins to hold them in. What you did was this." She loosened her hair and then stood and bent over so that her long dark hair hung over her head and brushed the rough boards of the porch. She gathered her hair in one hand and then stood back up, a high ponytail like Pebbles Flintstone or somebody might wear up on top of her head. "Then you take this ponytail and split it into four equal parts and roll each part onto a great big pink roller."

"A reason?"

"It was easy to sleep in and it gave long, parted-down-the-middle hair that kind of poofy *That Girl* look." She let go of her hair, and it fell around her shoulders. "For girls with frizzy hair it straightened; for girls with thin hair, it gave body." She came and sat beside him on the steps. "Come to think of it, it was a perfect solution for all people! Why did we ever stop doing it?"

"Why did you?"

"The shag."

"The dance?"

"No, the *Do*, it was the style! The shag did it, and then of course there was that awful wedge, you know like Dorothy Hamill. The wedge was hell to grow out. You probably met Sarah when she had a wedge."

"Wedge or wedgie?"

"God, you're as bad as Sarah says!"

"Sarah says I'm bad?" he asked. It had been a long time since he had talked about her in the present tense and it felt wonderful. "What else has she said about me?"

"First of all, the way she says 'bad' really means good, you know that. And, everything else she ever said was really, really good." She paused. "She said you were perfect."

"Did she have any doubts about marrying me?"

"No."

"None?"

"No fair!" June forced a laugh. "You're trying to get top-secret information. Sarah would kill me!"

"So she did?"

"Did you?" June asked, and he shook his head. "Sarah married you because Sarah wanted to marry you. Sarah loved you." Again the past tense stopped them cold but they didn't go through the motions of changing it.

"So who did she go to the prom with?" he asked. "That TomCat guy?"

"Yeah, Tommy Lowe. Nice guy. He's still around here."

"Yeah, he brought some flowers one day. Stayed maybe three minutes." He watched the woman next door come out and clip the weeds around the Madonna. "He never really looked me in the eye, never sat down; he went and stood beside Sarah, tapped her on the shoulder and then left. It was like he had decided not to *really* look at her or something. He tiptoed like she was just asleep." He started to tell how the presence of the guy had made Mack feel like he didn't belong in his own house. How he had felt this history settle onto his chest like a rock. Now that she had lost so much weight and was so plain and washed out, she was probably much closer to being the girl that Tom Lowe had loved. And Mack was struck immediately by his own similarities to Tom Lowe. They were about the same height, of a similar build, straight dark hair and light eyes. It was the first time in his whole marriage that he had actually stopped and wondered if *he* was the substitute, and now there was no way to know. Unless June knew. It was not the kind of thing he could ask her. He couldn't bring himself to talk about any of it.

Now June was watching the woman next door. She leaned in close and began singing "Let It Be." She nudged him with her elbow. "Mother Mary comes to me . . . ," she was singing in his ear, her breath and laugh tickling his neck. It was exactly what Sarah would have done, and before he knew it, he had his arms wrapped around her and had pulled her close. Her hair smelled like Sarah, her clothes. If things were different, Sarah would be over in the swing singing along with her. June would talk about the old boyfriend or a recent date, and they would say things like, "Excluding present company, men are just that way. . . ."

She hugged him back, and that's when he realized things were different. There had been no local dates, no mention of any new prospects, like she used to run by Sarah. She had brought dinner by on several occasions. She called him at the end of the day to talk about her fifth-grade class and to ask why she hadn't gone to law school. She was trying to fill in his empty spaces, and she was relying on him to fill in hers.

"So, that old TomCat is good-looking, why don't you ask him out?" Reluctantly he pulled away so that he could look at her.

"Nah." She sat back, her hands folded in her lap. "TomCat is an old friend, you know? It would almost be incestuous." The woman next door had gone inside and two of the children were running around Mary. It looked like Mother Mary was their base in a game of tag. "It would be like being with you!" She nudged him again and laughed.

"So Sarah and TomCat were that close, huh?"

She shrugged. "They were close."

"Her parents didn't like him?"

"Oh, I'm sure they did," she said. "I mean you'd have to like him, you know? Sweet guy with a hard life."

"So what happened?"

"In his life?" she asked, and he shook his head. Sarah had told him

much of that story. More than he wanted, really. Who wants to feel
waves of pity for the competition?

"They just grew apart." She looked at him as if to say, *You know all
of this, this is old news*, but she quickly changed the tone. "And then
you happened, Mack McCallister. *You* happened."

NOW MACK FINDS himself thinking of June when he's lying in bed
and at odd times during the day. He sniffs his shirt for traces of her
cologne. He studies the bathroom after she's been there, a single long
coarse hair occasionally in the sink over which she has stood and
brushed. Now there are nights when he catches himself thinking of
her eyes, her hips, thin and boyish, and he feels guilty. But it feels so
good to picture her, feels so good to rewind and replay words
exchanged between the two of them. He tells himself that he will just
let it all go, that he'll call Sarah's mother and talk to her, cry to her,
that he will call his own mother, and then the phone will ring and he
can't get there fast enough, or like now he will pick up and dial her
number as quickly and easily as Sarah always has. When the machine
answers and beeps, he catches himself sighing and then delivers in
practiced monotone how he so occupied her time today that they
never got around to talking about Ted, and how if she still needed a
friend he was here, and he hoped that she knew that he would love to
hear all about that asshole Ted.

"Mack? Is that you?" She is all out of breath. "Hold on, I was just
bringing in the groceries." He tries to imagine June in her own world,
but it's now been over a year since he and Sarah were over there. It
was a place Sarah usually went to alone. If there was a double date,
they usually went out or came here to his and Sarah's house. "Hi."

"Hi."

"What's up? Is everything okay?"

"Yeah, the same. I just wanted to say that I wasn't a very good friend to you today and I'm sorry."

"But you were. Really."

Mack sits now with his hand covering Sarah's hand. The sitter's needlepoint is in the chair by the bed; Sarah's parents had hired her to be there while he's at work. They had known her for years. They wrote her check. They came and paid the sitter, just as they had done years before when Sarah was a child and they went out on Saturday nights.

"Please let her come home with us," Sarah's mother kept saying, and there were times like now—June inviting him over for dinner—that he wishes he could.

"Of course you can't," June says. "I'm so stupid."

"No, you're not."

"I'll bring dinner there, how about that?" she asks. "It's just pasta and some kind of sauce you know. Easy stuff and a salad."

"Are you sure?"

"Yes. Absolutely."

"Thanks." He hangs up the phone and comes back over to readjust the tape on the feeding tube entering her nostril, makes sure there are no kinks in the line. This is when he feels guilty. Times like this when what he really wants to do is step out into the night and into his car and go for a long drive. No planning, no scheduling. He gently rests his head on her chest and listens to the dull thud, wishing with all his might that something would happen, that someone or something would intervene.

*A*mazing how slow a satellite post office can get, even during the vacation season. Wallace Johnson suspects that it all has a lot to do with busy, busy lives and a lot to do with computers. About once a month, somebody will come bustling in, all wild-eyed with a sack of papers, looking over that small room for a fax machine. He tells them that all they have is a copying machine, which *used* to be what everybody in a hurry needed, and overnight mail, which may or may not really make it overnight depending on when you sign off. It's a very different speed people live in now, even when they're on vacation. As far as Wallace is concerned, that's their loss. He would just as soon read. The paper. The tide chart. The little descriptions of all the stamps issued: lighthouses, comedians, Elvis and Einstein. If you can name it, it's probably on a stamp. And when he's all alone, like now, he likes to read the letters.

APRIL 1973

Dear Wayward One,
My whole life I have studied architecture. Not anything formal of course, just shapes and angles, windows facing east like the old-timey

graves. Let me see the sun rise on Judgment Day. Oh God, what if there IS a judgment day? It's starting to worry me a little. You know now people don't seem to give a damn how they're buried—one on top of another, right side up. I guess I always liked the notion of those mausoleums, but that's just because my whole life I have had a romance with little houses—playhouses, dollhouses, little dioramas like folks used to make out of a shoebox, a little wax paper window at a far end. I once made the Sahara Desert and my teacher said it wasn't anything but a box of sand. She was not what I'd call a real imaginative sort. I like the notion of dark little houses, little windows and lifeless curtains. I see such houses and I think of all the folks who pass them by without a single notice, because of that exterior paint or maybe because it's, say, over a business establishment or something. Imagine then that what you can't see behind those tired dirty drapes is a love-filled life: maybe there's a mama and a daddy curled up in their bed, and they are happy just because they have each other. And in the next room their children sleep and dream of ways to make those parents glad that they gave them life, glad that they have to work so hard to keep them all moving and growing and going. They have a plan and a purpose. I felt that I had a plan way back, when I sat under my house. I still do, though certainly my plans have changed numerous times over the years. You see, I thought we were like that couple in my dream. I thought we were that secret secret love—something pure and perfect beating behind the most sordid of scenes, or what would look that way to anybody just passing by and giving that old beach house a once-over. What will always give me a start is how I drove off, imagining you with that pillow clutched to your chest, your strong tan leg thrown over the blanket where I had been lying just moments before. Remember how I told you I had the hot foot, had to sleep with my left foot out from under the covers. You laughed great big when I said that my mama had a hot foot, as well as her mama before her. You laughed like a man who might roll over and invite me for another romp, a man who might get up and have a sip of liquor and then write some words. You might put on one of your albums and croon along, slow dance. That was not the laugh of a man who would in less than fifteen minutes blow himself to kingdom come. I drove away through that old Green Swamp that night with my legs shaking, that good tired shaking, and my eyes peeled for headlights coming toward me. I was concerned about some fool drunk driver crossing the line; I was concerned about getting home and into the shower so that my husband would not trace you on me. He still looks at me sometimes, and it's a look that leaves me wondering if he knows everything there is to know about me or if he knows absolutely nothing. And now I think you must have looked at me and seen those same possibilities. You were always saying how we were soulmates and how I could read you better than you could read yourself, but no, honey, not then, not now. I pictured you with a sheet wrapped around your waist, a cigarette glowing in your hand as you watched my taillights get smaller and smaller. And an hour later when I was showered and fresh, when I had told my husband all about helping this poor old soul with a flat tire and waiting and waiting all night long for the man from the Esso station, when he had asked me just enough questions that seemed to satisfy truth, then we were the ones all curled up behind still drapes. I remember falling asleep that way, my husband's hand drawn close between my thighs where he said I felt like a furnace. And all the while I thought of you stretched out in those cotton sheets, your lids fluttering with thoughts, ever racing, ever producing those beautifully brilliant thoughts. What I heard the next day was that your brains were everywhere. What brilliance. What generosity. Brains all over this godforsaken world.

$\mathcal{T}$om turns from the window where he has watched Quee oversee the trash pickup, and he drives the final nail into the molding at the top of the closet space. Quee didn't want a door on the closet. Said she preferred the curtain look. She had supplied him with the curtain already on a heavy brass rod and asked that he hang it in place once the closet was finished. The curtain was green, velvet she'd bought from that crazy old junk man she supports. She told Tom when she saw it she knew it was perfect, kind of a *Gone with the Wind* look to welcome Mary Denise. He figures a *Gone with the Wind* look means that if this Mary Denise ever finds herself with nothing to wear she could snatch down the curtain over her closet and put it around her. He laughs a crooked laugh, the last nail in one corner of his mouth, because after what Quee told him about this chick, the possibility of her wearing no clothes was quite possible.

He hears the stairs creaking and the key turn. Impulse makes him pull the curtain closed, and then she is there, this vision. Quee had told him that as far as she could tell the girl was sort of a dingdong, but that the girl's mama had been like a sister to Quee when they were growing up, and that loyalties never died, real loyalties, that is.

Quee said that even if she was a dingdong, she was college-educated and quite attractive, just what she wanted for the in-house therapist of Smoke-Out Signals. Quee said just because she undressed in the movie theater was no reason to condemn her; it might (if the whole story was known) even be a source of admiration for her. She had taken her clothes off, which is exactly what she's doing now. Tom watches through the split in the velvet, the thick dusty odor of the fabric making him feel like sneezing.

She slides her jeans down her hips and over her thighs; there's the imprint of the seam of her pants in the soft white flesh of her leg. Her cotton underwear is ripped up one side; her legs are hairy, knees knobby. The small indentations on either side of the base of her spine are deepened by her swayback stance. She looks at herself in the mirror, sticks out her tongue and then goes over to sit on the edge of the ruffly bed. She lies back and crosses her legs, hands behind her head. "It might just work," she says and laughs. "It's no Taj Mahal, but I'm no Sheba either. I'm just free at last, free at last, so fucking free at last." She begins to unbutton her shirt. Tom tries to look at the floor, to count the nails he has spent the morning driving, but he finds his eyes drawn to her, the last thing he needs about now.

She goes back over to the mirror and grins at herself, inspects her straight white teeth. "Who the hell are you?" she asks, and his heart freezes in his chest; but she's talking to herself again. "The Cheshire cat? The Runaway Wife? The Feminine Pee-Wee?" She turns and inhales from an imaginary cigarette. "What a dump!" She parades, dances, shimmies in her ripped-up underwear for what seems an eternity. Who would think that you could get bored spying on a nice-looking, near-naked girl who talks to herself, but here he is. She opens her suitcase and pulls a red and black silky robe from it. It's that kind of robe that looks Oriental or something; it makes her look a little hookerish. She pulls her hair back in a ponytail, sits cross-legged on the bed and pulls a tape recorder from her bag.

"Testing, testing . . . yoo-hoo. I'm home! It's an okay room. Quee is what I expected, not as big as Mama had made her sound, but of course to Mama everybody is BIG."

She stretches out flat on her back, one foot propped up on the wall.

"And she doesn't look so whorish to me. I like her hair long like that. I'm going to let mine grow that long. Her clothes are kind of weird like Mama said, but all in all I'd much rather be wearing Quee's muumuu than Mama's girdle, or whatever it is she wears to keep her butt looking so small. I like a big butt, a butt that moves a little when it walks. I'm thinking I might grow mine a little bigger."

She stops the machine and laughs great big and then turns it back on. "Now as for business. I've got a plan as to how to divvy up the clients. There are the anals and there are the orals. The one and only client here—let's call him the guinea pig—is clearly an oral. He talks all the time and even makes his living at it and it's clear that he eats a lot, and from the looks of the red nose of his I'd venture to guess that he drinks a bit. Clearly he's oral, but the Spandex Poet who is checking in this very minute is an anal. You can tell by the way she's way too thin. Eating disorders and anal control impulses seem to go hand in hand. Now what I know from experience is that an oral personality out of control is really bad news. My personal little episode of late is proof of that, but, honey, the worst news you can ever find is an anal *in* control. Let's just say, for example, if your spouse is an anal type who gains control then sex is mechanical, food is measured to a T, pennies are pinched, and much time is spent on the toilet wrestling with all sorts of issues that life may present. You are likely to find magazine racks and little mini televisions in such a person's bathroom. You are likely to find things in the medicine chest alphabetized; there's probably one economy size of the drugstore brand floss. The utilitarian bathroom. You could live there. There are people I wish would. For business purposes, I will refer to the As and the Os. Look out at the world, and it's easy as pie to figure. Like look at that show *The Odd Couple*. Felix is an A and Oscar is an O. Elvis was a cross between the two, probably because he was a twin. Quee is clearly an O, and I think I am, too."

By the time she has gone through just about everybody who has ever been on television or in the movies (Bette Midler is oral and Nancy Reagan is anal), Tommy catches himself dozing against the wall. What wakes him up is the sound of his own name being called, and Blackbeard's bark from the truck. He jerks awake and peeps out in time to see this raging dingdong hide her tape recorder under the bed and pull a pair of jeans up under that skimpy robe.

"Tom? Where are you?" There is a knock on the door and Denny goes to open it. Quee pushes right in the room, looking all around. "Now where did that boy go?" she asks, and before Tom can think, she pulls back the curtain and there he is like the Wizard of Oz, hammer in hand, nails in his mouth. "I guess you two met, huh?"

"No, no." Tom pats his top shirt pocket that has nothing at all in it. "I was wearing my Walkman, didn't hear a thing." He steps out and extends his hand. "I'm so embarrassed," he says and the whole time this Denny is giving him the once-over. She stares hard at his shirt pocket.

"What were you listening to?" she asks and pulls that awful-looking robe closer around her body.

"You mean just now?" He holds his hand up to Denny to pause the conversation and turns to Quee. "Did you need me?"

"I just want to see you before you leave, that's all." Quee stands there looking back and forth between the two of them. She always makes Tom feel like he's under a microscope, like she's taking in every square inch of him. It used to make him nervous, but now he knows she's just trying to place him among all the teenage boys who used to come to her back door. "So when you're all done, come on back to the clinic. I'm thinking we'll need to add a little salon before too long, you know, maybe just a room all by itself for the pedicures and such; dim lights, piped-in music, the addict can drink a glass of wine while getting a full foot massage and pedicure, doesn't that sound good?"

"I reckon." Tom looks at Denny. "If you're into feet."

"Well I *am* into feet," Quee says and sticks one of hers out into the air, twists it all around. Her skin is white and freckled and her toe-nails are painted a deep maroon. "I wear a size ten, and I have since I was fourteen. I had to drive clean to Raleigh to find any kind of fancy shoes and it always made me feel so"—she pauses as if struggling to find just the right word—"*unique, privileged. . . .*" She grins great big at both of them, the kind of grin that is wise and well practiced— *fake* some might say—her thin eyebrow sharply raised. "Lonnie always said that there was nothing in this world sexier than a great big sturdy woman with extra-large feet."

"Really," Denny says, just as deadpan as you can get. She looks like she is trying not to laugh as she pulls the belt of her robe tighter.

"Not to say of course that someone of your average size can't *also* be sexy." Quee cups her hand under Denny's chin and turns her face from side to side, looks at Tom as if to solicit his opinion as well. "I think she's quite fine-looking, myself. I have always thought, since the day she was born, that she was an absolute beauty."

"Well, I wear a size eight."

"Good, good," Quee says. "That's a start. If you ever have children you'll probably make it into a nine. Just hold on to that thought; I believe in the power of positive thinking."

"Yeah, your foot looks about the same as mine." Tom sticks his brogan out beside Denny's foot, and though there is a considerable difference in size he continues. "I bet we could swap shoes sometime."

"Oh, yeah, right." She looks up and stares at him with narrowed green eyes. Her eyes are saying *go to hell*, but there's play around the mouth, the softness of the person comfortable enough to strip down and prance around in raggedy underwear. "I still want to know what you were listening to in there and where *is* your Walkman?"

"I've got to go help Ruthie shred her cancer sticks," Quee says and eases out the door. "She's getting hysterical, and it's only been five minutes since she put out what I like to call *the final request smoke*. She was eyeing the dash of your truck there, Tom, you must have a stash scattered around in there. You're next on my list, honey." She points her finger at him. "I need a lot of things done around here, and if you always come in smelling of smoke, the addicts'll be asking to suck your clothes."

"Suck my toes?"

"She said *clothes*." Denny slings back the velvet curtain and is running her hand up and over each and every shelf.

"Worse things could happen," he says and grins, and Quee just laughs a laugh that makes the room vibrate, calls him *so bad*.

"I'll get you, Tommy," she says. "I'm gonna use you as the supreme example of the miracle of my cures."

"I hear you."

"Make yourself at home, Denny love." Quee flashes that same grin, complete with the affected batting of her eyelids before closing the door.

"Yeah," Tom says, his arms opened wide to the small cluttered room. "Make yourself at home."

"You were spying on me," she says now. "There's no Walkman." She has collected a bundle of clothes and now is holding them in front of her.

"Look," he shakes his head and starts to walk toward her, but she takes two steps back. "I am curious about what you're wearing. Would you call *that* a muumuu?"

"No, Mr. Eavesdropper, I'd call it a *robe* if I were to call it anything for your benefit."

"Hmmm." He shrugs and goes to get his toolbox out of the closet. "Why did you ask to begin with?"

"I don't know, just never quite saw anything like it."

"So?" She grabs up a big hard red suitcase and slings it onto the low double bed. Just last week, Quee had had him hang a big pink velvet curtain behind the bed, with the idea that it would make the plain-as-a-jail-cell room look fancy. "I'm sure there's a lot that you've never seen."

"Seen more today than I cared to." He laughs and extends his hand. "I'm just kidding really."

"No, I don't think you are kidding. I think you're making fun of me." She turns, holding the red satin lapels of her robe. "I mean what's so different about *my* robe except that you happened to *spy*"— she spit the word and took a step closer—"and see what was *under* it."

"Forget I said anything, really." He goes over to the door feeling like he got the best of that one for sure, only to turn and see her with a look so forlorn he can't take it. She looks a hell of a lot like his latest adoption, an abused cocker spaniel who answers now to Mary Read. "Really."

"Oh, just go on." She waves her hand and sits on the edge of the bed, legs stretched and crossed at the ankles, as she stares up at the odd overhead fixture that Quee had him install several weeks ago. It looks like a big lavender tit with a crystal pastie, again, a little accessory that Quee thought would bring elegance to the room.

"See you around," he says, but she sits there, barely lowers her chin in response. Nothing pisses him off like this kind of silent, "pity me" reaction; he doesn't even know her, and he'd like to put his fist through the wall. He should leave, just walk out, but he has always had such a hard time doing that. As soon as he did, she'd probably go to the closet only to have it cave in on her, decapitate her. *Tom Lowe was the last one with her,* they'd say.

"Look, what can I do?" He puts down his toolbox and takes one step back in the room.

"It's not you. It has nothing to do with you." She turns then with dry eyes and a whole new look about her. "I mean, yes, I wish you'd said you were in there looking at me without my clothes on, but you didn't." He wants to interject, to make a connection, to say that maybe this is reminding her of her little episode in the theater, but he thinks better of it and just stands there. "I mean it's not like you really *saw* me."

"No." He shakes his head and laughs, a full image of her body—the narrow shoulders and waist channeling into an ample rear—is firm in his memory. Before she even has time to question his laugh, he turns with Blackbeard's bark to look out the window where Ruthie, decked out in paisley spandex pants, is circling his truck. "Oh, you've got to see this," he says. Denny comes over there beside him, her robe still pulled tightly around her. He feels strange standing this close to a stranger, so close that he can smell the lemon scent of her hair, can see the pale blue vein in her right cheek.

"The Spandex Poet?" Denny presses her forehead against the glass just as Quee comes out into the front yard, waving her arms as if herding a flock of something wild.

"I mean it, Ruthie, I'm not having this shit," Quee says and grabs the woman's toothpick arm. "You are an addict. If you want to quit smoking, then you can quit smoking." Quee gives her another shake, and Ruthie starts sobbing. She flails her paisley legs and wails like a cat in heat. "I can help you, I can cure you." Quee practically lifts her up by the elbows, her arms folded in like she's in a straitjacket, her legs pedaling like she's on a bicycle. "I can beat your skinny ass if necessary."

"Man, she's crazy as hell," Denny says and backs away so that her breath on the glass won't interrupt the view.

"You got that right." Tom taps her on the arm, leans in close enough to whisper in her ear. "And you're her doctor."

"What will I do with her?"

"I think that everybody in this town has asked that question at least once."

"Really?"

"Really." He waits for her to say something else but there's just an uncomfortable silence. "Well, see you."

"In the clinic?" she asks and follows him to the door.

"Don't count on it." He's all set to go, but he finds himself taking the time to check her out from head to toe, the thick frizzy hair yanked back with a big yellow hair thing, those green cat eyes, the smooth near-flatness of her chest, no cleavage whatsoever as she pulls her robe tighter.

"What are you looking at?" she asks now, and in the background, from the other end of the house they can hear Ruthie's dramatic swearing to quit smoking, with Quee egging her on every step of the way.

"Something behind that preposition."

"Oh, smart. You're so smart."

"Yes, I am. Very smart."

"And that's why you're hanging curtains in a two-bit hodgepodge clinic." She twisted her shoulders as she spoke, a gesture he remembered girls doing in grade school; it was the physical movement that went along with nanny-nanny-boo-boo.

"Yes, the very clinic where you are the resident shrink, if I understand right." He stepped back into the room and closed the door. "Are we talking quality? Do you really want to?" He stares up at that lavender tit with the crystal pastie and catches himself picturing such adornments fastened to her. "Because you know I grew up here, my mom is here."

"So?"

"So, I didn't *choose* it. I'm part of it." He pats his chest. "You *chose* it."

"Well if you were any *good* at what you do then you would have had opportunity to leave." He laughs, waits to see if it occurs to her what she's just said.

"Oh, I'm good." He grins. "Anyone will tell you that."

Queen Mary Stutts was born in Fulton in 1925, the same year that her father, Seymore Stutts, an employer of the local ice plant, left home. She had never even seen a picture of the man, though people said she looked a lot like him, that she got his big bones, Greek complexion, and wiry black hair. Her mother refused to talk about him, saying only that he had taken shape and then dissolved, much like the blocks of ice he heaved and chipped with his cold metal hook. They were once told there was a woman in the next town, a married woman he ran off with, but the story stopped there. Her mother married Mr. Bradley when Quee was thirteen, and he was never like a daddy at all, more like an uncle or a neighbor. It was right after her mother married him that he took Quee (then Mary) to see the ocean for the very first time.

By the time she was fifteen, she had begun to call herself "Quee," much to her mother's dislike, and was anxious to go ahead and get married so she could get Stutts out of her name and move on to something new. The man she found was quite a bit older, Lonnie Purdy, the new church officer (an accountant by profession), who was known for his singing and his ability to speak Hebrew. Quee would whisper in his ear, beg him to speak some Hebrew to her. She said the word, stretching the last syllable so it sounded dirty. She had her mind on that name, Purdy, which she fully intended to have and one day change to pronounce as Pur-day, like a French name: Quee Purdé. Lonnie didn't get it, but he never had gotten anything, *nothing*, and when Quee pulled him down into the church basement on the pretense of finding some extra hymnals, when she pressed up against him in the dark musty closet, velvet costumes from some kind of pageant, her breath tinged with the licorice she was forever chewing (she liked to braid the strips and tie them around her neck like a choker), he started to catch on. She felt her way down his thigh, the crease in his pants so sharp it made her laugh to think of him or some old woman over at his boardinghouse spitting on an iron and pinching the fabric up that way. She reached for him, palm spread and pressed down in circular strokes. Behind her she could hear people coming down the stairs, everybody getting ready for Snak and Yak, stale sandwiches and room-temperature milk. "Let's have our own Snak and Yak," she whispered, his face as smooth as a baby, his starched pants stretching at the seams. "Church man, minister to me, oh save me, save me." She giggled and peeked out into the darkened basement.

"What has come over you, Quee?" he was asking. "What is it you need?"

"You don't get out much, do you?" She undid his belt buckle and slowly teased with his zipper. "Let's get you out for a spell." He closed his eyes at her touch, pretending like maybe nothing was happening. "Now talk some Hebrew or Greek," she said coaxingly. "Come on, now. Everybody's always bragging on you, I just want to hear it for myself."

"Quee, why me? What are you thinking?"

"I'm thinking I want to marry you. I want to get my naked body right beside you. I want to," she leaned into his neck and whispered. He strained to hear her every word and then turned suddenly and pulled her to the back of the closet where they stretched out on the cold hard floor. He moved on top of her, his hard shiny shoes tapping out a beat on the wall where there was a stack of tin basins and towels that had recently been discarded when the church women decided that their Wednesday night footwashings were archaic and should be replaced with a potluck dinner instead. Quee had once taken her mama's dark gray stockings and rubbed them in the fireplace soot so that when her mama got to church and rolled off the hose her feet were filthy. She was thinking about that, her mama coming home in a wave of fury with black splotches all up and down her white skinny legs, when Lonnie's breath became shallow and whimpery like a puppy. She felt his total weight on her then, and it felt good, like a flesh-and-bone blanket, a body of substance. "What have I done?" he asked after a few minutes. They were both suddenly aware of voices and lights in the basement, the women—her mama one of them— slapping those old stale sandwiches together.

"Looks to me like you might've proposed." Quee pulled out from under him and adjusted the waistband of her skirt. She pulled a piece of licorice from around her throat and popped it in her mouth. "I guess I'll give you an answer later on. And," she lowered her voice as if to issue a threat, teeth clenched. "I want to hear some of that Hebrew people have been bragging on you about."

Years later, she teased him about the look of horror on his face. She teased him about his modesty and the way that he would carefully remove and roll his socks, fold and tuck his briefs under his undershirt. One year of marriage and she talked him into leaving his post at the church and taking what she called "a job with a future," a job at the First Southern Savings and Loan. "People trust you," she told him. "People think you know some superior things."

"Speaking of which," he said. "How do you know all that you know?" It was a question he had asked often. "How did you know so much way back in the church basement?"

"I read a lot," she said. "And aren't you glad I do?"

Those years with Lonnie were some of the best, and even though the spark between them flared and sputtered off and on (at least as far as she was concerned), she could never have found a nicer person to set up shop with. He knew there had been other men, and he knew there would be after him. He knew that he had always been her sturdy stake in the yard, a father and a brother and a friend, a mouthpiece for the divine to get people off of her back. There were all kinds of rumors about her and what she did. People said she was a witch. People said she was a whore. Even now that she is known as a fully licensed massage therapist, people are still suspicious. The local chiropractor feels she's treading on his turf, and people around still seem to think that "massage" is a buzzword for blow job. She told a group of busybodies not three days ago that she was not in the business of giving lip service (Do you get it? Lip service? They were all in the checkout of the Winn-Dixie) to anybody. She said if somebody came to her looking for a blow job that she'd tell him to go straight to hell. She is a busy, busy woman, a business woman on the threshhold of a huge venture, and she didn't have time to help their tired old men get their rocks off.

"She's as wicked as ever," they said. "I don't know how she ever got such a nice man as Lonnie Purdy, rest in peace, to marry her."

"I am sixty-nine years old, ladies, and I was the best thing to ever happen to Lonnie Purdy." Quee held her arms out to the side, an avocado in each hand, and turned. "I look fifty-two. Your husbands like to look at me or *did* when they were alive. They always did. Those still breathing like to stop off at the shop and talk, get a massage or psychofoot therapy, which is something I invented myself after being inspired by the book *Feet First,* which was written by Laura Norman, the cousin of one of my dearest friends. I am a great reader, ladies; I'm a philosopher and I'm an inventor and now I'm curing the smokers. The people are coming in from near and far. I've had to hire a helper, that's how many reservations I'm getting. So . . ." She put her avocados on the conveyer belt along with a cartful of produce and several bottles of wine. "So, if any of your men take on a lean and hungry look, well you just better think long and hard about offering him a little massage yourself." She pulled her sunglasses down and watched while the fruit and vegetables tumbled down the belt. "You know I did once know a whore," she told them. "She taught me a lot of things, but none of what you're thinking. She had a big blank wall behind her dirty rumpled bed, and she'd reach up and make a little mark every time she screwed somebody. It was her tally card. She was a business woman, and she was proud of it." She started to tell them the whole truth that this woman who had taught her so much was none other than her own alter ego, fantasy self, but she didn't. It was enough that she had shocked them, enough that she had left them feeling dowdy and old, pinched in their little stiff clothes, their faces pasty with makeup, their hair lacquered in place.

"You'll get arrested one day," one of them said.

"For what, sugar? Servicing the underprivileged, or killing somebody I don't like?"

$\mathcal{M}$ack knew all about TomCat Lowe, or at least all that Sarah was willing to tell him. Maybe she told him all that there was, and yet still it always felt that there was something left out. Tom Lowe was the person who would haunt Mack's marriage. Mack had even considered turning down his father-in-law's job proposal just because the mysterious Tommy Lowe lived in the same town.

What he knew was that Sarah had slept with him, that she got pregnant when she was a senior in high school. She never would have told Mack that, he was sure, except that it was her bit of proof that she *could* get pregnant. For some reason, she seemed never to have thought about how this might make him feel; she had so taken the responsibility onto her own shoulders that she had never even considered that Mack might be the problem. She clung to the doctor's notion that she needed to calm down, relax, be patient. That's when she talked of the irony of it all; she told Mack how scared she had been when she realized she was pregnant. For hours she had sat perched there on the white canopy bed that is still in her room at her parents' home. A yellow-and-white panda bear won by Tom Lowe with skeeball tickets at the Ocean Drive pavilion is still on the window seat. She said that Tom took care of everything, that he promised her that no one would ever know. She trusted him completely, even after she was off at school and things didn't work out between them.

Then she met Mack. They were introduced to each other by Jones Jameson, a fraternity brother of Mack's. They had dated for a whole semester before they both admitted that they hated Jones Jameson (in college he had given himself the nickname *Moby*) and hadn't said anything because each had assumed the other was his friend. He was the kind who made it sound like everyone *was* his friend, which is exactly how he had always managed to come out on top, whether it was cheating on a college exam or being "the cool" disc jockey in a very small town. He did it as soon as Mack got to town, slapped him on the back with his *old buddy* talk only to ask five minutes later for a little *free* legal advice. The one bit of knowledge that keeps him from hating Tom Lowe is the story Sarah told about Tom Lowe beating the shit out of Jones Jameson in the eighth grade and again in the ninth. The current rumor in town is that Jones Jameson has left his wife, disappeared; the response that first comes to mind is *Good riddance to bad rubbish* and all those other little sayings that June has recently brought back into his life, compliments of the elementary school where she teaches.

Once when June was over visiting (they had just bought the house), she and Sarah were in the kitchen unpacking and listening to Jones Jameson on the radio; he was making reference to the nickname his frat brothers had given him and asking his listeners in between raucous hyena-like laughs if they could *fathom* (every day he seemed to have a new word that he used over and over: fathom, postulate, tantamount) how he got that name.

"Does he love Herman Melville?" June asked in elementary-schoolteacher pitch. "No, no, I think not. I'd guess, I'd *fathom* that perhaps he had a cucumber taped to his thigh."

"Except . . . ," Sarah turned from where she was standing on a chair and laughed.

"Except I've seen it," June screamed. "And so have you Polly Pureheart!"

"What's this?" Mack asked. "You saw Jones Jameson?"

"Oops." June acted like she was about to tiptoe from the room and then thought better of it. "Nah, streaking, remember? We saw everybody in high school, because all the guys liked to streak."

"I see."

"That's right," Sarah said, her face flushed with laughter. When he left the room, he could hear the two of them in there in hysterics.

"His poor wife," June said. "Imagine being married to that dick."

"Yes, a dick with eyes."

"A dick in loafers!"

"A dick in madras shorts and an Izod shirt."

"He did introduce us." Mack leaned into the room where the two were sprawled out on the kitchen floor, half-empty boxes and shredded newspapers all around them. "You look like a couple of crazed hamsters." This made them laugh harder. When he went back down the hall to the living room, they were still at it.

"A dick with an introduction!"

"Hi there, out there in radioland," Sarah was saying in a deep sultry voice. "I'm a dick."

"I'm a big dick."

"In loafers."

"Penny loafers."

"Bass Weejuns."

"Cordovan Bass Weejuns."

"Remember when everybody wanted palomino-colored loafers?"

"Ninth grade," June said. "I asked for a palomino horse, and my mother got me palomino loafers and a poncho."

That night the three of them had swapped Jones Jameson stories. It became a contest to think of the worst thing he had done. He was one of those awful people who, for some reason, certain women wanted to save. He was the kind of guy who would whistle at passing coeds and, if they dared look back, would wave his hand and say, "Hell, not you! Who would want you?" Everybody thought he was destined to marry one of the wealthy sorority types who would support him and his habits, but he never made it. He ended up with a quiet, average-looking social worker, who Sarah and June figured was either some really hot somebody in the bedroom or was simply an abused wife. As rumors circulated over time, it was clear that she was just a nice ordinary person who had made a horrible mistake. He made no bones about his activities and routine conquests. He liked to go to Myrtle Beach or over to Fort Bragg for a good time.

June told how once he invited a girl from one of the county schools to meet him at the movies. When she showed, he was waiting there, and he also had every boy in the junior high school lined up at the back of the theater, waiting for him to saunter up midway into the movie with a pair of white cotton underwear wadded up in his waving hand. "Come one, come all," he was calling. "Tour the Grand Canyon. Let your fingers do the walking." June was there with her big sister. She saw the girl whose name she couldn't even recall, Mary Laura or Marie Lynn, sit there until the movie was over; she sat frozen and staring straight ahead at where Mary Tyler Moore was having to decide between life with Elvis, the handsome inner-city doctor, or the convent. "She probably never got over it," June said. "He wore the underwear on his head to make all of those boys laugh."

Mack decided not to tell his worst story, simply told them that Jones had continued to do the same kinds of things all through college. He picked up women, got what he could, and then left them in the most humiliating way possible. Mack had, more than once, been the recipient of these stories, witnessed the evidence. He could see Jones pulling a pair of pink nylon panties from the pocket of his jeans and spreading it out on the table like a cat might lay out a half-eaten rodent. "Got some," he whispered. Then he reached into his other pocket and pulled out a flesh-colored elastic bra. Within minutes he had reached under his shirt and brought forth the girl's shirt, all neatly rolled up. By then he had identified her as that stacked nigger who was always at Happy Hour. "Left the jeans in the car," he said. "Left her with her shoes." He patted his chest and looked around the table. "Hey, I'm a nice guy. I said, Don't forget your goddamned shoes, honey."

"What?" There was nervous laughter around the table while Jones told again and again about how easy it was to get a little these days.

"You should have seen those great big white eyes," he said. "She looked just like what's his name? Buckwheat. That's what I was thinking, fucking Buckwheat."

All but a couple of the rowdiest guys were sitting solemnly, unsure of what to say or do beyond a nervous laugh. "I said, Oh honeychile, I really want to make it good; let's get out on the ground where we've got lots of room to play." He had to stop and laugh, all the while shaking his head as if in disbelief of what he kept calling her *ignorance*. "You should have seen her all stretched out on that blanket ready and waiting, and I was so drunk, you know, I thought I might fuck her, but then I thought wait, wait, wait, some nice girl who wants to marry me someday, you know how they are, is going to ask me if I

ever slept with a nigger, and there I'd be having to tell her the truth."
He laughed like a maniac, eyes glassy. "Is that classic or what?"

"You left her?"

"Yeah. You should have seen her hop up when she heard the
motor! She took off running behind the car like a goddamned dog."

For years Mack has thought of that girl out there making her way
from tree to bush. He thinks of the county girl in the movies. It could
have just as easily been Sarah or June; *You gotta meet this cute little piece
from my hometown,* he had said to Mack and pointed across the room
where Sarah was standing. For years Mack has wanted to find Jones
Jameson all alone someplace where he could walk up and confront
him, walk up and say what a lousy son of a bitch he is. Mack wishes
he were the one who at some time in the past had stood up to Jones
Jameson, beat the shit out of him.

Jones was at their wedding. He was IN their wedding, for christ-
sakes. If they had gotten married in any other town, there's no way he
would have even been *asked* to the wedding, but things being what
they were (Sarah's parents socialize with his parents), their hands
were tied, or so they were told and then weakly obliged in the midst
of all the other ridiculous decisions that had to be made, like what
color cummerbund Mack and his dad should wear. Sarah had also
invited Tom Lowe to the wedding, certain, she told Mack again and
again, that he would never come in a million years. "He hates things
like church services," she said. "But I really do need to ask him. I'd
feel really bad if I didn't."

Mack hoped she was right, that Tom Lowe would not show up. He
imagined a scene right out of *The Graduate*, Tom Lowe in the balcony
of the Presbyterian Church screaming "Sarah, Sarah," and her turning
and running to him, fleeing the church, barring the door.

He later discovered, on an afternoon when she was very quiet for no apparent reason, that Tom Lowe had not been there, that she had looked for him as soon as she and her father stepped into the aisle. It turned out that there was a reason she had gotten quiet. She had been unpacking and had found all of the letters he sent her when she first went off to college. She read one aloud to Mack, one where this Tom-Cat had written that he felt things had really changed between them. "The last time I visited you," he wrote, "I felt so out of place. It has nothing to do with that fraternity boy way of dressing, like you worried it did. Hell, if it was that easy, I'd buy a dozen Izod shirts and I'd stop wearing socks. I just felt so out of place, Sarah, you know? I was a fish out of water and I couldn't drive fast enough to get myself back where I belong. I said that the University was too far inland and of course that was a joke. But it is true that I feel better here at home where I do have the ocean and where I do feel like I know who I am. Being able to swim the fastest against the river current or swing the farthest from that old rope we used to all mess around with doesn't count for much up there. Guys like Jones for example. Around here people kind of knew he was a jerk. Around there he is really somebody. All of a sudden WHO you are ain't about being who you are. I hope you understand. It's not easy for me, either. Love, Tommy." She had read the lines slower and slower, voice a little shaky at the end. She took a deep breath, gave Mack a half smile. "PS, if you ever find yourself back in Fulton, I know you'll find me. I'll be the king of the hill at low tide. I'll forever be your TomCat." With this she shook her head, her face all twisted in an effort not to cry.

"I'm sorry, Mack," she said and came and buried her face in his chest. He stood, his arms by his side. He felt unable to touch or hold her. "Really, honey." She pulled his arms around her. "That's not really why I'm crying." She shook her head, and he knew again that they had

had false hopes, a late period, so late this time that she had actually come home with a tiny little cotton sleeper and a pair of socks. "Bad luck, bad luck," her mother had said the last time, when Sarah bought a blanket and silver rattle, so she only showed Mack—and, he suspected, June—before hiding the belongings on the top shelf of what would someday be the nursery.

Then he hugged her close, whispered that it would all be okay, and yet he still couldn't shake the thoughts of Tom Lowe. She probably often thought about what her life would have been if she had had Tom Lowe's baby and stayed in this town with him. Would she have been happy upholstering furniture or whatever it is he does for a living? Would they be one of those couples going to the all-you-can-eat salad bar at Denny's on Saturday night? Would she be happier that way? Even then, he began to think of her driving across town one day in search of him. It would be easy for her to find him, easy for them to pick back up where they left off. If they lived here forever such a meeting *had* to happen; he almost caught himself wishing that it *would* so that they could talk about it once and for all.

June had come over that same afternoon, and Sarah showed her the letter, then told her that she wasn't pregnant.

"Oh, Sarah," June said and shook her head. Her eyes were as dark as Sarah's were light. They called themselves the image sisters—one the negative of the other. "I'm sorry."

Mack stood by and listened, sensing that June's apology was for far more than a period. Even now he finds himself wanting to ask June, but he isn't sure how he would go about saying it. "Did Sarah still love Tom Lowe? Did she see him when we moved back? If this hadn't happened to her, would there have come a day when she packed a bag and left me?"

Dear Wayward One,

Remember how I told you that I used to climb up under the house and stay there for the afternoon like I might be some old stray cat? Well, what I didn't tell you maybe is how scared I felt many of those times. I would sit there and watch the light shift to the late afternoon while I dozed in and out in almost a dreamy way, my feet coated in the cool black dirt there. I can close my eyes right now and feel that buzzy cotton-headed kind of way, can smell the rust of our old pipes mixing with the scent of gardenia. My mother loved gardenias and when they bloomed in early summer, she had them all over our house, single blossoms floating in little silver bowls. I love the late afternoon light, the slant, the color, but for some reason it makes me feel so sad and lonely I could just curl up in a dark corner and cry. When I heard the news about you it was like I'd been waiting my whole life for a reason to feel the way I do. I have always felt a sadness deep within, an anchor that never allowed me to float too far. Even before I was ever really happy, I was afraid of losing happiness. I don't know how a person comes to feel so undeserving while at the same time feeling powerful, like she could beat up the whole damn world, but that's me. *The floors would creak over my head, footsteps walking around in a different world as far as I was concerned. My world was that other one; the one there under the house, the feelings I didn't have names for. What I did have was long, scratched-up legs and a broad freckled face. I had shoulders on me that would have put any old boy out on a field trying to play football to shame. Just yesterday my husband handed me a news clipping all about these little girls that are taking to the fields with their baseballs and footballs. I envy them even right this second because I think of how good it must be to be* told *to knock the hell out of something or someone, how good it must be to take off and start running, and then keep running, keep going till you have sweated away whatever anger and bitterness had found its way up and into your skin. Oh I can do a little workout, ride a bike machine or something but I'm too old by now to get it all out of my skin. It's like poison, those old sad feelings, and by now I guess I'm addicted to them. By now I guess I'm just the way that I'll always be. And isn't it strange—other than your bed, the place I most often wish myself is under the house with the cool darkness, the rich-smelling earth. Sometimes I picture you sitting there under my house instead of where you really are. You reach inside the little houses I have built by mounding the rich dirt over my foot, packing it tightly and then easing my foot out to leave a cave. From each you pull a prize: colored glass, cat-eye marble, ball of twine, some money I lifted from a big man's pocket when he told me to reach in and see what I might find. People are so stupid about what children do and do not know. You know that firsthand, don't you? You told me once that you feared your son was like a piece of sponge thirsty for anything you might have to offer. I see him around town from time to time and I'd say that somebody has offered him some goodness. He looks fine but of course you can't always go on that.*

My mother once said to me, "Don't we have a good life, darling?"
and she smoothed my hair back with her hand. "My but you feel so cool,"
she said, "like someone from a grave." By then I had washed my feet
under the old pump at the far end of our yard and she had no idea that
I had spent my whole day right under her very feet. I think of that all
the time lately. I hear my mother's voice saying like someone from a
grave *and I begin to think that maybe there has always been a part of*
me that was *dead, or a part getting ready to be dead. Those words come*
to me most often now at the end of the day, my favorite time of day.
Remember when we used to sit out on that old rickety porch sipping our
beers and watching the ocean? We might watch for hours, seeing the tide
all the way in, watching the sticks you had staked into the sand as
markers. The world would spin us right out into darkness and then it
was so hard to turn on the sobering lights, so hard to face the dirty
shrimp pot, pink foam crusted on its edge, and the dirty plates, empty
cans. All in the flip of a switch the dream ended. Wake-up call. I heard
it just hours ago when my husband came in from work and found me out
on the back stoop staring off into the pine trees that hide us from the
highway. And now he's waiting for me, there in the light of our bedroom
and here I am writing this letter. I thought I could stop doing it. I
planned to stop, but today is an anniversary. It's my birthday and I'm
just now starting to wonder how many more are ahead of me. Do I want
them? Sometimes, like right now at the end of a long hard day, I have
great doubts; but then by morning the doubts have retreated and I'm
feeling hopeful again, looking for a mission, a cause. These letters are
just another distraction, just another secret; most of my life is, you
know.

*M*ack has just gone out on the porch to wait when June drives up, her front wheel scraping the curb and horn blasting three short notes, which brings two of the guys from next door out in the yard to see what has happened.

"Mack! Mack!" She slams her door and comes up the sidewalk all out of breath. "That rumor is true. Jones Jameson *has* disappeared. Over four days and nobody has seen him. They have a bulletin on the radio!"

"Good!" Mack says, and then they both laugh. "He probably screwed some old lady, stole all of her money, and is now a gigolo in the Bahamas."

"Maybe some husband from out in the county caught old Moby in his bed and put a bullet through him." She hands Mack a bottle of wine and goes to put her bag of groceries in the kitchen.

"Keep a pleasant thought." Mack smiles and then leads her down the hall to Sarah's bed where they both fall silent; June smooths Sarah's hair, presses a cool cloth to her dry lips. He watches and then wanders out on the porch into the fresh air. Sarah is there, on the other side of the window. Sometimes when he is out here, the wall between them, he can almost forget.

"I hope Sarah *can* hear us," June says, startling him.

"What?" Mack turns sharply from watching the sunset, a clear perfect pink and orange sky.

"Jones!" June takes a long sip of her wine and sits down on the step beside him. They always end up here, on the steps, as if the swing, the rockers are too close to the house, too close to the open window. "I told Sarah that this is just what we've waited for since junior high, that maybe somebody has left *him* out in the woods without *his* clothes."

"What?"

"You know what he did in college." June nudges him now, a little too hard. "God, everybody heard that sick story. He told it a zillion times. I'm surprised he didn't take out an ad in the newspaper."

"You knew?" He watches her face to see if they're talking about the same thing. "About the black girl."

"Yes. And the white girl, and the red girl and the pink and green girl. It just so happens that the black girl has a name: Karen. Karen Stallings. She lived in my dorm freshman year. She trusted him because he told her what great friends of his Sarah and I were."

"Sarah knew?"

"Of course Sarah knew." June reaches for the wine bottle and refills her glass. "As a matter of fact," she gets up and goes and stands right in front of Sarah's window, leans against the ledge as if she is speaking for both of them, together, united. "That's why Sarah finally asked you point-blank what you thought of Jones, remember?" June takes a big drink. "It was a test."

"A test?"

"Yes. If you had said that you really liked Jones, that you thought he was a great guy, then she was going to break up with you."

"That easily? She was just going to break up that easily? I could have broken up with her for the same thing."

"But you didn't." June takes the rocker closest to the window and sits. There is a tension between them that he hasn't felt before, and he's not sure why. "And you never even tried to find out what she thought. You're one of those people who waits to see what someone else will say first."

"Such as?"

"Such as . . ." She waves her free hand out to the side. "Such as you always wait for me to say how I miss her. You always wait for me to wonder what she's thinking, if she's thinking."

"Like I don't?" He needs to stand up, to pace. "She's my wife, June. I do think about things. Nobody told me that I had to run it all by you." He goes and opens the screen door, the hinges whining in one long pitch. "I don't know what's happened to you all of a sudden, but I'm sorry. I'm really sorry if I did it." He goes in and lets the door slam, turns down the hall and stands in the doorway to their room; he is shocked by Sarah's thin silent presence, as if he's seeing her for the first time. The room is almost dark now and the glow of the circular nightlights light up the baseboards that Sarah had scrubbed with Spic & Span the last day. The lights are hazy in his vision, blurry, like underwater lights in a pool. He would love nothing better than for her to open her eyes now, as if on command, and call him to her. She would lift her head, turning toward the window, and she would say, "June? June, come on and make up now," as if they were children, the way she had done the time Mack got mad at June for knowing about the miscarriage before he did. Does she hear him? Does she see him here in the doorway? Is she locked there and waiting, forced to watch life as it continues to happen without her, or is she really gone?

"Mack?"

The whisper startles him and he rushes forward to the bed, leans close so that he can see her face, feel her breath, warm stale breath. He is about to call her name, scream her name when he realizes his error. It is June, there on the other side of the window whispering. He backs away from the bed, back to where he had been by the door. He pretends not to hear her, even when he hears her rocker tip against the wall, hears the door open and close, feels her hand on his back.

"Mack, I'm sorry."

He nods, refusing to look at her.

"Sometimes I just feel so lost, so lonely," she whispers, her hand still lightly circling his back. "And then I feel angry, and I don't know why. I'm sad and I'm furious. Like what Sarah and I would call 'on the rag.' 'PMS City.' Like I could squeeze the life out of somebody, kick a dog, curse a nun."

"Curse a nun?" he turns now, forcing the bemused look that would have accompanied that question, the question Sarah surely would have asked in all of that. "You don't even know a nun."

"That's very good," she says and nods over at Sarah. "You gave the perfect answer. You win the prize." She is avoiding his eyes, staring into his neck, her eyes watering, voice hoarse. Sarah once told him how when she and June were dancers in a local little theater version of *Oklahoma*, they were told to look adoringly into their dance partners' (old square-dancing men from the next town) faces, and June told her partner that she would have to look adoringly at his chin, that there was no other way she could do it.

"Are you looking adoringly at my chin?" he asks now and she steps forward, wraps her arms around him and squeezes. He can feel her shaking with stifled cries. He holds her, waits, his own hand now circling her back, combing through her hair. He turns his head so that his mouth is near her ear, those huge earrings she wears (the ones Sarah teased her about saying they were cheap and gaudy) getting in his way. "And what is the prize?" he whispers. It's like that game he remembers playing as a child: freeze, unfreeze. He waits, not wanting to turn and look at Sarah, not wanting to turn and look at June. And in the wait he feels her press a little closer than before; he feels her breath on his cheek. "I wish," she whispers, or it seems like she whispers. *I wish.*

"What? Tell me," he breathes back but the only response is that again she presses closer, and for a minute he almost forgets where he is, his hands squeezing and rubbing her waist, his heart skipping beats like a worn-out record.

"I wish I could, Mack. God, I wish I could."

esting . . . yoo-hoo. Day one has almost come to a close, and now I'm all locked up in this room that makes me feel like I ought to be in a brothel, all these velvet drapes and spangly light fixtures. It's what you might call faux whorehouse. I mean, when you get right down to it, a really serious whore would need a better bed than the one I'm sitting on. I think it must've been left out in the rain a few times; it slopes off to one side and squeaks if you breathe. Anyway, I checked to make sure that Quee hadn't left a nugget (pecan, peach pit, golfball) of some sort or another under *my* mattress like she did Ruthie Crow's. She told me that she had always done that her whole life, at least since she read "The Princess and the Pea"; she said most people never notice that it's there, which makes her able to honestly say that fairy tales *do* come true.

"It's just something I do, honey," she said and laughed. She has a way of saying "honey" that makes you feel like she's up to something. "Let's just call it a hobby. I am a woman of many hobbies."

"Better peas and nuts under mattresses than a cage full of children you're planning to eat, or spindles for people to prick their fingers on, I guess."

"Right, right," she said, tapping her pen on the table where she was writing out a chart of when I would hold my sessions. I might as well have been invisible. She might *have* a cage full of children, who knows? I know nothing about this place except that Gerald would be sneezing his fool head off with all the dust motes and balls and bunnies to be found. Right now I am feeling a teeny bit shaky, like I'm wondering exactly what it is I *am* doing. And that guy, Tom, who was here making my closet. Well, I try, but I can't seem to stop thinking of him; I mean, who could forget after what I went through in this very room? I can close my eyes and smell exactly how he smelled standing there next to me. His skin smelled hot, but in a good way, a *clean* suntan lotion kind of way that I found almost as exciting as William Hurt all perspired and listening to those wind chimes. And he's got a wonderful face, tan and smooth. He's taller than you might think if you saw him sitting down somewhere. He's lean but sturdy-looking, and he could not take his eyes off of my robe. I finally said, "So fill your eyes full, and then fill your pockets!"

"Sorry." He was about to leave for the second time (the first time he was telling me how *good* he is at what he does, like I might be fool enough to bite *that* hook), and it was odd but (like that first time) I didn't want him to.

"It's okay," I said. "Just tell me what it is, like am I green or something? Do I smell bad? Or is it that you can't take your eyes off of me?"

"The last one."

"Really?" I was believing him, and then he seemed to want to laugh. "What?" I said, "Come on, I need a good laugh. Really. I can take it. Hell, I just left a husband. Five years of my life sucked right down the tubes."

"It's nothing." He was acting like he wanted to leave, but I knew better, so I grabbed him by the shirtsleeve and pulled him back in. I closed the door.

"Was there ever a Walkman?"

"No."

"So you heard what all I said?"

"Yes." He looked me square in the eye as he said all of this, and I felt myself start to perspire.

"And you saw me in my underwear?"

"Yes." He tried to step away but I blocked the door. "But I tried not to stare."

"Why?" I tell this all on tape as an exercise to understand exactly what it was *I* was thinking. "You didn't want to see me?"

"I don't think there's a right answer to this."

Quee had talked this guy up from the moment I arrived. She had said how handsome and smart and what a sweet boy. She had said that she had wished for the longest time that he would get together with her assistant, Alicia, who, to the best of my knowledge, is married and also is about the mousiest thing I have encountered. I could send her flying with one flick of a finger. I think he's kind of *handsome*. I wouldn't vote for him over Harrison Ford, say, and for that matter I might not vote for him over Lincoln Preston, who I loved in high school. And yet, he's the kind of man who has this air about him, really, pheromones I think they're called, little chemical critters that make a dust mote look big, and yet they are some kind of powerful these pheromones, especially the kind this guy has that seem to say *sex, sex, sex*. People have said that I have quite a case of these pheromones myself, and I could feel my pores exuding that intangible scent as we stood side by side and watched Quee muscle Ruthie back into the house with the promise of a double martini and a full body massage. It was like a scene in a book, where I thought in that instant he was going to rip my robe from my shoulders and whisper what he wanted to do to me. I'm not saying the exact words even though I should be dead when you hear all of this. The "f" word is not one that comes to me easily in a sexual sense. Now isn't that peculiar. It seems to me *that* might merit an academic study. Who can and who can't.

Now for example I can say, "Oh, fuck, I burned up the dinner," or I might read an article about somebody in politics or somebody in academics like somebody I know and say, "What a fuck-up," but when it gets right down to the nitty-gritty, when it's time to tango, I can't say it. I have to like say, "Do it" or "You know." Well, maybe they don't *know;* I think that's a big problem out there in our society, all these people who think they do know, only they don't know. And here was this good-looking handyman standing before me, and I just knew that he was going to turn suddenly and take me, take me, take me. He was building up to it. He asked me if I had anything to drink, which of course I don't. I am someone who gave up liquor and I told him so.

"You don't like it?"

"No, I do like it," I said. "I like it too much. And I'm quite good at drinking it, better than most I'd say."

"Alcoholic?" For somebody who had been so quiet he was all of a sudden busting at the seams with things to say.

"No. But I coulda been, so I decided to beat the odds," I told him. "I gave it up for Lent."

"Catholic?" he asked, and of course I shook my head, and he had to go on and show his smarts by listing others who might be inclined to go for Lent.

"I don't know what I am," I said. "I grew up Methodist, and I like the idea of giving things up."

"Better be careful where you say such," he said, and it took me a

minute to get it. When you have lived with somebody who isn't
funny, your joke skills get a little rusty.

"Ha, ha," I said. "I believe in a little suffering from time to time,
you know, like when you run until you think your lungs might pop?
Or like when you floss your teeth really hard."

"You *like* that, huh?"

"Maybe I do," I said, and all the while I felt like he was locking me
into something I wasn't meaning to say. I hope I am dead if anybody
hears THIS tape. I think this one might have to be labeled "Guy Lom-
bardo Does Donny and Marie's Greatest Hits" to be on the safe side.
Anyway, then he said: "Well, maybe we can work something out."

I said, "Maybe we can," and I have to say I was feeling a lot like I did
in the movies that day and hating myself for it. "So back to where we
were, what do you think?"

"About?"

"Me! What do you think of me? Now that you've seen me, ratty
underwear and all, I deserve to hear. Otherwise I'll tell Quee you
were spying on me." I began talking to him the same way I had talked
to Gerald, matter-of-fact and direct. "I'll file a report of some kind."

"I think you're very pretty." He smiled when he said this, and I sat
down in my little bedroom chair and crossed my legs tightly. I tried
to angle myself so that he couldn't see that I had not shaved my legs in
ages. Gerald *despises* hairy legs, which of course is precisely why they
are in this state. "I'll confess I don't really like the robe." He stood
there with his chin cupped in his hand while he looked me up and
down like I might be some ancient urn.

Now here, dear tape recorder, and you, whoever you are out there
in recorderland, this is where I really screwed up. I mean why didn't
I say in low, guttural Kathleen Turner fashion: "Fine then, baby, I'll
take it off." But no, I did what I always do and have my whole life, I

got my nose out of joint and felt the need to defend myself, to state my case, to persuade him to look at it from my window. "Why? What's wrong with it? I bought it in Chinatown, and it wasn't cheap."

"It looks a little cheap, though, a little hookerish," he said and then, as if that wasn't enough, proceeded to let me know—as if I was interested!!—that he really sort of liked that All-American, sweet-girl look, he always had. "No offense," he said and then, "I'm just not into games."

"Oh no? Oh no?" and I realized that I was picking up the same anger I left behind in Washington and was finishing up the job. "Then what was all that about 'Maybe we could work something out' when I said I liked some suffering?"

"It was a joke." He pulled this innocent-as-all-hell routine and held his hands up in the air as if to ward off blows. "Just something to say." He breathed out, shoulders dropping. "Look, I'm sorry. I should have left when I started to. I haven't flirted in a while; the truth is, I really am not interested in flirting or being seduced or any of that."

"Like I am?" I was screaming by now, you can just imagine how pissed I was. "Why would I want to pick up some two-bit odd-job redneck? Who's coming on to who, Buddy?"

"Well, think about it, and you tell me. And you don't even know me. I'm not some redneck sent to serve your fat ass. I'm *not* a red-neck!" He placed his hand on his chest and stepped back. "Man, are you crazy. You're as crazy as Quee said you were. That's one lucky husband left to himself."

I froze. I literally froze. The blood stopped running, and I turned my back completely on him so that he wouldn't see how humiliated I felt. I hadn't felt so humiliated since my wedding night, when Gerald informed me that he felt he could get used to my being so flat-chested, that on his list of what he wanted in a woman it wasn't the only one I failed (he said the others were that I didn't like to drink cognac in front of a fire while he read aloud to me from his own work). I told him that somebody who chooses not to drink alcohol would not up and start slugging cognac, that nobody in his right mind would sit in front of a roaring fire in Virginia in July, and that his work was often too difficult for me to follow in the air, I preferred to read it for myself. On the day I left, I told him that his shit work was boring as hell, that it was almost as boring as he was, that it is so boring, somebody could sell it out as sleeping medication. And of course, being a know-it-all who had to get the last word, he told me that he had always found my body so unattractive, that dealing with my breasts was kind of like gnawing on a bone some other dog got to first (he said this in what he thought was a rugged kind of cowboy voice but really sounded like Liberace having a tantrum). He said that he had always planned to buy me some lovely big breasts. I told him to buy himself some, that it seemed to me he might be much better suited to the transexual life.

"I'm sorry." Tom was right up near me then, but boy there was not a pheromone in the place. The pheromones just up and damn croaked. Where have all the pheromones gone, long time passing? They were out of there. And I'll tell you right now, you whoever, archaeologist, visitor from another planet, museum curator, local cop, my butt is NOT that big. It looks bigger than it actually is.

"Quee never said you were crazy. Really." I didn't answer him, just stared at that old muddy brogan of his that probably *was* about the size of what my brogan would be if I had a brogan. "She told me what happened to you, that's all. I'm sorry, really." I just shrugged, because what else in the hell can you do. I planned to say nothing, but then it was like I snapped—it's like the absence of pheromones sent me. I said, "Fuck you, you fucked-up fucker." I said it several times, again and again and now it was his turn to stand there like a drainpipe. He let me finish, he let my breath slow back down; he didn't even tell me that during all of this my robe had slid open and I was standing there flashing him.

"Do you need a thesaurus?" he asked, reached and pulled my robe back up around me. When I made no move at all, he retied my belt and then stepped back several feet. He waited, eyebrows still raised with the question. All of a sudden I felt kind of good, like I'd up and let all of this bad stuff out of me. I felt lifted, unburdened. I thought of what a thesaurus might say. "Fornicate you, you fornicated-up fornicator."

He laughed.

"Copulate you."

"Sure," he said. I'm telling you that there are more pheromones to be found in one pore on that perfect face than Gerald could get if he was able to buy some at the Dollar Store. "Truce?" he asked then, and I nodded. I let him kiss my hand like I might have been the Queen Mother. Then he turned and told me he'd be back the next day to finish my shelves, that he'd be sure to knock first. Now maybe I'm reading too much into this, but it seems to me that he really lingered over kissing my hand. I think he was really attracted to me, and I wish you could talk, you old tape recorder, and give me some kind of opinion. I mean, would I be jumping right from the fire into the pan? I mean, I don't even know this guy, and here I was getting all worked up, you know? I mean, I don't know if that's *normal*, and I wish I did, seeing as how I'm going into the business of what's normal and what isn't. Oh, but Lordy, it was something to behold.

I felt the pheromones resurrecting. Immediately, all over the room they were springing back, crying out *Let me live, let me live! Let me do those things you said.* And I think maybe he felt it too, because when he walked out into the yard he walked right through the sprinkler, held his arms out and let himself get a nice long spray before climbing into his truck and giving his dog a great big kiss. I would swear that he was looking up at my window as he pulled off, and I know that he'll be back; he said he would. Now as a professional, I just don't know what I'll do about this. As a woman I have a few ideas. But for now I've got to go finish listening to Quee. Later when I talk to you, I'm going to tell all about some of my therapy techniques that I have developed; there's the jigsaw test and the battery of tests I think of as the Flora and Fauna of the Mental Landscape. But tonight we are going to rehearse my future speech that will target the impotence that comes to many male smokers. She says she has worked weeks on the ceramic learning aids to illustrate what happens. Lord, these must be some dim bulbs I'm working with if they can't imagine what a limp one might look like.

Part Two

Sometimes when Wallace Johnson takes his break in the afternoon, he angles himself so that he can watch the cars heading down Highway 211 to the beach, read a letter or two. It amazes him how he never gets tired of reading over the same words. It's like when he was a boy and buying pulps. Maybe part of what keeps him reading is because it's an unsolved mystery. During the twenty years since that first letter, this poor soul has lost her lover and then her husband; she's had boyfriends, but nobody she really cares about. No family really. She's one of those unfortunate ones who never really got to have a childhood. She was always working, always feeling responsible.

Now he turns his attention to the window where there is a steady gray mist. He'll take tomorrow off and Saturday and then he'll be right back at the crack of dawn on Sunday to start all over again. He doesn't mind at all. *Almost there, almost there*, sometimes he hears the words in his cash register or in the rhythm of how he stamps the postage. Retirement. It equals fishing and reading and building the deck that Judy has talked about for years.

The land alongside the highway here is known as Lamb's Folly, story being that old man Lamb built himself a huge beautiful ship, spent his whole life building it, only to then realize that there was no possible way to get it out of the clearing and to the sea without cutting down a forest of trees and all the homes that surrounded him. Old Lamb's Folly. Who knew if it was true, but it sure made a good story. Every time he drove his family on this stretch, which was near about every weekend, he'd say, "Did I ever tell you the story of Lamb's Folly?" And they'd all groan and moan and laugh. For years his sons begged him to take them up into the woods to search for the ship, but of course he didn't. In his mind there was no touching it. It was as big as the Ark. It was as fancy as the *QE II*. It was a myth, a legend, the kind of thing you can pin a life on if the rest of the world will let you.

He stares out into the rain and wishes that he could see the woman of the letters there in her red scarf. He wishes that she could pick her way through Lamb's Woods and that somewhere there, deep in the heart of it, she would stumble onto her Wayward One—that he wasn't really dead at all. He was there in this lost and hidden city waiting for her, waiting for a new life to begin.

Dear Wayward One,

It's three o'clock in the morning and I have driven myself down here to the beach to be close to you. It's kind of eerie as I sit here at the end of the pier, the light from a nearby post giving me just enough to see what I'm doing. There is no moon. I was hoping there would be. There is the occasional light from the Fort Caswell Lighthouse, that beacon searching the strand. As a young woman I was made to think it was searching for lost souls, calling the sinners over to a Baptist retreat, washing their stains with cold salt water. Now as I look down toward the point (I have a flashlight in my purse should I get up the nerve to walk down there) I keep expecting to see you there standing out on the top step. I guess you might know that the folks who own that house hate you for killing yourself there. I don't anymore. Tonight as I bent down and kissed my husband I had the strange sensation that I was two people living two lives, at least two! I think I'm really like an old alley cat, a big old pussycat with one life blending right into the next. I feel like I have been everything, done everything. I guess the only thing I never was was a mother by nature, but don't we all know that there are other ways to mother. There are mothers who have produced child after child in their stretched-out wombs; they have sweated and squeezed those muscles to push them out into the world and to someone like me it seems that would make a difference, that it would change them deep in their souls, but apparently not. My mother grew me in her body; I came head-first from between her thighs and then where was she? WHERE? All those times I needed her there for me and WHERE? There I was at the Ocean Forest and to all the world didn't I look fit? Didn't I look like somebody with a good life? I went from being somebody who practically lived up under a house to being somebody with a step-daddy who took me to spend a whole summer there at Myrtle Beach. You said you remembered meeting him. Well, a lot of people probably do; he was something, all right. My mother thought he was God. I never got over wanting my own daddy, the one I could barely remember by then. I knew kind sad eyes and I knew the scent of bourbon though as a child I could not have described either to you. It was just my way of knowing something. It's how I imagine people who have always been blind remember the world.

You know I thought you were God, for a time at least. I wanted you but then I also hated you for leaving behind a child who might grow up to feel just as I did about being left. I've seen your child playing ball over at the junior high and I think "Oh honey, you would hate me if you knew who I was. You would call me whore and witch." But instead he looks at me and smiles and waves great big like all the children do. He is beautiful, too. Perfect. There's a part of me that wants him. Not like you're thinking! I mean want him. I wish he did love me the way a child loves its mother. I wonder if it could ever happen? Your wife waves to me that same way. She hasn't a clue Dear Wayward One. I am sitting here looking for a sign I guess. I keep thinking that if there is something beyond this life, beyond my nine lives, that you'll find it and of course I know that if you find it, you'll let me know. I'll find a seashell in my mailbox or I'll find the rest of the note you were writing to me just before you died. Maybe I'll find my red chiffon scarf tied around my bedpost and it will smell just like you. The last time I was here you were beside me and it was at this same time of day. We weren't worried. If somebody saw us, they wouldn't know who we were, not at this hour, not here on the pier. This is a time and place for the serious fishermen, the ones who sometimes sleep here at the foot of the pier. The old men who know what they're doing and the teenagers who dream of catching a shark and drinking liquor all night. That morning there was a moon and we sat with it to our right, the sky lightening on our left. It was almost a full moon and you talked about how even though you knew that there was a flag up there on it, and that men had landed and walked and taken close-up photos that appeared in Life *magazine, you still felt complete magic when you looked at it. It had the power to take your world and shake it up, let the insignificant sift through like in those little plastic sieves the children play with at the beach; it still had the power to make you catch your breath and think how simple life should be. You wake and eat and sleep and love. Anything beyond this is unnecessary. I listened to you then. I believed your every brilliant word. I held your hand and stroked your fingers, pressed them to my cheek as you talked. We got corny then, remember? You said, "Here's old blue eyes" and you sang "Paper Moon."*

It was near dawn when I snuck into my house and there in my dark pantry I slipped off my coat and pants and was just as I had been hours before: white cotton gown, barefooted. And when I slipped into bed, my side so cold, my husband moved in close to me like he might be guided by sonar, like the dolphins you were telling me about. He sensed life, heartbeats, blood flowing.

And now I have to do that again. Now I don't even bother to hide my nightgown but wear it bunched up and stuck into my pants. I'm wear-

ing my slippers. It's strange but I still feel like I'm doing something wrong, like I'm committing some great sin, and when my husband rolls in close to me I'll worry if he can tell that I've been with you. You, the invisible, the dead.

WALLACE KNEW WHICH pier she was talking about in this letter. He knew by the angle of the moon, by the beacon she described, and the direction of the point. He had gone many times, right after that letter came. Since then Hurricane Hugo has slapped the end of the old pier into the sea and it's been rebuilt, the new wood golden blond and green next to what had remained. He had sat there at the end just as she had done, seen the world exactly as she had seen it. He felt compelled to call out to Wayward One in his own mind. Silently, in rhythm with the waves, the rolling pull and the whining give of the creosote pilings beneath him, he asked that if *he* was there, and if *he* could hear, that he please get in touch with that woman. "How could you do that to such a good woman?" he asked, a man who had enough sense to understand the power of the moon. And that was when Wallace began to wonder if everybody has a folly; if every life plan, no matter how carefully executed, doesn't overlook some important part. And now, gently folding the letter back up and into its plastic bag he knows that that is true. Something or someone is always overlooked, and it's only in looking back that it all comes clear.

When Robert Bobbin gets down to the Fulton police station, the first thing he does is pull the record assigned to him. His hands shake and his damp fingers leave smudges of ink. All of the guys are stalling before the day begins, doing what they do, which is pick on the newest guy, who happens to be a girl. "Did the department issue you those panty hose?" one guy asks and she turns around and shoots him the bird. She's really kind of cute, pixie-looking, with short frosted hair and a skinny little body, and everybody at the Fulton Police Department is trying to match Robert up with her. Apparently she has heard the news, because she turns and smiles at him as he passes. It's the first day to really feel like autumn, brisk wind and leaves flying, and she's all wrapped up in a regulation jacket that's way too big for her. She looks like some child playing school crossing guard, and he can't help but be a little relieved for her to know that by noon it will be one of those Indian summer days where the heat of the sun is in full swing and she will need to shed the wool. It's supposed to hit eighty later in the day, or so the weather guy said on the radio; he ended his segment with a silly jingle to the tune of Bill Bailey. *Won't you come home, Jones Jameson?* People all over town are

placing bets on where the asshole might be, and all Robert can think
about is the jerk's wife, a woman who surely doesn't need to be mis-
treated. Robert nods quickly and goes into his little tiny cubicle of an
office and begins reading the updated report:

> Jones Jameson officially disappeared on August 27th when he
> told his wife he was driving to Raleigh for a Disc Jockey
> reunion. Wife said they had not been getting along but that
> "that was nothing new and everybody in town knew it." The
> wife, Alicia Jameson, reported that he never telephoned her as
> he said he would. She said that it was not unusual for him to for-
> get to call home on his first night somewhere, but that he
> almost always called by late on the second day, if for no other
> reason but to see if he had any messages. She said that whenever
> she telephoned him on past trips she was greeted by party
> sounds, or more often, just the sound of someone in the back-
> ground. This time there was no record whatsoever of his arrival
> at the Holiday Inn in Raleigh. His parents also have not heard
> from him.

At this point in the police record, there was a break with a nota-
tion that Mrs. Jameson had broken down and cried. Robert wishes he
had been the one to ask the questions, that he had been there to touch
her shaking shoulder. The first time he ever saw Alicia Jameson, the
attraction was so powerful it left him tongue-tied and spastic like he
used to be and had been most of his life. She was beautiful in a serious, forlorn-looking way.

Robert reads on to find that Jones Jameson never showed up at the
meeting in Raleigh (turns out there was no meeting). State troopers
are looking for a gold Audi 5000. On the afternoon of August 30, the
wife came in and filed a missing person report after having called that

morning. When questioned about why she had waited, she repeated
that he had stayed away from home often and she had no reason to
believe that this time was any different from the others.

It is clear to Robert this is the first report the new girl has ever
written. It just goes on and on, telling what everybody was wearing
(Alicia wore a tight denim skirt above the knee and a black T-shirt).
Then she has what she calls "an aside note," such as "There was a big
woman with Mrs. Jameson by the name of Quee Purdy. She is the
wife's employer and likened the missing party to an alley cat out to
youknowwhat." On past occasions Jones had stayed away for as long
as two days without word. "Aside note: *son of a bitch* the big woman
said and the wife agreed." So does Robert. When asked why this
time warranted a call to the PD, Alicia said that she grew suspicious when she started getting phone calls in the middle of the
night from (she assumed) the girlfriend he had gone off to meet in
the past. It was a woman's voice but she was trying to sound like a
man and she kept saying "Jones, please." Finally, Alicia told the
voice she had no earthly idea where Jones might be and then this
voice called her a lying whore and hung up. In the report, "lying
whore" was typed in caps and underlined. The aside note said: "Big
woman says: 'Lying whore my foot—well, if that ain't the pot calling the kettle.'" Alicia called the department the very next morning with the encouragement of her employer, "the big woman:
owner and operator of Smoke-Out Signals, a place for nicotine
addicts to seek treatment."

Alicia had brought a picture of Jones Jameson. It is the photo the
radio station uses when he does a live show like at Tart's TV or Brew-
meister Palace (his most recent public appearances). The rest of the
report is all about the asshole's physical appearance, and the report is
way too personal sounding for police records, but Bobbin isn't going

to be the one to take down that little crossing guard; she'll figure it out.

The photo of the missing party shows a Caucasian male of age 40 with receding hairline. Hair is brown and buzzed close to the head. Head is somewhat elongated, some might say equine-like, and he also has prominent teeth to go along with above said description. He has big brown eyes which is why (wife said) he thinks he's something. (Though it doesn't sound very good and though a person might hate to admit it, he is downright gorgeous like somebody who could pose on a Stud calendar if you happened to be somebody who likes that sort of thing which I'll assure you Deputy Bobbin, I am not!) Wife also said that though you can't see it in the picture, his body is his strong point. He is six feet one and two hundred pounds. He works out on a regular basis and has a lot of body hair. When asked if he had any special identification traits, wife turned bright red and looked down. *Yes* she said but did not continue. After several rounds of questions she finally admitted to his being "endowed" at which point the big woman accompanying the wife burst into such a fit of laughter that she had to be asked to leave the room. (I hesitate to put this in the report but it could prove to be valuable information I'd think.) The wife then continued by telling that on the day he left home, he was wearing what he was always wearing: khakis, a white, all-cotton Izod shirt open at the collar, a salmon colored alpaca sweater (his golfing sweater) tied around his waist, loafers, no socks, Ray-Ban aviator sunglasses and a madras belt that she had given him when they first started going out. The Jamesons have one child, a son Taylor who is two. Wife can be reached at any time at home and/or her place of employment: Smoke-Out Signals, a place for people trying to kick the habit.

"So? What did you think?" The new girl pops her head into Robert's cubicle and points at the file on his desk, that asshole Jones Jameson looking up at him.

"About?"

"The report. My first report." She steps into the room now and in the light from the window, without all the guys gawking, Robert sees that she's right pretty, in a frail bleached-out way. She reminds him of somebody he used to have quite a thing for back when he worked in Marshboro and was the butt of everybody's jokes. "Why are you staring at me?"

"I'm sorry." His neck gets prickly. "You remind me of someone."

"Oh." Under her big jacket she is wearing full police uniform, except she's got on a skirt instead of trousers. The gun hanging off of her belt is about as big as her thigh. "Somebody good, I hope."

"Oh, yeah, she was, uh is. Great report." Robert stuffs Jones's picture back in and then pats the folder. "It's very colorful."

"I have a flair that way." She sits perched like a little bird on a wire, her head cocked to one side. "And"—she tosses an envelope on top of the folder—"here's the latest. A woman who says she saw Jones Jameson *after* his wife saw him. She's their neighbor."

WHEN PEOPLE ARE missing in Marsh County, the river is one of the first places to go. This was something Robert knew even before he came to work in this town. The men down at the station regularly drag nets up and down through that twisting brown river, one man in the boat designated to watch the branches of the live oaks for snakes that might sense the warmth of bodies below and drop onto them. It has happened many times. Grown men have peed in their pants, shot holes in their boats, and, on one occasion, shot a buddy in the leg. No, if Jones Jameson hasn't turned up before long, they definitely *will* drag the river, especially now that this morning a couple of old fishermen found his car hidden in a thick grove of pine trees not far from the Braveman Bridge, which is, or so Robert has been told, one of the best fishing spots along that part of the river. There was a change of clothes in the backseat, a white Izod shirt, a pair of khaki pants, and a pair of jockey briefs (red ones), like he might be Jim Palmer. Robert has thought of buying that kind of underwear but fears he would look like an idiot. Now the puzzle is that these clothes were tossed in the backseat and not there in the hanging bag where he had two more identical outfits—he had more briefs, a black pair and a paisley pair. If he's the average person who likes to shower at least once a day you can pretty much figure he was planning a two- or three-day trip. There was a tape of several of his own radio shows in the tape deck.

ROBERT HAS COME a ways since moving to this town, so maybe he *will* buy some briefs. He could walk into Belk-Leggett and do it. Why not? Everybody used to tease him without mercy because he was the teasable kind, the chicken bleeding all over the barnyard, but a couple of years ago he stepped up to a new level in life. It was like he'd done his time. He decided to stop going by Bob and called himself Robert. Robert Bobbin didn't tempt people to say shit like Bob Bobbin had. He got depressed, was the truth of it. After years of trying so goddamned hard to make people like him, he one day just said to hell with it. He sat one whole night studying his .38, holding it, the heaviness. He thought of all the famous people who had simply picked up a gun and fired. Hemingway and Del Shannon and Cecil Lowe, who was the closest this town had ever come to having a celebrity. And then he realized how quickly people forget. Maybe not Hemingway so much, but how often do you hear people talking about Shannon or, especially, Cecil Lowe? The local stories about his death circulated for a few years but then that was it, the stuff of old ghost stories and something to be told to a newcomer, something whispered when you pass by and see Cecil Lowe's son up on top of somebody's house putting on a new roof. It was when Robert realized that there was nobody who would really give a damn if he died that he put down the .38.

What happened then was amazing; when he stopped giving a damn about people, they started lingering at his desk, asking if he'd like a cup of coffee, asking him what kind of weekend he had. He took to renting foreign films and sat every night in his dark living room reading the subtitles and trying to follow what was happening. He didn't always follow, but what it did for him was take him off to another place. He was a foreigner in a strange land. If he got up to take a leak, he missed it all. He chose the movies by hit or miss, the same way he ran his life. Sometimes he got tired of reading and just watched it all happen, people laughing and crying and kissing and so on. He liked to watch with the sound off. Some of them were hotter in a sex way than anything he'd seen in English.

He'd go into the station and people would say, "Hey, Bob, uh Robert, what did you do last night?"

"I watched this Italian movie," he might say, interested that very rarely did anybody ask him the title, relieved, too, because he couldn't always remember. He had hated that one about the man who was so abusive: swept away, washed away; Goldie Hawn and Kurt Russell had done a funny one similar. He had actually LIKED that movie, but he didn't say it. He ate an occasional scone or croissant, and before long he had this new image. People looked to him as one of the "intellectual" cops. He was made detective. Alicia Jameson, who used to work as a social worker, started spending her coffee break with him, in spite of the fact that he was a nervous wreck when she was near him.

Now Alicia works at the slightly suspicious new business. Her photo was in the newspaper alongside Quee Purdy's. Alicia is known as "The Massage Therapist" and actually took a workshop somewhere. Her husband, asshole that he is, had said on the radio that he and "the old woman" had a lot in common. She was a "massagist" and he was a "misogynist." Several of the men sitting around the station had laughed at that one, but Robert sat silent with a pensive look, as he had learned to do. The truth was he didn't know what *misogynist* meant, but the answer came soon enough. There were call-ins.

"I hate you, you *woman-hater!*" one woman said, and for a minute it sounded just like Alicia. Robert's heart quickened and blood flooded into his neck.

"You love it. I know you love it," Jones Jameson whispered in garbled fashion, like he might have the microphone in his mouth.

"Who would have imagined you knew such a big word?" It was a male caller, highway noise in the background.

"I'm Phi Beta Kappa, boy." Jones Jameson let loose that hideous raucous laugh that he uses to introduce his show. "What's *your* education?"

The caller hung up, and it left the rest of them sitting there looking at one another, while Jones Jameson proceeded to play "Go Away Little Girl." Funny how the topic of education makes so many people nervous. Robert notices it especially when he's left to deal with somebody like Jones Jameson, somebody he knows he hates, but somebody who could beat the hell out of him in a game of Trivial Pursuit. It's been the curse of his life, this sense of inadequacy.

Now (speaking of inadequate) he is standing at the door of a house his own little house could fit into ten times. It's an old house on the main street of the town, and there's a sign in the yard that tells all about when the house was built and how, prior to the construction of the house in 1890, this was the site of a market house where slave auctions were held.

Robert takes his time before ringing the bell. He is at the home of Myra Carter, who claims to be the last person to actually *see* Jones Jameson. She was out walking her funny-looking dog, a shar-pei. She had called the police station yesterday afternoon with this bit of news. Apparently she calls them often.

Robert is taking in the front yard's neatly pruned privet hedge and circle drive when the door opens. He turns quickly and removes his hat to greet the old socialite whose picture appears so regularly in the local paper's social column. She has her ugly little dog all hugged up to her chest and kisses its head before inviting Robert in. The skin of her face is loose and doughy looking. She could go on one of those ads where the people look like their dogs. Robert doesn't know which one is more wrinkled. Myra Carter is telling him how her shar-pei cost her a little over a thousand dollars at a special dog store in Atlanta, which is where her sister lives and has since 1978; her sister can't wait for the Olympics to come. She tells Robert all about her sister's house and how it overlooks the Peachtree Mall, *prime real estate*, she says, and holds up a little plastic egg like what women buy hose in. The egg has been cut in half and there's a tiny cardboard building inside of it with a sign that says in glittered letters, Peachtree Mall. "My niece made me this commemorative egg after I visited her mama. You might know my niece." Robert shrugs. "Her name is Ruthie. Ruthie Crow. Never married." Myra nods with this information, studies Robert's face like he might be a bingo card. "Crow is a

name of her own choosing. You know she's a poet." Again she lowers
her voice and studies him. "Her rhymes don't always pay the bills, so
she has this little mini-egg business. It doesn't always pay the bills
either, but she's good to me, so what can I say?"

"Yes, now about—"

"All-occasion, too. The eggs I mean. From the Fourth of July to
Halloween is a real dry spell for her, so she takes a long vacation to do
poems."

After she's told him about every egg Ruthie has constructed, she
asks Robert to remind her to tape *Geraldo* if he plans to spend the
whole morning in her house talking and finally gets back to Jones
Jameson. It seems that little Sharpy had his wrinkled little body up
against a tree, leg raised (she gives Robert all the details—this was
the dog's first time raising his leg, which is why she remembers) at
about the same time Jones turned the corner in his car. She tries to
remember what kind of car but is having a lapse; she knows it's what
her brother-in-law, Ruthie Crow's daddy, once test-drove with no
intention of buying *that's how expensive it was!* but took the family to
the Tastee Freez in it all the same and then swore that he didn't know
why there was a dot of chocolate in the backseat upholstery.

"It's not important," Robert says.

"Well, the car dealer sure thought it was!"

"An Audi. We know that part already. It's been recovered."

"Are you getting testy?" she asks. "Because if you're getting testy
I'm not going to be able to talk. I have never been able to talk to a
testy man. You see, Ruthie's mama and I grew up with some money;
our daddy was a hard worker and a good provider, and then unlike my
sister, I just happened to marry somebody who was going to keep on
making it, which is what landed me here." She waves her arms out

into the immense room. "So you, like my brother-in-law, have no right to come here into my home and get testy."

"I'm sorry." Robert takes a deep breath, compliments the shitty-looking egg again, and then talks baby talk to Sharpy, which is what brings her back around. At this rate, he will be here all day.

"They found the car?" She is asking now, pulling on his arm like he's some kid with a secret. "Come on now, you, give me the news."

"I really can't discuss it," he says, but when she clamps her lips tightly and raises a crayoned eyebrow, he goes on to say that she will read all about it in the newspaper in just a few hours. He goes further to compliment the portrait of Mr. Carter there over the mantle. Dr. Howard Randolph Carter III, a doctor back when doctors knew how to do every thing and not just one. "That," she says and swings her arm toward the face of the stern-looking stiff, "is why in this county there are so many people named Howard and Randy, Randolph and Howie, Carter and Doc. He delivered them all!" She picks up a little feather duster off the mantle and brushes it all over his face; she slaps it a little harder than seems necessary. "He delivered Jones Jameson, for that matter, and it was a difficult birth to be sure, breach, and he came after Howard had already set a broken leg and pronounced somebody dead on arrival. I was kind of his assistant, and so I kept up with what happened in a day. We always felt that the Jamesons *should* have put Howard's name somewhere in that child's name, but no, they named him for his paternal grandfather, who was sitting around somewhere waiting and not doing a thing to help."

$\mathcal{Q}$uee's photo collection has evolved over a long period of time, beginning when Quee was a child. She was looking for a picture of her father, haunted by his image. She soon began collecting old photographs that somehow matched up with what little bit she knew of him. He was a big man, at least six feet four, and his feet were so large that his shoes had to be ordered. She wouldn't have known this, except that her mother told Quee she was built like him, the big bones and feet, that first time they had had to go to Raleigh to get shoes for her. People could not get over how she had grown, and for years she felt ugly and awful; she stooped down so she'd look smaller. When her mother remarried, something made her spine go stiff and straighten up, like she needed to stand up for herself and her invisible father. She was her own person. And then she saw the ocean for the first time, and it made her feel so small, so helpless in the grand scheme of the world that she decided the only way to survive was to be as strong and powerful as possible.

When she was first married, she studied Lonnie's family photos regularly. She would see his ears, his eyes on these strangers. And all the while she was collecting her own faces. People who resembled her. People she wished she knew. They became like secret souvenirs; she would find an old photo to remind *her* of a time or a place or a person, but no one else would have a clue.

When she was twenty, she needed something to remind her of a trip to the beach and bought an old photo postcard in a five-and-dime. The man with her made up the story to go with it: this picture of a couple strolling in their old-timey suits. "They are in love," he said. "But she's a good girl and so chances are they may never do anything about it. She may never feel his lips warm against her neck, his hand inch over her belly and down. They will see each other in passing and wonder what would happen if the conditions had been right."

She kept that card in the corner of her mirror and with every glance she thought of those imagined touches. At night, she touched herself, pressed as if she could hold in the urges, the natural flexing and release of muscle.

SHE BOUGHT AN old photo of a family picnic, with children lined up, hair plastered and parted, the little girls with lacy socks. There is a table heavy with bowls and baskets, and there is a man seated at the end of the table, suspenders and bowtie and tilted hat. The sleeves of his shirt are rolled up, and this alone is the only thing in his appearance that would suggest relaxation. He looked like her grandfather, a man she had loved, a man who smelled of tobacco and the starch of his shirt. And no sooner did she buy the photo but he died. Yes, he was old, and yes, he had been sick, but she believed it meant something. She had somehow glimpsed death coming.

Once she tried to explain to Lonnie how she believed if you could be objective about your own life, even for a split second, you would indeed be able to see patterns emerging; you would see signs and foreshadowings, you would know what was coming.

"Well, thank you, Jesus, that I don't know," Lonnie said then and stared long and hard into her eyes. The picture postcard curled into the edge of her mirror, and it seemed for a moment like the paper itself or the people in the picture might scream out, laugh to get his attention. "I don't ever want to know, Quee." He pulled her close, his arms squeezing the breath out of her. "Okay?" She nodded but as she looks back it seems that he was darkening and shrinking there before her, like a photo tossed in a fire, like a leaf in autumn. And when he was dying, she often thought of that moment as she watched death creep up his limbs, the skin of his legs mottled and darkening as the body reserved its blood and energy for the heart and brain. She couldn't help but be fascinated, to understand finally that it truly was possible to watch death pass over a body like a shadow; it was as simple as the sun setting, as simple as a shade drawn down against light. When Lonnie died, she pulled out all the photos she had secretly stashed over the years, and she spent hours cutting and piecing them into frames, arranging them in some sort of order. It seemed to her that if she could arrange them right they had the power to tell her story, maybe parts that she herself didn't know.

Now the photos fill every square inch of space in the hall leading to her room. She gives them lives and appetites, sex and dreams. She calls it her ghost wall—her orphans' collected souls, pinned and saved, each opening to her like a window or a door, an unknown world waiting on the other side. There's not a single one without some semblance of goodness, some form of redemption. There have only been a few photos she saw and refused, only a few that offered no trace of goodness. They were pictures of herself, real pictures from her real childhood—a tall, unhappy girl who pitied and loved no one, not herself, not anybody. The hateful ugly duckling who dear Lonnie could not believe existed.

The last time Tom saw Sarah seems long ago, almost like it never even happened. It was in the early spring—only three months ago—a humid, drizzly day, the kind of day the light stays the same from sunup to sundown. His windshield was streaked with mud, so he pulled into Doug Taylor's Exxon to borrow the squeegee. It was while he was wiping down the windows of his truck that he saw her standing inside the office. At first he thought he was seeing things, some other person just passing through town. She wasn't so special-looking; there were hundreds of thousands of people on the face of the earth who could be mistaken for her. Straight, shoulder-length, dirty-blond hair, sharp little features that prompted people to use words like "cute" and "pert," pale eyes too large for the rest of her, bringing to her face a kind of inward sadness like those pictures of alley cats and orphan children. He still got himself to sleep many nights with a picture of her eyes, her eyes during lovemaking, head rolled back and lids fluttering, breath shallow and rapid, her hands in his hair, on his neck as she pulled him in closer and tighter, harder, and then the slow motion opening of her eyes, her lids matching her slow exhalation.

But now that image was gone because when he heard the news, when he heard how she turned and fell, eyes rolled back, his sexual love, any craving, was replaced with an ache, pity, remorse. To imagine the taste of her skin, the flutter of her eyelids, was a betrayal of her life or whatever was left of it.

BUT THAT DAY, she stepped outside, leaned forward to see him better. He lifted his hand, and she began walking toward him, her hand self-consciously smoothing back her hair the way she'd done for as long as he could remember. It had been so long, and he felt a wash of guilt, as if she knew how he had mourned her, knew how he had pretended to sleep with her every night for years. She was his shot of liquor or sleeping pill, his way to find sleep.

"Hi." She laughed for no reason, a nervous laugh, a laugh that might've said, *Fancy seeing you here*, though that line would have been his.

"How are you?" they both asked, then laughed, shrugged.

"I live here now," she said. "Just moved back."

"Oh, really?" Tommy had heard she was back; sometimes he thought he had *felt* she was back, that some weird current had traveled from her house to his. So many people had mentioned that she was coming back that now he couldn't remember who had gotten to him first. "When did you come back?" He watched her as she gave him all the information he already knew: two weeks ago, moved into that wonderful old Queen Anne down on the corner of Linden and Fourth Avenue. He had grown up minutes from that house, had passed it walking to and from school his whole life.

"You liked that house in high school," he said. "I had forgotten until now." She looked away, and he knew what she was thinking. She was thinking that it was impossible for him to have forgotten such a thing;

she was thinking of all the nights that they had walked past that house and in their senior year driven past it on the way to Simmon's Beach, the only small stretch of the river with a real sandy shore and water tame enough for swimming. It was a place they had been warned about as children; every summer there was at least one drowning. With the building of the interstate, it was rumored to be a good spot for body dumping. Somebody could kill somebody in Washington before breakfast, dump him in the river at lunchtime, and be in Florida in time for cocktails. For teenagers, all that made the spot about as good as driving over to Wilmington to see the Maco Light, from the old ghost story about a man who searches nightly for his lost head. It was scary and exciting; it gave a reason for the high anxiety and rapid heartbeat that was tied to the question about whether or not you'd try to get in somebody's pants, and if you did try, then whether or not she'd respond.

One night Tommy had stripped down behind a bush and then dashed into the freezing dark water while Sarah stood on the bank and watched. "It feels great," he called out to her, struggling to keep his teeth from chattering. He swam out to the center and beckoned to her while treading water. The sky was cloudy, no moonlight. "I couldn't see you if I even tried!"

"What if somebody comes?"

"You mean like somebody coming to dump a dead body?"

"Stop it, Tommy." She was at the edge of the water, her big cloth purse abandoned up on the mossy bank where they had left a blanket and his cigarettes.

"Well, if you're out here with me, we'll swim right on to the other side and the bushes are so thick there they'd never see us." He consciously slicked his hair straight back the way she had once, in broad daylight, told him she liked it. She had said she liked seeing every tiny bit of his face. "But if you're way over there by yourself . . ." He let his voice trail off.

"Tommy? What?" she called out and he could hear the sudden fear mounting in her voice. "Tommy? Keep talking to me."

"Well, you know, like if a car were to suddenly pull up and say start dragging a body . . ." He watched while she ran off behind the big bush he'd used earlier. "I'll get you, TomCat!" she called. "I swear I will."

"Promises, promises." He waited, and then there was a flash of light and a splash as she made her way toward him. She was an exceptionally strong swimmer, her arms and legs as lean and almost as muscular as his. He reached out and grabbed her arm, pulled her over close, his legs treading hard and rhythmically, to keep himself upright while he wrapped his arms around her waist and pulled her in close. With each kiss they sank, and when he opened his eyes there was pitch blackness like at the planetarium when their science teacher had told them to hold their hands in front of their faces. Nothing. Space, void, emptiness. Those sensations scared him. Always had. But there in the water, her mouth on his as they surfaced and sputtered, he was not afraid.

That was the first night they made love, and it happened so easily there in the water—her legs wrapped around his hips, his toes digging into the slick muddy bottom to anchor them both—that he later wondered if it had in fact happened. It was their spot, their way. *Let's go to the river* meant much more to them and yet they could say it openly to one another across the high school cafeteria or in the parking lot. When it got too cold to go into the dark brown water, they stayed on the bank or in the car. "Careful, careful," she would often say, arching her back and easing out from under him just before he came; then he could sleep like he had never in his life been able to.

For the first time he had found in a person what he got from the ocean: she was a welcoming escape, and there was total comfort and safety. He could simply close his eyes and drift, disappear.

HE LOOKED UP suddenly with her question. "Is your car being fixed, too?"

"No, I just needed to clean the windows."

"Oh, I see."

"Car trouble?"

"Oil change." She threw a thumb over her shoulder, and he assumed it was in reference to the BMW parked there and not the rust-eaten Chevrolet truck. "He said it would only take a half an hour, but he hasn't even started."

"He's slow." Tommy laughed. "Always has been. Remember how people used to blow the horn?"

She laughed with him, her arms crossed over her chest.

"Remember how Jones Jameson used to blow the horn when the poor guy had his head under the hood?"

"Jones Jameson, now there's a name I've tried to avoid."

"He went to college with you, didn't he?" Tommy was stunned by the accusing tone of his words, the surfacing of the old anger he had felt when all those people packed up their footlockers and moved away.

"Yeah, my husband saw him more than I did." She seemed to mumble that word, *husband*, and she looked back over her shoulder at her car, then at her watch. "We've heard him on the radio, of course."

"He's as much of an asshole as ever." Tommy breathed in, tried hard to sound nonchalant. "So does your husband have a name?" As hard as he tried, the words seemed to stick and sound forced. Of course he knew all there was to know: Mr. and Mrs. David Hennesey request the pleasure of your presence at the marriage of their daughter, Sarah Elizabeth, to Mr. Charles William McCallister III, blah blah blah.

Tom went to the beach that day; he waited until long after the Presbyterian parking lot had filled and then emptied, until the country club parking lot had filled and then emptied to a spray of rice and the clanking of tin cans. The newspaper said: Mr. Charles William (Mack) McCallister III, graduate of UNC like the bride, native of Durham, where the two would make their home, while "Mack," good old Big Mack went to Duke Law School, alma mater of Richard Nixon. How could she have thought that Tom would want to come to her wedding. Was she feeling sorry for him? Why hadn't she felt sorry for him that weekend her freshman year when he went up to see her and all she could talk about was sorority rush and football games? Yeah, her husband had known Jones Jameson all right. Jones was in the wedding; they were in the same fraternity. Maybe Sarah's husband had also liked to fuck girls who *said* they didn't want to be fucked but of course really *did*, according to Jones Jameson. That morning Jones Jameson had told his radio listeners what the perfect woman looks like: *three feet tall, no teeth, and a flat head so you can rest a beer on top.* Surely people didn't understand what he meant or somebody would go after him. Tommy hated him and right then he let his hate spill over to Sarah's husband—hate by association.

"Mack," she said. "His name is Mack. You know I . . ." Her voice trailed off, and when he asked her "What," she said that she forgot. Forgot? He wanted to scream at her to finish the fucking sentence, complete one fucking thought during this lifetime, please. *You know I'm sorry that I ended everything so fast, Tommy. You know I invited you to the wedding, Tommy, so I know that you know what my husband's name is. You know I get so tired of waiting in gas stations. You know I wish the sun would come out. You know I never stopped loving you, TomCat. You know I sometimes still fall asleep pretending that you're deep inside of me.*

The memory that finds him most often is a night before graduation when she was so aggressive, desperate to tell him exactly how she felt, desperate to have him. When he picked her up that night, her parents' living room was cluttered with graduation gifts, sheets and towels and a little two-burner stove. Sarah's parents greeted him politely, but now there was this air of relief that she would soon be leaving, that he would no longer be part of their daughter's life. Sarah, picking up on the unspoken messages being sent, reached and took his hand, squeezed it, one, two, three. Her parents were going to a dinner party, and Tommy and Sarah were going to the movies, or so they said.

"What movie?" her mother asked while adjusting a little rhinestone butterfly pin up on her shoulder, like it had just lit there.

"*Rocky.*"

"Didn't you already see that?"

"Yeah." Sarah shrugged. "But we're going with some other people. Nothing else is on."

They walked out to Tommy's car, his mother's Impala, and drove away as her parents were leaving. "Good thing *Rocky* is easy to discuss without having ever seen it." She reached over and put her hand on his thigh, pulled herself closer. "I don't want to go to the river tonight."

"You don't?" He froze, preparing for some pronouncement. This is it, the breakup, the I-think-we-should-date-other-people speech.

"Nah, let's go back to my house," she whispered in his ear. "I'll show you my sketchings."

"Or etchings."

"Whatever." They parked his car two blocks away at an accounting office and walked back to her house. It was dusk and they went through the downstairs, then up to her room without turning on any lights. He had seen her room once before. It was the typical girl room. White furniture and canopy bed, pink frilly spread and pastel-colored quilt that she had had since birth. She went to her closet and within minutes stepped out in underwear he hadn't seen before: black and lacy, *purchased just for you*, she said.

He kept thinking he heard things, car doors, her father's whistling; he felt the eyes of all the stuffed toys and Barbie dolls that lined the shelves. Her parents could so easily forget something, return, walk in. His chest was pounding and even though she was licking around his ear, her hands fumbling with his zipper, he could not respond. His reluctance made her work that much harder, saying things she had never said, teasing him in ways that she had never done.

"What have you been reading, Sarah?" he whispered, but by then she had pushed his pants down and was rubbing against him, pulling him onto the pink silky surface. She straddled his stomach and leaned forward, and he saw her, the Sarah he knew pretending to be some-one else, wanting to be someone else.

"Are you mad at me?" he had asked, pushing her up so that he could see her eyes.

"Only about you," she said. "I am crazy mad about you." And he caved in, gave himself over to this plan of hers, the grown-up cha-rade. It was the best it had ever been, but then he was worried about her room, the bedspread, the smell of their bodies, no condom. He tried to pull out but she dug in with her knees and pressed harder, their hip bones grinding. It was like being in the middle of the river and unable to touch bottom; a rhythmic treading and gasping and then complete immersion. "I didn't get out," he whispered, and he felt her mouth breathe a weak "I know" into his cheek.

"IT MIGHT BE an hour or so," Doug Taylor called out from his musty garage. His hands were stained a deep brown from motor oil. "Had to get a tire change taken care of."

"Oh, dear," Sarah said.

"I could give you a lift home," Tommy said, and she looked up.

"Yeah? That would be great."

"Hop in." He opened the cab door, and she climbed up. He felt himself looking around as he circled the truck to his side. What would Jones Jameson, for example, make of this scene? Or her mother? Her husband? He got in and closed the door, brushed the dog hair from the edge of her seat. "I hope nobody thinks this is a rendezvous," he said and turned the ignition.

"So who cares?" She laughed and then fell silent. When he pulled into her driveway and stopped, no other car there, she turned in the seat and leaned toward him. "I know. Let's ride around. Give me the tour the way you used to. Show me what's new or different."

"Yeah?" He glanced up at her front porch all littered with moving boxes.

"Yeah! I'm tired of unpacking. I've been alone all day long."

"Where's . . ." He tried to say "Mack" but couldn't. "Where's your husband? Where's June?"

"Work and visiting the boyfriend, who sounds like a jerk."

"Which one's doing which?"

"You're the same old TomCat," she said, reached over and patted his thigh. He had not been this scared since they lay there in her childhood room, his underwear thrown and hanging over the head of a bear he had won for her at Ocean Drive.

"No, no, I'm not the same."

She got quiet, and he found himself able to look at her without blinking, able to return this stare she had fixed on him immediately. She looked a little older, around the eyes maybe; she looked tired.

"You look the same to me," she said. "Please, Tommy. Be the same. I'll be your best friend." The last time she had said that to him was when he went up to visit her in college and she wanted him to go to a dorm party where he was the only person not wearing Top-Siders and long khaki shorts. "Please. Please let me make things up to you."

He sat, hand on the gear but not shifting. What in the hell did she mean by that?

"You look surprised."

"I am."

"Why?"

"Because you're different, you know. You're married." He looked at himself in the rearview mirror. Reality check.

"We're still friends aren't we, Tommy?"

"It's been twenty years."

"So? Are you saying you don't want to be friends?" She looked at him then, eyes tearful. What had happened there in her perfect little cottage that now after all these years made her want him back in her life? Was she cracking up?

"Sarah," the sound of her name was so familiar in his mind yet it had been years since he had actually said it. "Think about where I am in all of this."

"Yes?" She sat and then a knowing look came to her and with it she promptly looked away. "Oh, of course, there's somebody in your life, and you don't want to botch things up."

"No." He shook his head and without thinking reached over and grabbed her arm, squeezed with each syllable. "There's someone in *your* life." He stopped just short of the presumption. It was so easy to turn such a line on someone. He had once been asked on a date only to be told upon declining, "Well, I only asked you to go for coffee. I wasn't proposing. Who do you think you are?" Now he stopped and waited for her to manipulate his meaning.

"I have someone, and you don't want to botch *that* up. Is that it?" She put her hand on his and squeezed back. "Mack knows all about you and how important you were to me."

"He knows *all* about me?" He pulled his hand out from under hers and played with the key chain that hung from the ignition, a silver dog whistle, remains of his last brief relationship, which had ended almost two years ago. *And how important I was?*

"Well not *all* about you," she said and squeezed his hand. "Really, Tommy, I need to ride around, take in the sights." She laughed. "Then you take me back to the Exxon and that's it, I'll never force you to take me for a ride again."

"That's what I'm afraid of," he said and he looked straight ahead as his ears and neck burned. He put the truck in reverse and backed down the drive. What he really wanted to say was "Let's go to the river." What he really wanted to say was, *Please just let me drown.*

Dear Wayward One,

It's our anniversary tonight. Twenty years since we had our own little ceremony out at the Holiday Inn on the highway. My husband always asks me why I love Holiday Inns so much. He recently tried to get me to stay in like a Marriott or something really swank when we went down to Georgia for a little holiday. Nope. Holiday Inn for me. He thinks I'm thrifty—imagine that! Oh no, love, it's the plain dull furniture, the same arrangement of everything bolted down, the same taste of coffee that he brought back to the room in a styrofoam cup, that YOU brought back to the room in a styrofoam cup that next morning. "To my make-believe wife," you said and leaned down and kissed me. My husband thought I was visiting my childhood friend and of course we did do that! In those days I just couldn't lie, not like I've learned to do lately. Now I am a professional liar. Watch out because you can't believe a word I say. I mean, maybe you think I'll tell you the whole truth and nothing but the truth so help me God because you are dead but honey, dead don't count. The truth is that I am just as drunk as I can be. I am as drunk as I got that time I wasted all of our screwing time throwing up there in a rented lavatory that smelled like old piss. *Oh dear, am I shocking you dead man? Am I making you feel bad? I can't imagine it feels as bad as being without a head. HA! I can't imagine it feels as bad as being the one left behind. I didn't mean for this to go this way. You see the truth is that my husband and I just got back from the most wonderful dinner out. We drove to the beach. We're AT the beach in a nice hotel and he has just fallen asleep after some of the best lovemaking I have done in my life. Eat your old decayed heart out! It's so convenient that we're here, because you see I don't have nearly so far to go to mail your little old shitty letter. I guess you wonder why I always go to that same old box. Well, first of all, it gives me a reason to drive down here and hear the waves and second, it is the closest box to where you croaked. SO THERE! If you are some ghost haunting your last spot, then this is as close as I can get to you unless of course I walk down to the point and go up into your room there. The house is disappearing you know. With every high tide, with every high wind, a little bit more is gone. Soon there will be nothing, no place for me to go and stand, should I ever get up the nerve, and no place for you to stand in some foggy stupid form, you stupid ass of a selfish man. Why weren't you like my husband, my real husband? What's funniest about that night all those years ago is how we were planning to keep meeting, to take that same trip forever. I did call my husband more than I probably should've. I was so nervous. You, you weren't nervous in the least. You put that styrofoam cup up to my lips and you said:* For better or worse, in sickness and in health, and forsaking all others, keep your private stock unto me till death do we part. *Well, we parted all right. And I hope you're jealous in your old dead state. I do. I do. I do.*

*A*ll the while Tom Lowe works on finishing off Quee's new deck, he plays the radio, listening like everybody else in town for news about Jones Jameson. It has turned into a hot day, and he has stripped down to no shirt at all and has a bandana tied around his forehead to keep back the sweat. He has yet to see the dingdong doctor Denny, though he finds himself thinking of her off and on, checking every time Quee's door opens. Most of the visits have been from Ruthie Crow, who is as agitated as a person can get without needing to be put in a straitjacket. She keeps eyeing the pack of cigarettes in the pocket of his shirt, which he's hung on a lagustrum bush. "Uh-uh-uh, Ruthie," he says. "Don't you be a bad girl." This was kind of flirty, he realizes, but she's too addicted to nicotine to be thinking of sex.

Sometimes when Tom is working, he thinks back over the old pirate stories; it's like he's being read to in a pirate brogue. He loves when Jack Rackham thought Anne Bonny had taken up with another man only to discover that it was really Mary Read in disguise. *You? You? Why, you little wench!* They were some tough-ass women, to be sure. Unlike their male companions, they didn't get strung up by the neck because they were pregnant. Supposedly the three oldest professions were medicine and prostitution and piracy. Quee had told him that one day when he was telling her stories about Blackbeard. They'd begun talking about facial hair, and nobody had more facial hair than Blackbeard. Quee said, "I'd pick prostitute."

"I'd pick pirate," Tom had said, though clearly he wouldn't. Oh, he could take the part with the boat and the ocean; he could take the stealing and looting. What he couldn't take was the murder. That's when he told Quee the pirate superstitions about drowning and how nobody ever tried to save anybody because it was thought to be interfering with the underworld. Drowning pirates would scream for help, and their friends would yell back, "Give in, matey, it's meant to be." Now he keeps hearing *Give in matey, it's meant to be*, with every scrape of his handsaw, every slam of the hammer. Ruthie is back inside now and since he no longer needs to stand guard over his cigarettes, he can drift along, turning back again to Sarah, wishing, as he does every time he thinks of the day he saw her at the Exxon, that he could have done something to keep her future from happening.

HE DID FINALLY agree to drive her around, for old time's sake, to prove that he could be her friend, and he had driven several blocks, Sarah's hand still just inches from his thigh, when he asked where she wanted to go.

"Show me where you live," she said, and plucked some dog hair from her shorts.

"In my mind or for real?"

"Do you still go out to your lot?" She relaxed and stretched her legs, leaned her head back on the seat. He felt her watching him and nodded. "Do you go every day?"

"No, not every day."

"Anytime I think of you, that's where you are." She paused. "I love that you do that; I love the story, always have."

"Is that what it is? A story?"

"A wonderful story."

"A story you told in college? Maybe tell at cocktail parties?"

"No." Her hand is there again, patting and then covering his hand on the gearshift. "It's a story I guess I keep to myself."

The memory of the river was so strong it pulled him away, although she sat right beside him. He had planned what he would say to her, things like: "So, I guess we broke up, huh?" or "You are some kind of fickle highfalutin bitch" or "How many guys have you fucked since me?" He has also imagined himself *at* her wedding, there in the Presbyterian Church. She would change her mind at the last minute and together they would run to his truck and head for the beach. He could see her in her long white dress, thigh deep in the ocean. Her arms around his neck pulling him down.

"How about where you actually live," she said, just as they passed the bank and the house where he grew up. His mother had recently added a sunroom and the new brick didn't quite match up with the old. He didn't look to see if his mother was there; he would see her soon enough, and he'd hear about how he needed a real job and a real house, a wife and children. She would say, "No woman, or sensible woman I might add, will ever put up with all those mongrels."

"Why?" he asked, once his mother's house was two blocks behind them.

"I don't know. Seems fair. You know where I live."

"Yeah, well, I used to like my neighborhood, but it's gone down quite a bit." He pressed the accelerator, making it through the yellow light at their old elementary school. "A lot of people have moved in and driven down the value of my property."

"Oh." She laughed. "Now most people would argue that your property value has gone up since all those people moved in."

"Depends on your definition of value." He turned into the subdivision, pausing at the big brick pillars to give her the full effect. "If you value trees, frogs, privacy, well, you might say something has been lost." He drove slowly past the houses and yards, three-car garages, and little islands of landscaping. "You might want to duck. I bet you know most of the people who live here. And if you don't, you surely will soon."

"I've been here several times," she said. "The realtor was determined that we buy a house out here."

"She probably tried to sell you the one right across the street from my mansion."

"Yes," she nodded knowingly. "Yes, she did, but I had no idea that you were the person."

"The person everybody out here hates?" He turned into his drive and then bumped into and beyond the pines that hid his trailer completely from street view. There were only six dogs then. "Home Sweet Home," he said and offered her what he thought later sounded more like an apology than he meant for it to. "I was here first."

"You really *haven't* changed, Tommy."

"I'm sorry."

"I'm not." This time she grabbed his arm with both hands and inched her way across the seat. "You look the same, sound the same." She leaned in close. "You even smell the same."

"And is that good?"

She nodded and then pressed her nose near his collar and breathed in. "Let's see, there's tobacco and puppy breath and ocean salt and a little sawdust." She moved up his neck, her warm breath covering his ear. "Prell Shampoo."

"Why are you doing this, Sarah?" Now he refused to look at her. He stared straight ahead, his hand gripping the door handle.

"You brought me here."

"You asked me to."

"I didn't make you, though." Her hands were on his back, first lightly and then palms pressed flat and circling. She pulled his shirt out of his jeans and moved her hands back up.

"Your car will be ready," he whispered, his heart beating so hard he was sure she could feel it against her breasts as she pressed in closer and closer.

"No, not yet."

"Your husband might look for you." That got her attention and pushed her back. "Really, Sarah. This is kind of crazy."

"Just show me inside. Then we'll go back. Show me your dogs, okay?" She opened her door and stepped out into the wet, soggy straw. The door creaked louder than usual when he stepped out, and it seemed the whole neighborhood had fallen silent, there were no birds, no crickets; it was so quiet he believed he could hear the mist that was shrouding the world. He opened the door to the leaping and barking of the three dogs. Blackbeard's tail alone could do considerable damage, which is why Tom stored his dishes high up on a makeshift shelf.

"Home Sweet Home," he said and grabbed the big bag of dog food to lead the three outside for an unexpected meal this time of day. She stood watching him, her arms crossed over her chest. He barely got back in the half door before she locked her arms behind his neck and pressed against him.

"Why Sarah?" he whispered. "Why are you doing this to me?"

"*To* you?" she stepped back with a wounded look. "Is that how you see it?"

"Yes, yes I do." He moved away from her and pulled himself up to sit on the side of the bed. "I'd offer you a chair if there was one," he said.

"I would have gladly offered myself the bed if you didn't feel you were being taken advantage of."

"Sarah." He watched as she stood staring at his belongings all lined up on what was supposed to be another bed. She ran her finger up and down the spine of his giant *World Atlas*, the same book he had used to tutor her in geography years before. What a joke. Even then he knew what a joke it was; he tutored her and yet she was the one going off to a new life.

"You don't have anything to lose," she said without turning, and before she could complete the words he was standing, holding her arms and forcing her to listen.

"I have everything to lose," he said. "And I'd be losing it again."

"Oh, Tommy, I'm sorry." She leaned into him and cried. "All this time I've just wanted to make things up to you."

"It can't be done," he said and then softened. "What I mean is we can't change anything."

"Can we pretend? One minute?" She kissed his cheek lightly and ran her finger around his lips, pressed to silence any rejection. "Do you ever think about what we would have been like?"

"No," he lied.

"We would have a nineteen-year-old," she whispered, "somebody older now than we were then."

"I can't imagine that."

"We would have slept this close for nineteen years and there would have been no hiding, no slipping." She moved her hands up under his denim shirt, flat palms circling, her cheek pressed against his mouth. A slight turn and she spoke again, her lips not an inch from his. "You never think of me, TomCat?"

"Never," he said and then "always." When they kissed it was as if they had never been apart, the familiar ways of touching, her hair wrapped around his hand as he pulled her face closer.

"I want you, Tommy." She stepped back only two steps and there was the bed. "Please." She had that same desperate look he had clung to all those years. It spelled need, need that seemed to go far beyond the physical. And there was a pull like swimming out and then letting go, letting the current pull and pull; there was the fear of drowning in the undertow, forever lost. Then he was on top of her, her hand guiding him in when Blackbeard began barking, his tail thumping against the camper door.

"Don't leave, Tommy."

He swung his legs off the bed and rubbed his eyes. He heard the mail truck on the other side of the thick pines as it rattled down to the next house. "Do you love your husband?"

There was silence, and then a weak *yes*.

"Do you think that you might one day soon leave him and join me here in the camper?" He forced a laugh without looking at her.

"I hadn't really thought about it."

"So what have you thought?"

"That I want a baby." Suddenly she was sitting up with her shirt pulled up to her chest. "For four years I have." She began crying, openly, loudly, the same kind of crying she did when they broke up. Something clicked inside him.

"Is that why you're here?" He shook her by the shoulders. "Yoo-hoo, was *that* what you were thinking?"

"I don't know," she said. "I don't know what I was thinking. It's been so hard. It's so frustrating, I mean I know that I *can* get pregnant, right?"

"Yes, that we can do. But Sarah." He pressed his hands on either side of her face, kissed her forehead. "I ain't your guy, honey. I'd only want the baby if I got the mama." He kissed her again, this time on the lips; this time he was in control. "In that way, nothing has changed."

"Do you wish that we'd had a baby?"

"No," he said. "Because you would have hated me before it ever had the chance to grow up."

"Are you positive?"

"Yes." He didn't offer her any of the ideas he'd had, things he would have done to make it work. Why should he? There would have been no guarantees. Maybe she would have grown to despise him, to blame him for existing in this town. And now, as she slipped back into her clothes and dabbed at her eyes with a tissue, somewhere in this town the young Mack McCallister was probably wondering if it was all going to work; wondering what he could do to hold it all together.

TOM PULLS HIS shirt, warm from the sun beating down on Quee's bush, back over his head. He hates himself for having not given in to her. If he had the chance to go back he would not be so stubbornly practical and moral. He wouldn't give a damn about Mack McCallister or the mailman or the confused dogs. He sits down and lights a cigarette.

"Hey, you."

He looks up to see Denny leaning out the window of her apartment.

"Are you talking to me?"

"Of course." She is grinning now. He's not sure if he has the energy for her. Surely if you give this one an inch she will flat take a mile. If she were a dog, she'd be one of the high-maintenance varieties like his little Anne Bonny or even Blackbeard, one that has to be stroked and groomed or else winds up dull and matted and looking like shit.

*J*ones Jameson didn't even glance Myra's way when he passed that morning, and she had been so relieved, seeing as how little Sharpy was taking care of other things and she found this terribly embarrassing, which is why she tends to walk the dog so early to begin with. It was six-thirty in the morning (Sharpy's bladder is more punctual than any clock), and Jones Jameson was driving fast. Gravel sprayed as he raced past on West Seventh Street, and it scared Sharpy. She stood and watched him heading towards the downtown area.

Sharpy perches on Myra's lap the whole time she gives all of this information to the *seemingly* nice young officer who is seated in her living room. He is sitting in the chair that poor Howard used to sit in, and just seeing a body in that chair, seeing a MAN in that chair makes her furious all of a sudden without warning; she would like to smash something. These feelings come to her suddenlike and have since Howard died. She called it grief for five years and then in her head began calling it relief. She was glad when he died; she was tired of having to share her belongings. She had *shared* her whole life, and she was sick of it. She was looking for a good therapist to tell this to. I am so glad he's dead, she wanted to say, what a relief, what a blessing, what a load off of my back. She would also tell that in secret she always listened to Jones Jameson's radio show, that she didn't necessarily *like* the way he chose to say things, but the ideas behind his words, ideas like that the Negroes had been given enough free handouts and it was time for deserving whites to get a chance. Yes, and she agreed with him about all these women out there wearing suits and trying to pass themselves off as something with a *you know what*. Jones Jameson had said the word. He had said "penis," and despite herself it had made Myra laugh a little. *Damn right* she said in her head, "Stay away from what's mine."

"Jones and his wife did fight from time to time," she tells the officer.

"How do you know?"

"I have ears." She says this and then pauses for effect, like she has seen people do on *Oprah*, people who say things like *I am in touch with a ten-thousand-year-old Indian.*

"I do hope that smart young man isn't dead," she says, not meaning to think out loud; it's something that begins to happen naturally when you live alone. "He needs to improve his manners, but he has a lot to give this world. He would make us a fine mayor or senator one day."

"Why do you say that?" he asks. "Any reason?"

"He was Phi Beta Kappa. He is for equal rights to the white people."

"No, I mean about him being dead."

"Well, because that's the first thing you might think when somebody's missing now isn't it? Like that Exxon man who disappeared from his very own driveway? Isn't that why you're here?" She smooths out some wrinkles on the dog and then lets the loose folds of skin fall back the way they do, like an accordion. "A lot of people stopped using the Exxon after that little spill, but I always said, well it was an accident. Little accidents happen." She pauses and stares at the young man. She bets he was one of those children people thought were so ugly they didn't know what to say to their mama. He looks okay now but, you can just tell he was that kind of child. "Now take Howard's accident."

"Excuse me, but I'm going to need to leave now." He stands. "Is there anything else you needed to tell?"

"Well, not if nobody's listening."

"What kind of dog did you say that is?" He maneuvers his way through her living room, where she keeps a big pasteboard box full of eggs for Ruthie.

"A shar-pei," she says slowly. "Sharpy is a shar-pei." She is suddenly desperate for company. This man would not be her number one A-plus choice, but beggers can't be choosy. "I can see how he could be dead, you know?" This gets the officer's attention. "I mean, my Howard seemed to die so suddenlike, and they never quite figured what had brought it on." She stops and smiles at him the way her Sunday school leader, Connie Briley, always does; it's a smile that says, "I'm perfect and you are not; if you touch me, I will knock the ever loving feces out of you." Myra hates Connie and would love to see her up and stricken with a hemorrhage; sometimes at night she gets herself to sleep with an image of Connie blue in the face and pop-eyed with that smile still intact. She thinks this, too, is something that she would like to tell a therapist. She would like to be reassured that such thoughts do not mean you are not a good Christian.

"You know, arsenic is real big in this state," she tells the officer, but surely he knows this. If he doesn't, then he doesn't deserve that badge he's wearing on that bony chest. "There was the woman on death row back a ways. That was a sad one. A Christian grandmama gone bad. That's what the newspaper said. Said she was on drugs. And who would have thought? And her coming from such a nice little town, too." Oh, she has the officer's attention now. She might even be able to get Ruthie a date with him before it's all over. Ruthie would say he wasn't "her cup of tea"; Ruthie would say what she has been saying for years: "But if your backdoor neighbor ever gets a divorce, I'll be sitting there on his steps. Mmmm, mmmmm, mmmmmm." Myra is still convinced that that's why Ruthie has enrolled herself in that foolfangled smoking clinic. Ruthie wants to rub shoulders with Alicia Jameson and work her way into their lives. Why else would she be there? Myra warned her over and over about that Quee Purdy, about how nobody who was a good decent person would pass any time with her. She told Ruthie that for years people had said she was a W-H-O-R-E; she told Ruthie how Quee Purdy had attacked Myra right there in the Winn-Dixie less than a month ago.

"Are you saying that you think Jones Jameson could have been poisoned?"

"Anything's possible." She beckons for him to follow her into the kitchen. It's kind of exciting leading a man through her house this way. "Then there was another woman not too far from here, did the same thing. Arsenic." She stops to point out the portfolio of when Ruthie was wanting to be a fashion model way back. "Ruthie has always had big ambitions," she says, and shows him one of Ruthie in a macramé swimsuit. Myra thinks she looks like a skeleton with her cheeks all sucked in like that. "Isn't she something else?"

"Absolutely."

Myra doesn't tell him that the agency in Raleigh told Ruthie there was more to modeling than looking like a starved refugee, even though Ruthie herself will tell of how her *disappointments* in life led her to her present vocation of spilling her emotions onto the paper. Ruthie talks so often of spurting and spilling and spewing that Myra sometimes thinks she ought to keep a mop by the door.

"Ruthie's single, you know."

"Where did these women get the stuff?"

"Now son, you should be ashamed of yourself." She shakes her head and pulls out her favorite photo of Ruthie; she's dressed up to look like a little girl with her hair in braided pigtails and short, short dungarees like that girl with the big bosoms on *HeeHaw*. Howard loved that show, and Myra used to always tell him that if breasts were something good, then the Lord would have given big ones to more of the *good* women. He nods and she pulls out one with Ruthie trying to look like Greta Garbo turned backward and looking over that bony shoulder. Bones and More Bones. This might be the man for Ruthie. "Arsenic is so easy," she says. "Ant killer. Rat killer." She fans herself with the photos, suddenly feeling quite girly and coy though she can't for her life say why. "Those women just decided to go for the big pests."

"Is Jones Jameson a big pest?"

"Oh, no, like I say, he's a darling boy. He was handsome the day he was born. Now he might drink a bit too much on occasion, and of course his language and those jokes on the radio are just awful, but you know his mama, who I have known my whole life, says that that's all part of Jones's image down at the radio station. If he's to make it big, he HAS to do those things."

"I see," the officer turns to write on his little pad. "And what about Mrs. Jameson?"

"What I can gather," she says, "you know from bits and pieces I've heard over the years. Um. How can I say this? I'm afraid I might blush."

"Please," he says, "it's very important."

"She just wasn't satisfying him. And we all know what happens when a man is not satisfied."

"What?"

"Like you don't know, a big fella such as yourself!" She snatches the
photos and puts them in the envelope. It's coming back, the anger,
like a great big dark wave breaking over her head.

ROBERT FOLLOWS MYRA Carter into her kitchen for coffee and a
snack before he wraps up the questioning. There is a joke around
town that people who go to visit Myra Carter sometimes disappear,
that she talks them to death. The paramedics who came when her
husband died said that they were wanting to die, too, before they
could get out of there. Alicia once defended this very issue; she
called it "the widow syndrome." She called it loneliness; her work
with lonely widows is what got her hooked up with Quee Purdy in
the first place, though people around town will quickly tell you that
"lonely" and "widow" are two words that do NOT fit Ms. Quee
Purdy.

"You know, they live practically in my backyard," Myra says and
points to the window over her sink where she has all kinds of knick-
knacks: little Dutch children kissing and a bird that bobs his head into
a glass of water, a little tiny wooden outhouse that holds toothpicks.
"From the window you can see the deck and their family room. Get
to the far end of my garden in the new potatoes and you can see their
bedroom."

Robert gets up and follows her lead. He leans close to the window
and, sure enough, he can see the back of Alicia's house. He can see
the deck where he was once invited to a cookout where he was way
out of place and out of style. Alicia was hoping Robert would enjoy
meeting some people since he had just moved to town. Maybe that
was her way of letting him know she had a life that didn't include him,
that they could be friends but nothing else. Before the night was over,
right there on that deck, Jones Jameson announced that he had

knocked up Alicia. She was sitting beside Robert, and he saw her jerk to attention.

"See? You want let's walk outside?" Myra pushes herself out of her chair. Her hair is a brassy strawberry blond, like somebody used the wrong bottle of solution when she went in for a rinse. "I'll give you the tour. Besides," and her voice gets high and squeaky, "Mr. Sharpy has to wee-wee." The dog waddles over to her, his rolls wiggling in excitement. "A weedle-wee for Mr. Sharpy."

Robert hesitates as he stands there in the afternoon sunlight, looking out over Mrs. Carter's backyard. As boring as it is listening to this woman talk, he is oddly comforted by her surroundings, soothed by the smell of pine paneling and oilcloth, coffee and toast. The little junk bits she's collected over the years. Robert has already learned not to comment on anything; there's a whole long story behind whatever it is. It will begin with something like: Well, my Howard had just returned from *the War*. . . . Everything began when Howard returned. What on earth will Robert use to measure his life? Has it already happened? Was it when he took to croissants and for-eign flicks?

He follows her outside. It's so hot, like being wrapped in a thick heavy blanket, his eyes blinded by the brightness. She makes a funny clicking sound, and Sharpy waddles right beside her, lifting his leg on a fence post as she opens the garden gate and leads Robert in. The smell of the garden is overwhelming, rich with newly spread manure and the acrid odor of tomatoes and marigolds. The garden is perfectly manicured, not a weed to be found and, Myra boasts, she does NOT use weedblock, as do all of her young careless neighbors who might think they "garden." One compliment and now Robert is getting the full garden spiel, how she uses tin cans to protect her tomato plants' roots, and how she orders her topsoil from down near the river, where there's lots of decay and the soil is slightly acidic.

"I have a load coming the end of this week," she says. "I like to really feed my plot of earth every fall."

"Now where are the potatoes?" Robert asks, straining to see into Alicia's backyard where Taylor has a plastic log cabin. It makes his chest swell and ache to see that little house. There's something about kids living in a shitty household that tears him up. He imagines Alicia trying; he sees her out there putting that house together, lifting and connecting the pieces while that lousy bastard husband was probably inside jacking off to some magazine or a picture of himself. Robert flushes with his own thoughts; he is ashamed when he uses bad language and yet, so often there's no other way to do justice to an idea.

"The far end." She gives the dog a look like "Is he stupid or what?" and then shoos Robert on down the path. "Now walk around the hills, please, there you go." She waves one hand as if presenting the back of Alicia's house, the deck, and yes, a window, the shade drawn.

"Oh, well," she says. "Late one afternoon, dusk really, I was out here working and I saw them having an awful fight. You know dusk is the best time of day to see *in*."

"Do you know what it was about?"

"Well, he didn't want her working, which I can't blame him seeing as *where* she works." Myra pats her thigh for Mr. Sharpy to come back to her. "I've had several run-ins with that awful Queen Mary Stutts Purdy, myself. She can call herself Pur DAY all she wants, but she is nothing but a Stutts and folks around here know that."

"And?"

"And what?"

"The argument."

"Hmmm now, let's see if I can remember." She looks at her watch and tells him she's going to have to think it all through again, that she has got a thousand things to do today and so he best be on his way. "I know. Why don't you come back tomorrow, and I will have remembered by then."

"All right." Robert takes one last look at the back of the house, the rubber ball, the plastic wading pool, Alicia's bathing suit hanging over the railing of the deck. He would give anything to talk to Alicia right now, just to see her, but she had specifically asked that they not bother her until there is new news.

"I do hope Jones isn't dead." Myra hands him a little brown paper bag full of cherry tomatoes and dirty cucumbers that smell of pesticides and hustles him back through her dark house. She stands in the doorway, her television (she flipped it on in passing) now blaring in the background. It's time for Oprah Winfrey. "You better check the river," Myra says. "Especially now that you've found that old fancy car like what my brother-in-law drove to the Tastee Freez. Check it for prints. Do your duty, young man. Did I even tell you what my brother-in-law did buy?" She calls out to his back, "One of those Gremlins. Can you believe that? A Gremlin. *He's* a gremlin. When you come back I'll tell you why."

$\mathcal{T}$esting . . . yoo-hoo. Day four and I just don't know how long I'm gonna last here in the twilight zone. I mean, this radio guy I told you about? Not the one staying here who tries to flash his fat ass at you if you'll let him. HE spent his whole therapy time talking about how he knew he was capable of having some extramarital activity, it was just that he hadn't found anybody who was worth him risking all that he has. Quee told me later that what he has is a wife who tells him exactly what to do when. Quee says she's all for a powerful woman all right, but she has no respect for the man who doesn't give her a good fight. Man oh man, I wish you could see Quee's face when she gets going on something. It's like her whole face quivers, like all that loose skin starts trembling with a life of its own. She clenches her teeth and flares her nostrils and, other than that, all of her emotional reaction is there in the skin, especially the skin around her neck. She said the other day that somebody could snip away what was there under her chin and fashion two rather sizeable breasts.

"I'll take 'em," Alicia said though as far as I can tell that is the one and only thing that she does have, and Lordy she's another story, which is exactly what I'm building up to. She is downright pitiful. If the greased-up addicted radio guy is (to quote Quee, of course, because I have never made a habit of using the "p" word and certainly not the "c" word—only the "f" word) "pussy-whipped," then it's for sure that this Alicia is pecker- (a "p" word I do find myself using quite often) whipped. She looks like somebody who ought to be walking around with her mouth hanging open. You might name her Pitiful Pearl or Sorrowful Sue if she was a baby doll. I'm into such names right now because part of my made-up therapy is to have folks look at a baby doll and then name it. It's kind of a modernized Rorschach. I mean, do they see sadness or joy, loneliness or horniness, as suggested by Mr. Radio Lard-Ass. I try to pick babies whose expressions are not so obvious. Then I pull out the hard part of the test. I hold up a stuffed animal and I say: "What gender is this?" Quee kind of liked this one because she herself is also somebody who has always been able to know the sex of a stuffed animal. It's just instinct; it's the same way that I'm very good at knowing someone's sexual preference, like when I was set up on a blind date with a man I knew would much rather be with the man friend who set us up. My date, of course, didn't know that yet, and neither did the friend who set us up, but I did. It was like being struck in the head with a car jack; that's what Quee's forever saying, *Struck in the head with a car jack*—sometimes she says, *Well, hit me with a concrete slab*, the same way my ex always said, *Wow, I could've had a V-8*. He is so original, somebody should give him a prize. That's what I'd always say to him. I'd say, *Yuk, yuk, that's about as funny as Elvis singing "What's eatin you, Babe" on a leprosy ward. That's so funny, when Columbus told it to the Indians, they shot him.* Well, I knew those two men were in need of two men, and you might as well say four divided by two and just stick those that are left together, which is what I did, and they are living happily ever after to this day, still amazed that I knew they were gay before they did.

I mean, it was like I was saying earlier, you know about how I just have intuition about things, which is why people come from all over for my expert advice. Come out, come out wherever you are. Shit or get off the pot. Don't put off till tomorrow what you can do today. Life is a terminal thing.

Anyway, you would see Alicia and you would say that she had been beaten to a pulp emotionally. She thinks she's ugly, and she thinks the world is ugly. The only thing she seems to think is cute is that old handyman Tom, always hanging around here, and who wouldn't, I ask you. Still I'm trying to talk myself out of thinking so, because for one reason he doesn't even live in a house! Besides, it seems he's all moonie over somebody who fell into a coma, a *married* woman who fell into a coma I might add. AND, Quee seems to think that if he ever gets over her that he might come to ask Alicia out. Another married one! Quee said all this about how men find Alicia so much fun to be with. There's Tom Lowe, who always stops after building a closet or some other big brain-requiring feat to ask how she's doing and to play with that child of hers who looks too old for diapers if you ask me, and then of course there's that tall skinny cop who looks like he might be in the poultry family with that Adam's apple of his and those white, white, almost gooseflesh-looking arms. He's the kind of man you might see and then say, "Did I see a ghost? Is your name Caspar?" You would NOT want to see this man in swimwear.

I won't be surprised if I swing around and DO see a ghost one of these days, what with all these awful-looking people that are long dead staring out of their dusty old frames. As far as I can tell right now, the only thing that Alicia and I agree on is that these old photos give us the creeps. Alicia seems to think that some bad karma might get out, but Quee just laughs and says, "Oh, honey, you'd know bad karma if you felt it. But I was in real estate long enough to know that it doesn't happen very often." Now how can you let her tell that little bit and then stop? I mean, there that child of Alicia's was hanging on to her and smelling like a polecat, and Alicia was wanting to hear a story. So of course I asked if she'd ever encountered "bad" karma (worse than what I'm feeling right now, I wanted to say but of course didn't). She said that once she was trying to sell a house that's known as the murder-suicide house, and that yes, when she went in and there was still the smell of death, blood in the shower stall and brains on the light fixture, that there was some bad karma. Alicia was looking like she might vomit with this part of the story and excused herself to go change that old diaper where there's a diaper pail that keeps the whole back of the house smelling like something died and went to hell. "But a little steam cleaning and Clorox, fresh paint, and all the bad karma disappeared."

"Or was covered up," I said and she just smiled, her skin quivering, and *that's* when she said that about she could take what's on her neck and make somebody some boobs, that is *if* she believed in boobs. She said that she was starting to think that women should have them removed as soon as their childbirthing days are over; get rid of all those cancer caves, she said. Alicia gasped when she heard this. Some people shy off from that word *cancer*, like the word itself might bite you. I suspect they probably had somebody in their childhood tell them that if they had ever eaten or touched a crab (also known as Cancer in the zodiac) that they would die from that very disease. A boy in third grade told me that but of course I was too smart to believe him; I did however tell him that he had ancestors and that his epidermis was showing and that everybody knew he had slumbered in his sleep, and he cried to the teacher, who spanked my hand with a ruler and never once asked me *why* I felt the need to say all of that to him.

So Quee says, these men just take to Alicia "like a fly to honey."
Now if Alicia has a pea in her head, she knows that Quee is just trying to build up her ego. I mean, her husband is missing. Gone for
days. Not a trace, except that car of his that if I was Alicia I'd've gone
and claimed and be driving. "It's impounded," she said to me slowly,
like I might not have all of my chromosomes. "They are thinking
there might be foul play." Her husband was probably bored to tears
like me and just had no choice but to pack a bag and run like hell. So,
anyway, there I was with Mr. Radio in the therapy room, and he's saying all this about how he might have his fat self an affair if he finds the
right person, and there Alicia, who's sitting there rubbing out his
hairy-monkey-looking feet, thinks he's making a play at her. She said:
"Really, Barry," which was the first time I'd heard him called anything
other than the Radio Guy. She said, "Really, Barry, why don't you just
go home and do something nice for Wanda?" Alicia glanced at me as
if to say, "Why don't you shut up with your little dream interpreta-
tion and let *me* take care of things." I waved her on. Fine, fine as wine.
I am not going to beat my brains out in this little job. I mean, it is like
the handyman said, I *do* have a choice about being here.

"She's a wonderful person," Alicia said. I had seen a photo of
Wanda when I rooted through Barry's top drawer in search of guiding info while he was in "the sauna," which really means he was in "the
shower" with the doors closed. Mr. Fix-It had nailed up a big piece of
Plexiglas between the doors and ceiling to hold in the steam. A person could probably suffocate in there or drown if it was to suddenly
fill up with water like in that *I Love Lucy* episode where Lucy and Ethel
get stuck in there and are swimming around. I have always *loved* that
episode. It always reminded me of that little pool at church where I
got baptized. My ex, brilliant man that he is, said that watching things
like the Nickelodean or Ted Turner channels, which is where I find all

the shows that I like best, was an activity that he did not understand. I told him that any activity that involved being with him was an activity that I couldn't understand. I guess this Tom Lowe guy might not even own a TV, can you imagine that? What would you do all night? Anyway, as I was saying, I went peeking in Barry's drawer, kind of like the way the wizard goes into Dorothy's purse, and I found that photo of his wife who looks all right, not wonderful like Alicia said, but all right. Normal-looking.

"Wanda will be so proud of you," Alicia said. "You know Jones still smokes."

"Yes." Barry twisted his foot out of her hand and sat forward, his hairy stomach lapping over his towel. He touched her shoulder, and I was about to say, "Well pardon me for conducting my therapy session"; I opened the bottom drawer and got my hand on the visual aid for impotency, deciding that if they got all mushy-mooshie, I'd just whip out that limp number and see what they thought of that. "You're right, Alicia," he said and sighed. "I'm not Jones, and it's about time I stopped trying to act like I am."

"That's good, a positive thing from what I hear," I said and decided to close the drawer back. It occurred to me that it might be a fascinating study to ask the clients to name *that*, since a lot of couples out there seem to engage in such a thing. My ex was forever trying to get me to call his something, I can't even remember what by now. What I do remember is that I told him that I felt about his penis the way I did about a person, and when it was unattached to the blood and oxygen supply and living on its own then I'd give it the decency of its own name. Until then it was just a part of his body and deserved no more special treatment than his feet or nose.

They both whirled around and looked at me like I might be a slug instead of the therapist in charge when I mentioned that no-good husband of hers. All day long, that Alicia talks about how awful he is, but, oh no, don't let anybody else do it.

"Do you know Jones?" Barry asked me and I said no, but I do know that everybody is always saying how he acts just like Howard Stern, how they call him "the preppy Howard Stern." I said that I personally listened to *Imus in the Morning* or *did* when I lived in a civilization with good radio.

"We have good radio," Barry said. "We *do* have good radio." He got red in the face and looked real agitated. I mean, that is what the clients, who now consist of Barry, Ruthie Crow, and a seventeen-year-old boy from the halfway facility, who Quee gave the Smoke-Out Fellowship to, have in common. They are all real agitated and snippy. Quee says the lack of nicotine going to the brain causes this reaction. When they get snippy, she sends them out on the back porch to squeeze out cotton batting that she has soaked in wet ashes. She makes them sing: "I'm gonna wash that soot right outa my lungs." Then she makes them hold and smell raw beef liver as a way of making them consider their internal organs. That poor seventeen-year-old that she has taken into the clinic most recently (free of charge, too!) spends all of his time out there. From the looks of him and that design of a skull shaved on the back of his head, I'd say that smoking is probably the least of his problems. Ruthie Crow stands out there with him a lot of the time because she has become obsessed with finding the best way to describe his skin color. When she held out her little pad where she had written "brown like the suede coat on the cover of the Bloomingdale's catalog" and asked if he wanted to see what she had so far, he hitched up his long raveling shorts and asked if she wanted to see what *he* had. Quee said that he is a good boy, that she has known him for years; she took him to see the ocean when he was in the first grade and that they have been friends ever since, especially when his mama who was raising him ran off and left him with some relatives who cared about as much for him as they did one of the cats that stayed up under their old lean-to house. Quee said it was no wonder that he had tried his hand at abusing some substances.

Lord, don't I know *that* story. Nobody could've ever lived in the marriage I was in and *not* have abused something. Anyway, it's clear that Barry is a bit of an abuser of wine and peanut butter on Saltines. He is forever spewing crackers and licking those sticky fingers. Quee got herself some of those skinny mirrors like they have at some of the department stores and like I've heard they use at some of these posh girl schools where these girls try to see who can come the closest to starving herself. I'm being facetious, of course, for those listeners who are *not* informed about bulimia and anorexia. Bulimia is the one I find most disgusting. These folks eat and eat like there's no tomorrow and then they go and vomit it all back up. We suspect Ruthie Crow of this particular malady, though in four days now I have not smelled vomit on her once, not to mention that I am somebody people just naturally like to tell about their sicknesses. My ex had a friend, a fat divorced hypochondriac sort, who used to give me reports on this virus or that. I called his phone calls the vomit-diarrhea report. He would tell me exactly how many times he had had diarrhea and exactly how many times he vomited and what was in it. I think he thought that I surely must have some kind of special insight into the appearance. Anyway, that old Barry just wouldn't let it rest and kept right on talking; I'll do my best to re-create his exact words.

"We get public radio, too, you know," Barry said. "And I get letters all the time about my show."

"Oh, I've heard your show is wonderful," I lied. "I've heard that you are truly brilliant with the top news stories."

"He is," Alicia adds.

"Well, thanks." He finally nods and sits back, relaxes. *If one of these guinea pigs drops dead with a heart attack, Quee will get me for sure.*

"Oh my, yes, I didn't mean to imply otherwise. You know I just know that Alicia here is hurting, and so it was natural of me to bad-mouth her husband to make her feel better." I had their full attention then. "I mean, haven't we all said something about a friend's partner while she was fussing, to make her feel better?" They nodded yes, and then of course I had to go and finish out the story, like about how many people then later find themselves without a friend when there's a reunion, and then the friend remembers what you said.

"Well, I won't do that to you," Alicia said then and patted Barry's greasy foot one last time before slipping it back into the slipper socks that Quee has everybody wearing. They are white tube socks but she has colored in the toe with black permanent marker so that they look like stubbed-out cigarettes. "I mean, you're absolutely right. People say awful things about Jones. I say awful things about Jones." Her eyes got all wide and glassy, like she might burst into tears any second. "The truth is that he's an awful person and probably, probably . . ." She glanced out in the hallway where Taylor was playing with a little fire truck. "Well, I'm sure he's off with someone. Either that or some-body's husband finally caught and killed him."

"God." Barry took this as a personal threat and pulled his robe a lit-tle bit tighter, crossed his legs. "Do you really think that?"

"I wouldn't be surprised." Alicia looked at me then and it was like every muscle in her face relaxed. "I'm glad you think of me as a friend. Certainly Quee is my friend, but over the years I quit having friends my age because they either hated my husband or they slept with him, sometimes both."

"Is this something you'd like to talk about?" I asked her, mainly because I'm in such a habit of doing that these days, and she said that, yes, she thought she would, only not right this minute, maybe later.

"It's Barry's turn," she said and stood to go out in the hall. "Besides, Ruthie is waiting to get her facial and head massage." When she left, I realized that I hadn't had any girlfriends in a long while either. It sure wasn't because they would have wanted my husband. If they had, then I wouldn't have wanted them for friends! No sir, I was ashamed for them to see how a lively and smart person like myself had been reduced to a substance-abusing space ranger. Sooner or later a friend would say, "But *why* did you marry him?" and the honest-to-God truth was that I had no idea.

"Where were we now, Barry?" I asked and he reminded me that we were discussing dream therapy. Well, he was no help at all, said he couldn't remember a single dream, and I was furious about that. I mean, Ruthie Crow had dreamed that she went to Yellowstone National Park to see Old Faithful.

"That's it," she'd said.

"Well that's a shitload," I'd told her and then resumed my professional demeanor. "Listen to this. I know you watch TV late in the day, because I hear it turned way down low. What's more you watch cartoons. Yogi Bear, Jellystone, Yellowstone? Then we get to Old Faithful. This is either sexual, which I don't have to explain, and it refers to your constant man searching OR"—I didn't pause for a beat because I could tell she was mad that I said she was *looking* for a man—"it has to do with your ever faithful body and your own efforts to control what goes in and what comes out of it."

"What do you mean?" she asked and narrowed her eyes.

"You tell me."

"I know what you think," she said.

"And?" I waited, tapping my pencil until she broke down and
sobbed. Bingo. I should have been a lawyer.

But with Barry. No dreams. Here I was, dying to spout off all that
I had taken in from my reading. I mean, if he dreamed of water, birth,
or death, or sex, I'd know what to say. But nothing. So I used our
dream time instead to try and find out what I could about Alicia's husband. Barry had been torn up over Jones Jameson for years. There
was a part of him that so admired his handsome face and firmly
toned physique; he thought Jones Jameson was such a quick wit and
certainly had a vocabulary that outdid everybody down at the radio
station.

"But," he finally said and looked down at his stomach roll.

"Yes?" I used my most sensitively controlled voice. "Please go on,
Barry."

"He never really wanted to be my friend, you know?" Barry looked
up now and his mouth was quivering. "Wanda and I had them over for
dinner at least twice, and they never asked us back. I don't blame little Alicia for this, of course, I mean he tells everybody down at the
station that he makes all the decisions in his house. I could tell he
didn't think I was worthy of his friendship."

"How?" I asked, even though I was sitting there thinking how sitting here watching this pitiful plump man cry was about the hardest
thing I'd ever done, especially when right outside my window I could
see the handyman working on the deck of the new "fitness room,"
which is, in fact, a little prefab outbuilding where Quee is going to
have two stationary bikes, a treadmill, and a NordicTrack, all of
which she has already ordered. He saw me in there and kept looking
and grinning, shaking his head like what *he* was doing was somehow
better than what I was doing. That ill-kempt dog of his was right there

at his feet. His feet were in black Converse high-tops (no socks, laces loose and loopy), and he was wearing a pair of old faded-out nylon beach britches, like were in style about a century ago.

"He never looked at me when I was talking," Barry said, and I realized that I wasn't looking at him either. I mean, can you blame me? It was hard to, especially when that idiot was out there showing off, first slamming his thumb with the hammer and then filling his mouth with nails like that was something new. "He never asked me what was going on in MY life. It was like he thought nothing could go on in my life. He treated me like I might've been one of the women instead of a man just like him." Barry paused and sighed. "Well, not just like him, but I am a man!"

"Yes, you are."

"I wanted him to say to me, 'Barry you are truly a man,' but he never did it." Barry leaned forward and put his hands up to his face and while he was that way I waved my fingers at the handyman, who looked surprised that I did that.

"How did that make you feel, Barry?"

"I got to where I hated him."

"Yeah?"

"Yeah." Barry stood and paced around with just that towel tied around him and the handyman brushed his two fingers in a *shame on you*. He took the nails from his mouth and made a face like "ooohhh-hhhhh." "Are you a real therapist?"

"Of course I am."

"Well, then you'll be able to appreciate this."

"Okay." My palms got all sweaty, and I wasn't sure if it was because my self-education was about to be tested or because of the shape of Tom Lowe's mouth making that "ooohhh" sound.

"I wanted to kill the son of a bitch!" Barry sat down in the

La-Z-Boy and swiveled himself toward the wall. "I hated him. I kept thinking, I'm a hell of a lot better than that guy. I kept thinking, so why is *he* the big disk jockey and I'm not? I kept wishing that something would happen to him. . . ."

"Yes?"

"Well, so now it's starting to look like something has." Barry looked up, all red-eyed. "Do you think I made it happen?"

"The question, dear Barry," I said and watched Tom Lowe pull off his T-shirt and drop it onto a bush. His back is very lean and tan. There was a stripe of white ringing his hips where his shorts were falling a little lower than they should, but what was the truth was that I liked them hanging down that way. "Do *you* think you made it happen?"

"I think it's possible," he said, and then we wrapped up therapy, and I wanted to lean out the window to say that I was *not* amused by the floor show, just in case he thought I might be. I mean, good God, where does he even do laundry? This place where he lives, well, it must be infested and awful. All those dogs and thus, fleas and lice and probably some field mice and an occasional dead possum. I was thinking of all this and trying to convince myself that there was nothing whatsoever appealing about this yard man out my window. I did that for about the next hour or so while I was writing up all of my notes. Now I'm here, in my room, talking to you and looking out the window where he is *still* down there, working away. Alicia has left for the day and all that's left for Quee and me to do is what we jokingly call "vespers," where everybody gets to drink (except the youngster of course) and talk about their addiction to nicotine. Speaking of which, the handyman is puffing away this very instant. Listen to this; first I gotta raise the window:

Hey, you.

Are you talking to me?

Of course.

Yeah?

When are you gonna give up that habit?

When I get ready. When are you gonna give up your habit?

Which is?

Entertaining married men in their towels.

I'm a professional.

Yes. That's what everybody in town is saying.

And who's everybody?

Everybody.

I *am* a professional.

That's what I said. It's just that people aren't sure what word comes after that one.

Therapist.

Oh. I see.

I'm a good one, too.

Oh, I'm sure you are. Probably as good as your taste in clothes.

Oh, yeah? Well, I can cure you.

Of?

Addiction. I can cure you of smoking, and I can cure you of mooning over somebody who doesn't even know you're around. Somebody who doesn't even know she's around.

What do you mean?

Oh dear God, why did I just now say that? Wait. Where are you going? I thought you'd let me work on you. You can come to our meeting. You can stay for dinner. Really. Please don't leave. I was teasing, you know? I don't know anything about you or anybody in your life. Quee is gonna be furious with me if I'm the reason you're not finishing that work today. Please.

OH, SHIT. WELL, let's pretend you didn't hear that. I think that's what you call bombing, screwing up royally. I think that if I analyze this, what I see is that I said those words out of some kind of strange jealousy that I'm feeling for a very sick person who I've never even met, about a man I really don't know at all. Lordy, I think that I need some therapy. Tom Lowe's truck is already out of the drive and heading down the street, his denim jacket there on the banister. I'm feeling like crap now, dear tape recorder whoever. Why did I say such a stupid thing?

I was going to tell you about my dream interpretations and my new kinds of therapy like the flora and fauna, but now I'm out of the mood. The gist is pretty simple anyway. Some people like tightly pruned privets, and some love ramblers tumbling from the trees. Need I say more. It's not so different from the orals and the anals; it all eventually becomes sexual, just like all the dream stuff with water and trains and guns, like you know when Ruthie Crow told me that she dreamed of a slippery path, I just automatically said *vagina*, which made her furious. And the jigsaw puzzle test is just to see who can walk away from one and never go back. I suspect if you can, then you can also leave parts of your life undone. I used to be somebody who could do that, and now I find myself feeling like I want to finish a few things. If nothing else, I want to finish the Radio Guy's therapy. If I have to see those fat feet once more, I might out-puke Ruthie Crow and then turn on this machine and report every bit of it. I want to finish the argument that I just started. I want to say to Tom Lowe those words I have always found difficult to say, *I'm so sorry. Sometimes I find that I can't help being a bitch. It just happens and I don't know why.*

Mack sits on the porch and watches the lights go out in the houses around him. The house to his left has long been dark, the children who run screaming all afternoon tucked into their beds and sleeping peacefully. He imagines the tired mama with her feet propped up, belly swollen, dim lamp swaying overhead. Even the college kids have turned in for the night, the only window lit being the stark white bathroom that glares in full view. Sarah used to wonder why they didn't get a shade, a curtain; instead, there was an all-day parade of young men with their backs turned to the world outside.

Mack sits and sips his wine. He's had far too much tonight, and about an hour ago he was even contemplating going and buying a pack of cigarettes. Why not? What's the worst thing that happens? Of course, then he might wind up in that redneck two-bit Smoke-Out trap on the edge of town that is being advertised on the local radio station along with constant bulletins regarding the whereabouts of one Jones Jameson. That was the topic that got him through the rest of the night with June. They were actually able to spring back to life and laughter after a near collapse.

Even now when he thinks of standing there in the doorway with her his heart quickens. Was it excitement or guilt? All of the doctors and nurses who he's met in passing have stressed he should assume that Sarah *can* hear him and does know what is happening around her. There are even cases where people are locked in what looks like a coma but respond with blinks—open, close, open. But Sarah's eyes are always closed, aren't they? He leans his head against the porch post, drains his glass and reaches for what's left in the bottle, the second bottle, that is. June was pressing closer and closer, and he knew in one awful moment that she could feel him pressing back, that she could feel him. It's the kind of story most people, at least people with any moral tact, never tell, and yet it is exactly the kind of story that June would tell Sarah or vice versa. "We were just standing there," he can hear June's voice, Sarah's eyes wide with anticipation, "and then like all of a sudden the guy has an *erection*." She would whisper the word and then they would both fall out laughing as they always did— literally, physically, dramatically lying back on the floor or a bed, with feet in the air.

But June didn't react at all tonight. She fell silent—froze—and waited for him to speak first, to do what she said he never did. And all the while he imagined Sarah there behind him, opening her eyes, stretching her arms, rising up behind him like a ghost.

"June," he had started, but then there was a ring of the bell and a whirling of action like a storm blowing in and there was Sarah's mother, clean linens clutched in her arms, a plastic grocery bag slung over her arm. When she came down the hall, Mack and June were apart but he knows that they both looked guilty. They both were flushed and breathless; he had to turn and adjust his belt, thrust his hands deep into the loose pockets of his pants.

"What happened?" she asked them, eyes wide and moist as she

rushed to Sarah's bed. She leaned over her daughter, kissing and talking and smoothing. "Why are you here in the hall?"

"Talking," Mack whispered, and entered the room to stand beside her. "June brought dinner."

"Oh. So did I." She handed him the bag filled with deli containers, placed a fresh box of baby wipes under the table by the bed. "June, you seem to be here every time I come."

"Yes," June said. "I check in, but I'm leaving now."

Mack turned suddenly, disappointed and grateful at the same time. "Oh, I hope I didn't shorten your visit."

"No, no, I have a date," June said. She was still in her cut-offs and big shirt, moss-green Birkenstocks.

"Really?" Sarah's mother had turned her full attention on June then. "Someone Mack and I might know?"

"No, I don't think so," she shook her head. "He's a teacher from out in the county. We met at a workshop recently."

Mack had wanted to participate in her lie, but he suddenly found himself unable to participate. He couldn't help but wonder if there was any truth whatsoever to her story. He walked her to the door, all the while feeling Sarah's mother's eyes on his back, feeling her ears straining on the other side of the porch wall. "I'll talk to you tomorrow," he said, trying to read her response, but she was looking everywhere except at his face. "Okay?"

"Okay."

"And I'm sorry."

"For?" Now she looked up, her eyes red, jaw clenched. He shrugged and she smirked knowingly. "For wishing I was Sarah?"

"I don't know."

"I feel guilty, too," she said and walked out to the curb, away from the house, and he followed. There were cars lining the street. It looked like a pre-formal gathering, all the kids coming and going in ridiculous-looking tuxedos and strapless cocktail dresses. The children from next door sat in the middle of their yard watching, oohing and ahhing with each sparkly dress. "I feel lonely and confused."

"Yes."

"Yes?" She opened her car door.

"So do I," he said and then on impulse, "I'm sorry for what happened just now. I can't explain it."

"I can," she said and put her key in the ignition. "I can explain it a hundred different ways. But you know what, Mack?" she rolled down the window and pulled her door to, faced straight ahead as she spoke. "I just don't want to."

"Mack?" Sarah's mother was out on the porch then. "Can you come and help me?"

He lifted his hand to her and then patted June on the shoulder. In all of the years before, he would have leaned in and kissed her, hugged her, but now all he could do was pat her at arm's length. He stood watching her drive down the street, turning the corner just as he mounted the porch steps.

"I want to bathe her, and I need you to help turn her," her mother said as soon as he entered the house. "You know she has to be turned on a regular basis." There was accusation in her voice, anger in her eyes.

"I know that," he said. "The physical therapist was supposed to come today and then didn't. I'm sorry."

"I really want her with me, Mack," she said, grabbing his sleeve to keep him from entering the bedroom. She pulled him off into the living room where she continued to stand while talking. "We can do better for her until . . ." Her voice trailed off and she looked like she was going to cry, but then with a firm shake of her head, she looked back up. "There is a very good chance that she's aware of everything."

"Yes."

"Well, you remember that." She was staring at him then, and he wanted so badly to look away. "She's a very intelligent woman and a sensitive woman. She knows things." He couldn't tell at this moment if she was talking about Sarah or about herself. Was it possible that Sarah sent her mother messages, emotional pleas in the very air she breathed?

"I know that," he said. "I'm doing the best that I can."

"Yes," she lowered her voice. "But her father and I can do better." She turned and went back into the bedroom and stood waiting for him to join her at Sarah's thin body rolled to one side, a pillow—his pillow—propped under her back to keep her from rolling into the same position. He thought then of King Solomon entering the room and offering to rip Sarah in half. He had no idea what the right answer was.

And now, in the middle of the night, he still has no answer, and no excuse for his behavior with June. Right now he feels only anger and hatred. He feels robbed. He understands the mood that might send someone out into the streets not giving a damn about what happened—not giving a damn about the consequence of actions. He hates what has happened, despises his life, and yet still, in all of this feels a flicker of hope. In all of this, he knows that he won't start smoking, that he won't get this drunk every night, that he will get up in the morning and go to work. He will do everything that is expected of him and then some, and the goddamned insane question behind it all is why? Why will he continue to do such normal things?

Dear Wayward One,

What an odd dream I had last night. I dreamed of your feet. I came into your house and the wind was ferocious, like hurricane weather, I came to tell you to get out, to run. I was screaming your name but you never answered and then I stepped into your room and I knew with one quick look that you were dead. I knew it was you by your feet. The big toe was so obviously your big toe. It was like I had super-vision; it was like I could see the fine little white circles of your print, your genetic code like a road map. I wanted to scrape away the cells from your toe and then grow you, cultivate the life back into you. I wanted to grow you like a little test-tube baby and I said as much, even knowing that that would never be enough for me. I needed the man, you. And as I was standing there taking in your toe, the wind suddenly blew everything away and I was left squatting near a creosote post with a scrap of paper in my hand. It was your handwriting, your last words written to me. And isn't that funny, how reality enters in. There in that dream I saw a bit of my life played over like a movie. That foot part would be right up your alley. You'd say, "Ooh, foot fetish," or something like that. Well, you know why I thought it. I mean didn't I always give the best foot rubs now? Was it you who said there was nothing sexier than a woman with great big feet? No, no I guess it wasn't. It seems that lately sometimes I confuse you two and it's so odd. I can't help but wonder if you ever confused me with somebody else. But how could you compare me to your wife? I wish I could see your toe right now, foot, hand, neck, thigh; I would recognize and welcome any part of you.

Sometimes when Tom is out on the beach he thinks he sees his father; he might bend to pick up a stick to toss to Blackbeard, and there, out of the corner of his eye, he sees a flash of white like a shirt. Now he sits back in the damp sand and watches the water. It is low tide, and the beach is peppered with people, their voices offering the droning kind of background noise that Quee has with that noise machine of hers. The sand is warm to his hands and feet. The warmth pulls him into lying back and closing his eyes against the sun.

The first time he saw the ocean, his instinct had been to run out into it, to give in and let it pull him, suck him away from the shore. He still wonders why his father didn't choose that as the way to die; he could have simply let his lungs fill with the warm salty liquid. He could have taken in the water, breathed in the water. Drowning would have been much more natural. But no, he had to leave something, a wine-stained piece of paper shredded to bits, pieces that Tommy should have left in the wastebasket where his mother found and then returned them. "He couldn't even leave a real letter," she said when she called Tommy away from the bedroom of the small beach house his father had been renting. "This is what I meant to him." She shook the pieces of paper and then let them go. "All the pieces aren't even here." She waved her hand, saying she would have nothing else to do with his filthy sheets and clothes, his filthy life. She told the policeman standing there that she didn't even know why she had been invited to this *lovely* house party. She walked out with that remark, the screen door slamming on rusted hinges, and while the policeman followed her with apologies Tommy ran and scooped up all the pieces of paper, or what he thought was all. As he sat up late that night piecing the letter with scotch tape, he realized that he was missing something, and the following Saturday when he mounted his bicycle and rode the twelve miles to the ocean, he found the house locked tight, every window, every door. Even now he wishes he could just let go of it, that he could toss the remains into the water; instead he has it in his wallet neatly folded, the ink is smudged, the paper is the texture of worn cotton.

> Dear Betty, Here at the end I beg your forgiveness. I know that you will probably never give it to me but I beg nonetheless. Here I finally tell the truth for once. Don't you see that
> wish I'd seen sooner. We have a nice boy. I wish we had had a nice life.

"No, Dad, tell me what she doesn't see," Tom thinks now as he lies there. Maybe she didn't see that he never loved her? Maybe she didn't see that his type, that "gifted" type, couldn't afford to be tied down. How many times as an eleven-year-old had he looked out at the world and the other fathers and thought of his own: "Why doesn't he just fuck himself and die?" And he did. He up and fucked himself or somebody else and died. It was a hard thing to forget, this image of his father in that bed on those sheets. "You should have seen it all," his mother had whispered to a friend. "Filthy, filthy. An old rag of a mattress thrown on the floor and it looked like he had drawn all over the wall behind his head, marks like a prisoner might mark off days."

Tommy had imagined it all many, many times. His dad got up from the bed, the sheet wrapped around his waist and dragging the sticky dusty floor. He stood at the window in full view of anybody on the strand. He thought he was a regular "Brethren of the Coast." Aye, matey, you'll never catch me. I'll run myself in so that you don't. He fired the pistol and when he did his head went through the big window and was sliced clean from his neck and the hair on his head, the neglected facial hair, burst into flame just like in the story about Blackbeard.

This is how Tommy had described the scene to the school nurse when she asked him what he knew about his father's death. He told her that his father's head burned and rolled a path to the sea. He told her that if you go to the beach late at night you would see his father walking the shore, a headless gray figure in search of his head.

"Really, Tommy." The nurse sat frozen and pale, tears in her eyes. "That sounds more like the Blackbeard story your teacher says you're always telling, that and the Maco Light."

She waited, but he made no response. He watched his mother as she stood on the other side of the glass partition of the principal's office, her back to them.

"If you *do* want to ever talk," the nurse said, "you know where I am."

"He was drinking and fucking," Tommy said to the nurse. The words out of his mouth felt good like a rush of cool clean saltless water. "Always drinking and fucking." He rapped his knuckles on the glass where his mother and the principal were staring, faces white, mouths open. Not so soundproof after all. The principal offered to handle this discipline problem so that Tommy's mother wouldn't have to. They had already had such trouble with him, splitting the lip and smashing the nose of Jones Jameson, who wouldn't tell what he had said to prompt such a beating. He had sat there in the school office and lied, said that Tommy attacked him for no reason except maybe jealousy. Tommy wasn't involved in all of the school activities that Jones was, after all, and he guessed the girls didn't like Tommy like they liked Jones.

"Your old man was a fucking loser" is what Jones Jameson had said right up in Tommy's face. "People say all he did was fuck whores." And even though Tommy hated his father and had thought those same thoughts, he would not hear it from somebody else, not from somebody like Jones Jameson. He would have killed him if the assistant principal hadn't come and pulled him off Jones. He spit in Jones's bloody face, and then he punched him, over and over until the blood and spit mixed and smeared like thick paint.

Then the principal went for him, ten swats with a wooden board with holes in it that had been a gift to him from some fraternity. Boys who had gone on to graduate had signed their names there like it was some big deal to have had your ass beat by some shitty principal who had to show he was tough. Tommy took the paddle, his face like fucking stone with every swat, while Jones Jameson and a crowd of boys watched. It was like a public hanging, there in the hall right in front of the cafeteria, girls hiding their faces with every strike. The one time he dared look out into the crowd he saw Sarah there, her shoulders hunched, arms hugged tightly to her own chest as she watched. He had known who she was from the first day everybody poured into the junior high school from various elementary schools around the town and county, but chances are this was the first time she had noticed him. He wanted to impress her that day, and so he took it without a flinch. But he wasn't going to take it again, not the next time, not in front of his mother, and when that son of a bitch got his little fratty paddle off the wall, Tommy went for him with all he was worth. "I'll beat the shit out of *you* big man," he screamed. "You're so tough aren't you, what a tough shit man?" The principal motioned for his assistant and another male teacher to come and help, but Tommy got in one hard swing to the side of the bastard's head before they each grabbed an arm and forced him face first into the cinder block wall. The school nurse stepped in to beg, but they pushed her away with a wave of the hand. Tommy's own mother said she couldn't bear to watch and turned and walked down the hall and outside, the large blue door slamming behind her.

"Now what did you say?" the principal asked.

"I said I hate your rotten guts," Tommy spit. "I said that you are a hateful son of a bitch."

The first crack landed above the belt, stinging his lower back and knocking the breath out of him. "Some places this is illegal," he gasped.

"But not here," one of the men said. "Not in this school, son, and not in this whole big state."

"Are you going to apologize?" the principal asked after two more hard licks.

"No," Tom said, and so, after another round, they suspended him for two weeks. Two weeks of zeros and Fs. Two weeks of working in the yard and sneaking off to the bowling alley to smoke cigarettes and an occasional joint when some of the older kids offered. Two weeks of his mother not speaking to him, or worse, telling him how she hoped he wasn't going to end up like his father. Even when he walked into church that Sunday, nobody sat near him; nobody spoke to him. The first person who did say anything to him on his first day back at school was Sarah. His goal then was simply to get promoted to high school; he had to get the F grades up to Ds so he wouldn't have to repeat the year. He had already decided that he'd drop out before he spent another year at that slumhole. Sarah didn't really stop; she barely even looked at him. He was at his locker trying to cram in his jacket, and she slowed just long enough to whisper, "Welcome back." Her lips were shiny with something that smelled like peppermint, and there were fat strands of yarn like a sailor's knot, tied in her long hair.

"Thanks," he said, but by that time she had turned and was walking away with her friend June, their heads pressed together as they talked. He never talked to her again until late summer, when they both wound up parked at the river. He was with some older kids from out in the county, and she was with June and a couple of high school basketball players. Somehow the two of them wound up sitting on the bank just yards apart while all the others swam against the current like they were on a treadmill. She was probably the only sober person there. It was one time when he didn't think about what he was saying or doing; he got up and went and sat beside her, asked her if she wanted to run away with him.

"Forever?" she asked and laughed.

"Forever, an hour, you pick." He watched her profile then as she stared out into the river. She waved to her date, somebody Martin, everybody called him Sky. Tom didn't really have a "date" but more or less was expected to fool around with Theresa Dobbins later. "Or maybe I could call you sometime."

"That would work."

"Really?" he asked and reached for her hand that was inches from his. She nodded then ran out knee-deep to where June was motioning to her. For the rest of that late afternoon and early evening, he entertained the crowds by swinging from the highest vine and dropping a good fourteen feet into the deepest part of that stretch of the river. The other boys tried but they hadn't practiced like he had. He knew every limb of every big oak there along the bank and could scramble out to the highest limbs without even paying attention. She was watching the whole time. Finally he got way out on the highest branch only to look and see the car they had come in disappearing down the muddy twisting road. He was abandoned and ridiculous for all of his showing off.

Now the memory makes him shudder as he sits on the damp and cold sand; the tide is coming in, claiming his past. Someday, when he is forty-one, he will breathe a sigh of relief because then he will know there isn't something genetic to make him go out and buy a gun. Who's to say it couldn't happen? Who's to say there isn't something perched and waiting in his brain, something that would send him out of this world in a goddamned burst of flames.

He wonders about the sensations. How does it feel to know it's coming? Or do people really believe it is? Whole cities have been unearthed to expose people frozen in their everyday lives as if a big plug were suddenly pulled. The people on the *Titanic* kept dancing to the orchestra music and drinking. Those who survived told how passengers tidied up their state rooms, fed pets, fixed their hair; by the time they knew to panic, to throw themselves out into the icy water, thousands of screams at once, it was too late. And the person gasping for a last breath knows, doesn't he? Doesn't he think *this is it, this is it?* Or is there something that keeps the brain hoping, against the odds, against the predictions? If Sarah were to suddenly wake, would she remember the last day he saw her? Would she make him swear never to tell, or would she beg him to let her try again, and then beg him never to tell? Chances are pretty good he will never know. He will know no more than one of the survivors he read about, a woman whose last memory of her father was his lifting her carefully into a lifeboat. Then she drifted through the icy water away from the beautiful *Titanic* into darkness and into a life with a big hole shot through the center. She probably spent all those years wondering what he did next. Did he straighten his tie and talk to someone about his business? Did he say "Some vacation, huh?" and get a round of nervous laughs. Did he pull out his wallet and show his daughter's picture? Did he think of her at all? Or did he simply embrace death because there was nothing else to embrace?

Tom gets up now and walks back over the dunes to where his truck is parked. The hot sand squeaks under his feet, the low-growing flowers—"Indian blankets" is what Myra Carter had called them when he did some work on her porch and she spied several on the dash of his truck—spreading around him in every direction, their blossoms protected by the sandspurs mixed in. He hears Blackbeard behind him, smacking saliva and panting, and behind that he hears the constant rushing of the surf and beyond that he thinks he hears someone whispering "Aye, matey, it's a good day to lose your head," and he keeps walking, faster and faster, fearful of turning around to see someone there, a man, a monster, a vision. He's afraid he might see some truth he has yet to see.

Part Three

$\mathcal{F}$or Myra Carter there is nothing quite like a big load of topsoil from down near the river where the moss and ferns have been growing and shooting their spores into that thick musty air. The only thing better is a nice big load of manure, practically steaming from some old cow's bottom. She likes to think of that, the steamy plop that she had watched as a girl on her grandparents' farm. Those cows would stand there and stare you right in the eye without a single change in expression as they raised their tails and delivered a fine dollop of fertilizer. It is so exciting to think of fertilizer; she feels embraced by life and filled with energy. It makes her think words like "fecund." Now what would a therapist make of that? Well, she won't ever know because there's not a therapist on this earth who can understand Myra Carter. Howard couldn't, and he might as well have been a psychiatrist, he was every other kind of doctor in town. It is the curse of Myra's life that her husband knew what everybody—man and woman, boy and girl—looked like without their clothes on. Ruthie sure can't understand her; Ruthie can't even understand herself these days, she's so man-crazy.

Myra breathes deeply over the new topsoil that Mr. Digby left first thing this morning. If Mr. Digby weren't forced to live such a lower-class life, she would envy him his property there near the river bottom. If they were of the same kind of people, she might even invite him in for some tea some afternoon just so she could sit there near him and breathe in the dirt and manure and river rot from his clothing.

Fecund, fecund, fecund. She sings in her head while she digs in with her shovel and tosses loam to the wheelbarrow. She tried to get Ruthie to use "fecund" in a poem, and Ruthie chewed on her pen, which is her main food source, and then said after about two hours that she couldn't think of a single thing that rhymed with "fecund."

"Well, does everything *have* to rhyme?" Myra asked, to which Ruthie shook her head and laughed, said, *Who is the poetess in this room?*

Fecund, fecund. The shovel strikes a rhythm; dig and toss, dig and toss. Fecund. Fecund. Dig and toss. Deacon. Beacon. Dig and toss. Myra stops and rests, takes a deep breath. "Rhymes," she mutters, and Sharpy runs over to her. "Miss Crow will say that my words don't have a 'd' on the end and therefore can't work." It makes her mad and she grips that shovel harder and gets ready to set into some serious damn digging. She dares anybody to match what she can do with a shovel. Howard couldn't. Ruthie can't. Dig and toss. Dig and toss. I'm the boss. I'm the boss. Take that Connie; take this shovel in your big wide grinning mouth. Tell us how like Jesus you are now. Myra is just getting up to a full-fledged rage when her shovel strikes something solid. If that Mr. Digby has camouflaged some trash and brought it to her yard, she will have his poverty level reduced to subpoverty. Probably if he worked harder he wouldn't *be* poverty level to begin with, this is America after all. She keeps pushing in with the shovel, striking like a snake and every time hitting something solid. She is red in the face and getting winded, so she throws the shovel to the side and gets on her hands and knees to start digging. Sharpy thinks she's playing a game, like when she sniffed around the yard and taught him how to lift his leg like a man dog ought to, and he runs over to help. And Sharpy is the one to get there first. Sharpy is the first one to find skin, pale and pulpy, bluish gray. Sharpy's natural instincts make him back off and growl deep in his throat.

"What is this?" Myra is demanding. "What in the hell, pardon my French . . ." She reaches in and grabs with both hands, pushing against that pile with all the strength she has. She rips off her gloves so she can get to whatever it is, dog corpse or chicken or old rotten fish. The smell is there now hitting her like a two-by-four in the face. She would probably vomit and pass out if she wasn't so furious that her wonderful fecund dig-and-toss afternoon has been ruined. Now she's reached something hard and solid, and she locks her fingers around the edge and pulls and pulls. There's resistance. It's big. Whatever is in there is big and she feels like the top of her head is about to fall off when all of a sudden the pressure gives and she falls back flat on her back, a soggy weight clutched to her chest, the noonday sun burning black spots into the world, and in one of those spots she would swear she saw Howard, and he was grinning; he was looking just like he did that day that she came up on him talking to that old Mary Stutts. *Medical matters, dear*, he said to Myra later when she questioned him, *medical matters, confidential*. He's saying it right now, plain as day, his face blinking and twitching in the sun, like it might be covered in ants or termites, and she has to close her eyes against such ugliness, *It's confidential information*.

$\mathcal{E}$ver since they found Jones Jameson's car a few days ago, Alicia has been as jumpy as a flea. Quee is doing all that she can think of to calm her, to relax her. Quee has even given Alicia a massage in hopes that she would fall asleep and get some rest. But, rest? Lord Jesus, who can rest around here? Old Denny forever spouting some bit of an idea she's come up with, old Mr. Fatass Radio ringing his bell, Ruthie Crow in front of one of the skinny mirrors reciting, and the orphan child always having to stand out on the back stoop. "Jason, honey, you need to find a girlfriend," Quee had told him just yesterday, to which Ruthie Crow responded that she did so wish he was a teensy bit older, that she'd wait for his goose-pâté-colored self if he wanted. He turned where Ruthie couldn't see him and looked like he might upchuck.

Quee has got to speed up the curing process and move these folks on before they make her have a breakdown. What a nuthouse. And Denny. Lord, if Quee had known how really way out there Denny *is* and how the child cannot shut her mouth, Quee might've thought long and hard before hiring her. She wishes all of her clients could be as nice and easy as the young woman who just checked in; she doesn't even *really* smoke but has come as sort of a little vacation from her husband and young children. She is perfectly content to just sleep, watch a little television, and read. She has told people all over town that she was a closet smoker but finally cracked under Quee's questioning. "It was cheaper and more convenient than a spa or a breakdown," the woman said. Now everyone has become kind of interested in the ghost wall, so Quee agreed to give a little tour.

"THIS IS A little girl by the name of Sally," she says and points to a small oval frame. The child in the photograph is dressed in a sailor dress and holding a kitten, squeezing it up to her chest. "She is not an orphan, but she has always felt like one."

"Why?" Jason, who has to keep moving to get away from Ruthie, asks.

Quee shrugs. "Well, her real father disappeared and then her mother went into a kind of second childhood where she wanted this little Sally to be like her friend or little sister. You know, she'd say things like 'Sally, come help me braid my hair,' instead of worrying about whether or not Sally had herself any homework. Of course, Sally *did* her homework, because she knew from even before this picture was taken that she was going to grow up to be *somebody*. That's what she would say to herself every single morning: 'I am somebody.' Then her mama remarried a man who pulled them on into a new life, a very different life, one that this little Sally never felt fully included her."

"That's *my* story you're telling," Denny says now, because it is impossible for her to go any length of time whatsoever without talking. If Quee ever went to church, Denny is somebody she'd like to see sitting there, because she can't imagine that Denny could make it through a whole sermon without a question, or comment, or as she always says, a little psychological insight to add.

"That's a story that belongs to many of us, honey," Quee says and forces her sweetie smile. "And from that story I could go into a step-father story, and there are many different varieties there."

"Yes, mine is a nice one for sure," Denny says. "I mean, he's not handsome like my real daddy, or tough like my real daddy, but he is nice." Quee just nods and moves on down the hall. Denny has tried to wriggle information out of Quee since she landed here: What was my mama like as a girl? What was my daddy like? Did you go to my daddy's funeral, Quee? Were you there when the military planes flew overhead and dipped their wings and then the whole Fulton High School Band struck up and played "When the Saints Go Marching In." With every question, Quee has wanted to call Denny's mama and give her yet another lecture on how to tell a *good* lie, how *not* to go overboard. You don't just go from having an illegitimate child that probably belonged to somebody else's too-hot-for-his-britches step-father, up to having fallen in love with and married a decorated World War II hero. But then again, these are the stories that have probably given Denny the confidence or whatever it is that enables her to talk all the damned time.

"You see—Sally there was somebody who just naturally felt a kind of energy with the world," Quee continues quietly. "If you look for signs and listen to what is happening all the way around you, then you just automatically know which way to go."

"Well, I need to have my eyes and ears checked," Alicia says and walks ahead, stops in front of one of Quee's favorite photos of all. It's Baccalaureate Sunday at the Piney Swamp School of Personality in 1902, and there are twenty-one stone-faced young women dressed in white, each holding a daisy. Their teacher is all in black and looks like she might be a hundred and a voodoo queen, when really she was probably only thirty or so. "What's your story here?" Alicia asks and lifts little Taylor who has come and grabbed hold of her thigh.

"Well, that one there in the center?" Quee points to the one in black. "The teacher? Well, let's just say that she has been teaching these young women a lot more than about how to have a good personality." Quee laughs great big, her eyebrows arching up in an *if you know what I mean* kind of look.

"Tell us, tell us." The radio guy has stepped into the hall and joined them. He has just come from the sauna and there are little rivers of sweat running down his old hairy chest and plump belly. He's got one of those big white fluffy towels wrapped around his waist and Quee makes a mental note to go heavy on the Clorox next wash.

"Well, it's not what you're thinking," Quee says. "It's not S-E-X," she whispers and rubs Taylor's head. He looks at her and meows to continue what she calls the pussycat game. She meows back and turns to face Alicia, Denny, and Radio (Jason has wandered back to his room and is playing his music louder than she usually allows).

"These young women," she points her arm at the long blurry photo. "Are training in medicine. They have learned just enough medical procedures and cures to venture out into the world and do goodness."

"Goodness!" Radio waves his hand in dismissal and waddles on down the hall to where he has some books waiting. The way he says *books* everybody knows what kind of books. "I don't want to hear about women and goodness; I want to hear about women and badness."

"That sounded just like something Jones might say," Alicia says quietly, and Old Fat Toad stops midroute. At first, there is a satisfied look on his face, mission accomplished, he too can go out into the world and be a disgusting pig shit sort, but then he seems to think better of it.

"I'm sorry," he says and rather than be quiet so that everybody is left to watch that fat can rolling down the hall, Quee calls them over to another, a tiny three-by-three black-and-white photo like what might come from an old box camera. Most of the picture is the ocean, a seascape with sea oats lining the dunes of the foreground. A woman sits there, scarf on her head, legs hugged up to her chest.

"I love this one, always have," Quee says and slips it from its frame, turns it over so they can all see the fine brown lines of writing: "It's not Heaven but it's as close as I've ever come."

"We've all felt that way from time to time," Quee says. "Not heaven but as close as you can get."

"It's been a long time since I felt that way." Alicia sidles up closer to Quee, Taylor clutched close; she looks like she might cry, which is precisely what Quee was avoiding when she started this whole gallery tour. I mean it ain't like she doesn't have thousands of things to do!

"But you will again, dear heart," Quee says. "You will."

"Promise?"

"Cross my heart and hope to . . ." Quee calls Denny closer and whispers. "Hope to spend eternity with Ruthie and Radio without any television or liquor in the world."

"That's a promise, all right," Denny says.

"Yes, that's a promise." Alicia wanders back toward the kitchen where Quee is about to start heating up some more oil.

"This is like a school of sorts," Quee says. "Let's just say that I'm the teacher. Let's just say that I am here at the School of Personality to work on you girls. I can teach you some procedures; I can cure your souls."

Myra is still flat on her back when a neighbor whose name she doesn't even know walks up in the yard to ask if she can help. Sharpy doesn't even bark at the woman or her snotty-faced little girl, and Myra makes a mental note to work on that with him; she will teach him aggressiveness and anger direction like she herself never quite mastered.

"Are you okay?" the young woman asks and then her face goes pale and she grimaces, shudders, steps back.

"Stinky dog." The child reaches her arms for her mother to lift her.

"I must've fainted," Myra says. "I pulled . . ." she pauses, brushing and wiping muddy dirt from leather. "I found this shoe in my topsoil, and then I guess I fainted."

"What is that?" The child points to where Sharpy is now reluctantly sniffing. It seems Sharpy has done a little digging during Myra's spell, and now there is what looks like a foot, torn and discolored yes, but a foot nonetheless.

WITHIN MINUTES OF the 911 call, the police come and uncover the rest of the body that goes with the foot. It is naked and muddy. Myra tries not to look but can't help herself; it is just like when Oprah or Geraldo has something on that is sick and not very Christian and she has to watch it anyway. What she sees looks like a sponge—soggy and bloated. The policeman (the same young one who had come around the other day) has gone inside to vomit. He said, right before covering his mouth in as polite a way as possible and running, that it looked like the fish had had a pretty good time with the deceased.

"Do you think?" she asks as soon as he returns, pale and slick-looking. "You know." She nods her head over toward Jones Jameson's house.

"Could be," the man says, and as Myra looks at his sometimes handsome face she is trying to decide if Ruthie would appreciate his needing to wretch from the inside or if it would make her not like him as somebody to go out on a date with. "We got a lot to do." He holds out his hand to her, and she keeps thinking there's something she's supposed to tell him, something about a gremlin. "I will be needing that shoe."

NOW THAT ALL the excitement has passed, and Myra has spent the whole afternoon inside with her feet propped up and a cool cloth on her head, she thinks of that naked body with its one shoe. It's kind of like if Alfred Hitchcock did his own version of Cinderella. Now it all gives her the creeps, and even Sharpy with his warm little wrinkly body isn't making her feel better. She would call Ruthie, but she's at the Whorehouse getting cured. Can't call Howard; he's dead. So there. The truth is that she has nobody to call. All of her money and refinement and gardening talents, and she has no friends. She almost calls that cop, that Bobbin boy, but then she thinks better of it. What if he was to start thinking she was somehow involved? She *did* after all tell him all about arsenic the other day. *I am the doctor's wife,* she thinks now. *Of course I know all about anything like that!*

She is nervous all over, twitching nervous. She goes and gets herself a little cooking sherry with some vanilla extract on the side, which tastes awful but nonetheless soothes her, and then she sits with her robe pulled tight around her and stares at the telephone. Does she dare to do it? She dials and then sits there twisting to the point that Sharpy moves over to another chair. "Hello, Connie?" She makes her voice real slow and sweet; it's what Howard always called her Sunday school voice. "Connie, the Lord has really tried me today. Uh-huh, yes. The Lord caused a dead man to wash right up into my yard."

"Oh, my," Connie says. "Well, did the Lord *speak* to you? Did he tell you *why* he was doing this?"

"Not directly, like what you might get in a phone call."

"Oh, when I get a message from the Lord . . ." Connie pauses so that it will look like she's a polite person. "Well, never you mind, hon."

"Are you telling me, Connie, that the Lord will sometimes just up and speak out to you?" Myra makes herself laugh with a little picture in her mind, a picture of Mr. Sharpy lifting his leg and wee-weeing on Connie's powder-blue ultrasuede suit that she bought in Southern Pines.

"Oh, yes," Connie pauses and Myra can feel that stretched-lipped smile clean through the telephone. "When Mama passed, the Lord came and whispered to me, *Fear not*. Now what did you get, love?" Connie sounds like a child who might be comparing what Santy Claus brought to her to what the old guy brought another. But then, that's how Connie lives her whole life, by comparison.

"Hmmm." Myra stretches the phone cord and goes over to her window where she can see the light on in Alicia Jameson's bedroom. While she is watching, a car pulls up and stops. A figure gets out and walks to the door. Maybe Jones is home! She strains to see better.

"What, dear?" Connie asks. "I can't hear you. Do you think I need to come and sit a prayer vigil with you?"

The light on the Jamesons' front porch goes on and in that instant Myra sees the stark bit of truth that ends the day. "No, dear, I'm fine alone," she says. "But the Lord did speak to me. I wasn't going to tell it at first, because I didn't want anybody thinking that I'm crazy, but since you too on so many occasions have heard the Lord speak so clearly, I can tell you. The Lord said, 'Myra, you're a good-looking smart woman and so I have decided to do something that's going to call a lot of attention to you.'"

"He said all that?"

"He said, 'I have put the body of Jones Jameson in your topsoil as a message.'"

"Jones Jameson? He's dead? Does his mama know?" Connie is going a hundred miles an hour. She wants to know if the family is having a visitation, will there be a service? But Myra says a quick good-bye and hangs up the phone. She stands there in the dark watching the house next door, waiting to see what will happen next. Maybe it was a sign, only she didn't see God at all; as a matter of fact she saw somebody as far from God as you can get, she saw Howard, and exactly how he looked that day he was whispering with Old Mary Stutts Purday. Maybe all this was meant to happen in some kind of grand scheme. Maybe Mr. Digby will bring her a new load of topsoil to make up for her discomfort. He said he would, didn't he? He said he would, along with a little cow manure for good measure, manure so good and strong that it would burn some of the more tender plants if she wasn't careful.

Now Alicia Jameson is out on the porch, and that officer is still hanging around. They look like children at the end of a date, not at all like a cop who has come to say that her husband was dead and buried in the muck along the river. Alicia is in his arms now, their bodies intertwined right out there in the yard, and there is a voice (not Myra's voice, of course!) saying *Kiss her, boy, kiss her. Show her what a man you are.*

"Who is saying that?" she asks the ceiling. "Who?" And Mr. Sharpy perks up his ears and twists his little wrinkled jowls from side to side so that he can hear, too.

Kiss her! I said, Kiss her you fool. Show her what you've got.

*T*esting . . . Oh God, oh man. Ruthie Crow's aunt dug up a
foot today, a damn *dead* foot that happened to be attached
to a body, a damn body that just happened to belong to Alicia's husband. Everybody in town knew that it was him because he was wearing one loafer, which apparently is his trademark and has been since
he was a fraternity man—not one loafer but just loafers, period. He
wore Bass Weejuns and always had. Alicia said he bought three pair at
a time and then rotated them. One pair always had pennies in them.
They were always oxblood or *cordovan* as Ruthie (who is quite insis-
tent on which word you use for what) kept stressing. As soon as people heard Bass Weejun, they knew, but of course the police had to do
all kinds of investigating. Myra Carter, Ruthie's aunt, had told her that
the body stunk worse than anything she had ever encountered, worse
even than the time all those field mice got into her heating unit and
got fried. She said that the body was all bloated and looked somewhat
pickled. The loafer didn't have a scratch on it. Myra had spent ten
minutes of telephone time telling Ruthie how this single loafer would
make a good poem, how Ruthie should just sit and wonder where the
other loafer might be. Ruthie was visibly shaken anyway. She told

Quee that she had always felt a bond with the man because of the way he always looked at her like he was seeing right through her garments. Quee told me later that that's how the lousy son of a bitch looked at everybody, and it was in that moment I started thinking of all the radio guy had had to say about Jones Jameson as well as Alicia. For the first time since leaving Washington, I was thinking that my bathtub there would have been a nice spot to retire. It's amazing what you can convince yourself sounds like a nice life sometimes.

Quee said, "Go get Tom Lowe and bring him around here."

"Why?" I asked, but she didn't seem to have a real reason.

"Just go get him," she said, "while I call Alicia and ask her and Taylor to come and spend the night with us."

And so here I am, following these scratched-out directions into this great big neighborhood where there are great big houses in every direction. I'm hoping my car can make it around these streets without backfiring and/or screaming when I put on brakes. I know I shouldn't feel ashamed of what my car does, but I do. It's the exact same feeling I used to get when my ex would go on and on about the sneezers. When I hear a car squeal in public, I try not to look at the owner, who I'm always sure is just hangdog embarrassed. Oh, my Lord. This is looking worse than even Quee said, and there are mad dogs everywhere. I will sit right here in my car, and let Mr. Lowe come right out here. I'm gonna beep the horn twice, and that's the best I can do. If he doesn't show, fine, then.

I have brought his old denim jacket and have it right here on the seat. It smells like him. I'm not wanting you to think that I'm some kind of weird chick who is into sniffing out folks' garments, but at the same time I want to give you a full picture of what's going on. I am also trying real hard to distract myself because it's so dark once you get down here on his driveway and because God only knows what's out in these woods. I mean there *is* a murderer loose in this town. It reminds me of that story people used to tell in high school about Hookarm and how he hooked himself up to the door handle when a couple was out in the woods parking, and then there's that other one around here that folks are always talking about, *the Maco Light*, where an engineer lost his head and still searches the tracks looking for it.

Oh God! Oh Jesus! Are you trying to give me a heart attack?

No, but you're bothering my dogs. Did I hear you talking to yourself?

Dear Wayward One,

I have started a new business and nobody has any idea what it is I do. You see I have this notion that I can make a difference in the world. I have this idea that just because I failed with you doesn't mean that I am a failure. No, I'm a winner and deep down inside of me I know it. I hope you will wish me luck if that's possible, if you're out there in the universe just blowing around. I have days when I wake up and I think just as clear as a bell: There is nothing beyond this very second. The memory of a life is all that lingers. And then there are other days like today when I think that I see and hear you everywhere. I eavesdrop sometimes in the grocery store, and sometimes it seems that the very words I hear are meant for me. Now don't get all worked up, I am not crazy, not hearing voices in some weird psycho way. I do not think that I'm communicating with aliens through the fillings of my teeth. But I do think that a human soul is too powerful to simply vanish in a puff of smoke. I believe the energy has to fly somewhere; into the throat of a bird or the limb of a tree. Like whenever a butterfly or fly lights any-where near me, I say in my head: "Hello there, you old so and so." I can make a difference in this world. Either way—if there is something beyond this world and if there is not—it's the best thing that I can do. I can make a difference and I just hope that someday I'm out there with you looking out on it all, or UP on it all, depending what the case may be. For all I know, you have become a lichen on a tree deep in the forest of the Green Swamp; you are a conch shell, tossing and rolling, whistling on the shore. And I am your ear, dear one. Speak to me. Please, speak to me.

*T*esting . . . testing. I'm having to whisper because Alicia and Quee are still wandering around downstairs. What a night. I don't even know where to begin with it all. It's not bad enough that I get sent out in the boonies to *fetch* Mr. Fixit Jesus, but then he goes and scares the ever loving crap out of me. He popped up out of nowhere, asking if I was talking to myself.

"No, it was the radio," I said, my heart still going double time. I unlocked my door and handed him his jacket so that he wouldn't think I'd been sitting out there in the dark fondling it while talking to myself.

"Thanks." He took the jacket and put it on. "Is that why you're trespassing?"

"Trespassing? Trespassing?" I asked and wanted to close the door but he propped that big workboot of his alongside my seat. "Is that what you call driving up to somebody's house?"

"So this is just a social visit?" He laughed and his eyes narrowed into slits. He was just as stoned as he could be, his body saturated in the rich sweet smell. "Well, well, well, I'm honored," he said.

I said, "More like stoned."

"Whatever." He shrugged and started walking along a weedy old path to his camper, which, by the way, looks like it's been through a couple of hundred hurricanes. He got to his door and stopped, slapped his leg so that all those dogs ran forward and practically stood at attention. "Come on in," he said and lit a cigarette. "Let the visit begin."

"It's not social," I yelled after him. "I can tell you right here from the car." But instead of turning back he went in and got an oil lantern; he brought it outside and set it on a small wrought-iron garden table off to the side like he might be hosting a campout. Things looked a little better in this light; there was a trellis and some pole beans growing up a bamboo tepee in the distance.

"Aw, come on in," he said with a fake accent. "My cleaning staff was just here. The place is impeccably spotless." He started moving toward me. "Come on, now, don't be shy. You weren't so shy when you were butting your nose into my business now were you?"

I told him again that I was sorry, that I didn't even know his coma girl and that I never should have mentioned her. I got out and stood right by the door of the car.

"No, you don't know her," he said and by that time he was so close I could have reached out and touched him. "And chances are you never will know her." He was trying to see in my car. He asked what I was listening to while out there spying on him. When I said nothing, he looked like he might suddenly reach in and steal this tape so I locked and slammed the door.

"So why are we here?" he asked, and put those farmer hands on either side of my face. When I said Quee wanted him, he laughed great big. He said, "At this hour?" and honest to God this is about when I started losing a sense of myself and what I was doing. "She must be thinking of a different kind of service," he said.

"What? What do you mean by that?" I asked.

"Night service," he said like a vampire and then sauntered back over to his little table and the circle of dogs. I told him that Alicia's husband is dead and other than that I didn't know *why* Quee wanted him.

"Dead?" he said. "The son of a bitch is dead?" He lit another cigarette and took a deep drag. He could make anybody want to smoke, he made it look so good. "Well, I'll be damned."

I told him all about how Jones Jameson was found in a load of topsoil that got delivered to Ruthie Crow's old aunt. I told him, all the while walking closer and closer like I might be in a trance. By the time I finished my sentence, I was sitting in the little webbed yard chair across from him. Even right now, repeating the story of that topsoil again gives me the heebie-jeebies. He laughed again and said that he guessed old Mrs. Carter must've had a fit; he said he was surprised she hadn't dropped dead when she found him.

I sat there petting the big head of the dog who was slobbering all over the knee of my jeans. "So are you coming to Quee's?" I asked like I might be impatient, when really I was thinking that I'd like to stay right where I was for a while.

"Yeah, I'll do that," he said.

"Now?" I jingled my keys to let him know that I was about to leave, but it didn't seem to faze him.

"Soon. After I give you the tour."

"The tour?" I asked. "I don't want a tour."

"No? Come on. Have the tour." He grabbed me by the hand. "I mean a person who knows so goddamn much about my life should definitely have the tour."

"I said I was sorry."

"So prove it," he said and pulled me up to the little cinder block stoop and half door. "Come inside." I followed right behind him, so close that I could breathe in the smells of his jacket, wood smoke, cigarettes, marijuana; I thought that he might suddenly disappear in one big poof of smoke, so I put my hand on his back and held on to his jacket. "This is it!" he said and spread his arms. He clicked on the little battery-powered lamp in his hand. On one side there was his bed, a rumpled mess of pillows and a quilt; the other wing was filled with stacks of books and cassettes. He has a tiny refrigerator, a small flip-out table, and a cardboard chest of drawers. It's all cheap-looking, but kind of cozy.

"It's nice," I said, which wasn't an entire lie. "Really."

"It's okay," he said. "Someday I'll build something, but it's okay until then."

"And you could," I told him. "Build something. I mean you *are* a carpenter after all."

"Don't try too hard," he said, and I was amazed that he could see through my fake nice voice, which has fooled people my whole life. "I said I forgave you," he said.

"*You* forgave me," I said and leaned down to look at his books: ships and pirates and ghost stories like what you might find in a child's room. "But you have yet to say that *you're* sorry for all the rotten things you've said about me."

"Such as?" he asked.

"You said I was crazy."

"No, I said someone ELSE said you were crazy." He took a beer out of the little refrigerator and popped the top. "You want one?" he asked and barely gave me a chance to breathe and answer before he went on spouting all that he knows about me. "Oh yeah, I forgot, reformed." He took a long drink, making it look real good, too. He could get a job as Satan and I almost said that but thought better. "I guess you don't do anything then, do you? Talking is your only vice," he said, and then without missing a beat he asked me how old I am.

"Thirty-five," I said and looked up to find him practically standing on top of me. "How about you?"

"Thirty-nine."

"So where is your bathroom?" I asked. It seemed like a good time to exit.

"Outside. I have three acres of bathroom." He said this so seriously, of course I believed him. I asked how he ever took a shower, or did he just *not* shower. He said *not* and then laughed and pointed out the little mesh window where there is a small wooden building the size of a single-car garage. He said it's all plumbed and wired, a lit bathroom, complete with newly installed Jacuzzi. He said not to tell anyone because it would ruin his image. Man oh man, we were standing close enough for the pheromones to return and they did, big time. Without even meaning to, I slipped my hand into his and nuzzled into his neck. What was I thinking? Nuzzling in like a goddamn pony.

"Sorry," he said, like he might be a priest and leaving me to feel like a complete idiot. "I took a vow of celibacy."

I said, "Oh, yeah? Well so did I."

"You?" he asked, like that might be one of the wonders of the world.

"Yes, me. What's so hard to believe about that?" I said and got myself over near the door so I could get the hell out. I said, "So what are you doing, anyway? Going out for the priesthood? Is your goal in life to be a celibate carpenter? Are you trying to be Jesus or something?"

"I said celibate not virgin." He laughed like I might be stupid. "Besides, now correct me if I'm wrong, but I've never thought of

Jesus as being somebody who might smoke a little dope. And, just in case you're wondering, I certainly am *not* a virgin."

"I was being facetious," I said and pushed to get out the door. "You are as far from Jesus as that jerk they dug up in the topsoil." I had to move quickly so I didn't start crying from humiliation or something, and I set off a chain reaction of barks in the process. "You are *not* a nice person, I don't care what Quee says about you. Maybe you do *service* her."

"Celibate."

"Oh, yeah, right." I wanted to say something that would hurt his feelings right back but couldn't think of anything that didn't involve the girl in the coma. "Well, I'll tell Quee I gave you the message."

"Give me a ride?" he asked then in a sweet voice, probably his fake nice voice. "My truck is on empty, and"—he paused—"as a rule I don't like to drive this way."

"What way?" I asked. "Celibate?"

"Oh, this way . . ." He held his arms out to the side, like he was being made to walk a straight line. He said he was fine, but if he got pulled wouldn't be.

So what could I do but wimp out and let him ride. I hid the tape recorder in my purse while he walked around to the other side. As soon as he closed the door, I turned on the radio, and what's playing but a call-in show for lovers sending mushy messages across the country. I was about to say something, offer some explanation for why I suddenly felt so attracted to him back in the trailer—I thought I might say that for a second he looked just like a lover I have in the D.C. area—but I was interrupted by a broadcast report about Jones Jameson. No suspects. No leads. The story was being repeated for the second time—this time with an address of the radio station if a lis-

tener wants to send money to the Jones Jameson Scholarship Fund—
when we saw the police car parked in front of Quee's house.

When I turned off the car, he reached across the seat and picked
up my hand, squeezed like he meant to hold me in place for another
second. "Come back when you're not stoned by second-hand smoke,"
he said.

I said, yeah right, that I was sure that I would. Everybody likes to
be rejected by somebody who thinks he's the chosen one.

"I hope so," he said and kissed my cheek. He said that was an invitation that he doesn't give often. And of course then Quee was peeking out the window and motioning us to come on in. I know I should
have said something back, but right that minute I couldn't think of
anything that sounded smart. Anyway, it doesn't really matter because he was out the door and up Quee's sidewalk in no time. As
soon as we got inside, that skinny white cop who puts me in mind of
a turkey was standing front and center in the living room while
relaying new bits of info about the death. I got this real paranoid
feeling like *I* might be the one stoned out of my gourd. I started
thinking, oh, God, what if old Mr. Lowe decided to tell Quee I made
a play for him, and they set in laughing over my pitiful plight, the
way they always do Ruthie Crow. And the funny thing, you out there
in recorderville, is I'm *not* sure why I all of a sudden turned and
grabbed him, and as if that's not bad enough it's like the urge hasn't
left me. If anything, my urges have gotten worse, especially right
now, sitting in this room all by myself and feeling creepy about being
here.

The cop told how Jones Jameson's alpaca sweater was being worn
by a scarecrow in a tobacco field not more than a hundred feet from
that grove where they found the car. Now imagine that, a cold-

blooded killer takes the time to stroll through a field and dress up an old straw man.

"Well, it might have been somebody else that done, uh, did it," the cop, Robert Bobbin, said. "Maybe some kid found the sweater in the woods." His neck and ears flamed bright red with his grammatical error since not five minutes before, the lardo Radio Guy was going on and on about his awful replacement and how the least a person could do was learn to speak good English. He had been talking poetry with Ruthie all night; he had made a little game of trying to make everything rhyme. He said: I'm a healthy bloke, no need to smoke, to which Ruthie raised up her third glass of Chardonnay. I know from experience what she was feeling. She was feeling like what someone of my chemical makeup might be feeling after a bottle plus a glass or two. She was feeling good, but teetering dangerously close to pass-out/cottonmouth/hangover land.

Tom Lowe was sitting there red in the face trying so hard not to laugh over the scarecrow—of course he *had* laughed over Ruthie and Radio's stupid talk. "I'm sorry," he finally said, shaking his head. "But folks have been dressing up that old scarecrow for a long time now."

"God, but yes," Quee said. "Honey do you remember when somebody put a lampshade on its head? Or what about the Shriners' hat, back during one of their little conventions."

"Here's a question," Ruthie said and eased herself down on Quee's big velvet ottoman. "Was there blood on the sweater?"

"Nope." Officer Bobbin moved closer to Alicia anytime the actual crime or body was mentioned, like maybe he could protect her from whatever words were let loose in the air. "No blood. Clothes must've been removed before he was killed; they don't show any tears or signs of struggle."

"All but the shoes," Ruthie said. "My Aunt Myra said that was one stinking sight."

"Yes, it was awful." Bobbin moved even closer to Alicia, his hand right on the back of her chair while he glanced over at where that child of hers had fallen asleep with a grape popsicle in his hand. It had dripped all over Quee's heavy old damask slipcovers, but she never said a word. It seems that child can get away with anything in this house, just like its mama, but Lord, don't let me talk too long at one stretch or prop my feet up on that big piece of wood there by the front door, the *antique hall tree*. Bobbin was playing daddy, now that Jones Jameson is dead. What we know for a fact is that Jones Jameson drowned. Now there was a bump to the side of his head. It could be that he was all by himself, decided to go for a swim and fell, or it could be that he was struck with something kind of blunt.

"Like a rolling pin or a leg of lamb?" Quee asked. "I've seen both of those used in the movies."

"Like a baseball bat? boat paddle?" Tom Lowe offered this question in the most serious way possible, so serious that Bobbin stopped to think about that. "Because why would he swim in shoes?"

"We just don't know," he said. "His wallet was missing, so it could have been a robbery. But Alicia doesn't need this talk."

"It's okay." She patted him on the arm and stretched out those skinny little legs. Alicia made Ruthie Crow look like Miss Piggy, and I was thinking of pointing that out but then thought better. I mean, I look like the Amazon warrior next to the two of them. And Quee? Well, let's just say something like hippo or rhino. But who looks better? Well, of course me and Quee (no rhyme intended).

"I was just telling what my aunt said." Ruthie's speech was getting very slow and her eyes were all droopy, making her look even older and scrawnier than she is. "But if nobody cares what I have to say, that's fine."

"We care, Ruthie," I offered, certainly not because I care, because I don't give a rat's smelly ass for her, but you know it's part of my job to say those things and I'm flying on autopilot. I patted Ruthie and, even though I hated to, I touched Radio on the shoulder and suggested they get a good night's sleep. After all, they would be going home the next day. The truth is that Quee had to try and let out some britches so that the Deejay could fit into something other than a great big towel.

At the same time, Officer Bobbin lifted the kid up in his arms and carried him down the hall to go to bed. Alicia followed right on his heels like she might be a ghost.

"Finally," Quee said and stretched out on the sofa, propped her feet up on a rose satin pillow. "I couldn't take any more of that talking."

"So why am I here?" Tom asked. "I mean there I was, having a nice quiet evening at home and then she drives up and parks like some kind of spy." He pointed at me like this was the first time he'd ever even seen me. "She scared the hell out of my dogs."

"I thought I might need you to go get Alicia."

"Why didn't I just go get Alicia?" I asked, but of course the answer was clear. She had in her mind that Tom Lowe needed to be fixed up with Alicia. There old Jones Jameson with his messed-up body is barely hauled over to Tucker Funeral Home and all tucked into a box, but what Quee is matchmaking. "I mean, it seems to me that Alicia has somebody who is very attentive to her needs."

"Yes, it does," Quee said.

"We all need for someone to be attentive to our needs," I continued. Quee and Tom looked at each other and laughed. "Psychologically, I mean." I went on to tell them about what a pleasure it had

been working with the woman who lied that she was a smoker and
checked in purely for a couple of days of peace and quiet, television
and back massages. That woman had told me that she didn't understand how anybody with a job and children had the time for an affair.
She said that her fantasy was a day without a word spoken, a hot bath,
and something like the *Bob Newhart Show* on the television. *Now*, we
were talking. Of course I *could* understand how a woman without
children might have plenty of time for an affair or whatever she might
be able to get, but Bob Newhart? We both love him. I hope that if
these tapes of mine are like a little time capsule then I can do some
good for mankind by telling the secrets to real happiness as we discovered in that very therapy session where, I must confess, I did most
of the talking. Ben and Jerry's and Bob Newhart.

Well, by then Bobbin and Alicia were back in the room and so with
the idea of lightening up the terribly dark mood, I began telling about
this game I used to play in college all the time—sometimes in a
group and sometimes right by myself—a game called "Hi, Bob,"
which is really very simple. You see, you just go and buy yourself
some beer or whatever it is you like to drink, and then you get a
comfy seat and tune in to Bob Newhart. Every time that somebody
says "Bob" you have to drink, and every time somebody says "Hi,
Bob" you have to chug.

"You'd be amazed how many times they say the name Bob on that
show." I turned to the officer. "Does anybody ever call you Bob?"

"Once in a while."

"I mean, Bob Bobbin is like a tongue twister." I thought somebody
else would speak up, laugh, something, but nobody said a word until
it was clear that Mr. Fixit couldn't stay quiet any longer.

"Well I'd think you'd have taken Tongue Twister in college right
there along with Hi Bob." Tom Lowe stood and stretched, his T-shirt

rising with him just enough to show a strip of his hard tan stomach. "Did you want me to hang out anymore?" he asked, and of course Quee said no, looked at me as if to say "Hop to it, drive the boy home." He told Alicia again how sorry he was, shook Bobbin's hand, patted Quee on the shoulder, and then there we were right back where we started in the car with the radio playing so that we wouldn't have to talk.

"Wonder who got him?" he finally asked just as I was turning into the dark stretch of road that leads to his trailer, as if that wasn't creepy enough. "I mean, somebody did. Don't you keep wondering, like did this person make him strip or what?"

"Maybe he was doing something *with* somebody and somebody else walked up and caught him."

"Possible." He leaned in close to me as if to guide me down his dark little road, pine twigs snapping beneath the tires. "That would mean there's a witness. Could be that somebody had been watching him for a while. Somebody could have been stalking him, ready and waiting." He lowered his voice, and I felt a chill up my arms. "Or maybe it was just a random robbery."

"Any ideas who? I mean if it *was* someone around here."

"It would be easier to guess who it wasn't." He ran his finger along the gooseflesh of my arm making the little hairs stand up. "I've got this idea for like one of those K-tel albums. . . ."

"Albums?"

"CDs, whatever, *Songs to Stalk By*, whatta you think? 'I'll Be Watching You' and 'Run for Your Life.'" He laughed. "Songs for the discriminating stalker."

"Nice." I didn't add to his little game even though ever since I've been hearing that old Beatles' song "I'll Get You" over and over inside my head.

"Or what about the Tragedy Theme Park?" He pawed my arm for a response like he might be one of those mongrel dogs of his coming and going. "You know, like there's a simulated Space Challenger, Guyana Juice Bar, Waco Golf instead of Wacky."

I think he was wanting to make up for the way he'd treated me earlier, but by then I felt just like I was made of stone. I mean there was a part of me with ideas connected to the book depository and Ford's Theater, but there was also a part of me still back there in Quee's house trying to picture what had happened to Alicia's husband. I mean he was (in the words of Bobbin) nekked. I felt sorry for Bobbin because he never noticed that saying "nekked" wasn't the right choice; and there he was being so careful of all of his grammar in front of Alicia, whose husband, though mean and dead, *was* Phi Beta Kappa, and in front of Ruthie and Radio, since they considered themselves the literary leopards (Gerald always called himself a "lion," so a spotty version of Gerald sounds about right).

"Come on." He tugged on my arm, then moved his hand up to my cheek. "I'm trying to make up." He leaned in closer so that there was no mistaking those big eyes staring right into mine. "You're not making it very easy."

"So come back when you're not stoned."

"Okay." He slid over and opened his door, and all I could think of again was that old Hookarm story. I waited and watched as he walked in front of my lights, froze there with his hands up to his head like antlers; then he came to my side and rapped on the window.

"Yes?" I asked, and that's when he said that he had come back, that he was not stoned. That he'd really like some company. My first thought was of Quee sitting here at the house waiting for me. Imagine, my first real worry at such a moment was what Quee would think of me for spending a little time in the flea trailer rather than that

I was being propositioned and that somewhere roaming about in the night was a murderer. It was a real toss-up, but before I could even think, I had taken his hand and gotten out, followed him right back in. I warned him that I might start sneezing and wheezing any second, but he said if I did we'd leave. I told him that I couldn't imagine living the way that he did in that cramped little space, and all the while he reached for my hands and pulled me closer. A little tiny red-headed poofy dog looked at me and bared its teeth.

"Anne's a little jealous," he whispered and pulled me over to that rumpled-up mess of a bed.

"Why are you doing this? Why are you all of a sudden changing your mind?" I asked all of this, but he just kept hugging and kissing and pulling until I was up on that wing of a bed and my blue jeans were unzipped. I said, "Are you an octopus or what?" I said, "Is this a joke?" I said, "So you're getting out of the Lord Savior business?" I was flat on my back looking up into the low canvas ceiling where there was a little mesh skylight. It looked like something he had designed himself, the edges ratty, and right there above us was the moon, coming and going behind the clouds. I had a second there where I felt snuggly and safe, like I had been able to make myself feel as a child with the right blanket and stuffed toys, the things that smelled like home. "Where do you do your laundry?" I asked. "And how can you possibly work on those ship models in this itty bitty space what with so little ventilation?" He raised himself up, hovering over me with a tired look on his face. "Did you ever sniff glue?" I asked him, because I never did. I knew some boys who did. Now I did sniff mimeograph fluid—I loved that stuff, do to this day and I liked to smell that thick white paste and of course rubber cement. He sat off to the side and took the liberty of rezipping my pants and buttoning the top buttons of my shirt.

"What's wrong?" I asked. "It *was* a joke wasn't it?"

"No." He lay back beside me, his shoulder touching mine. "The mood just came and went."

"Mood or moon?"

"Both." He cupped his hand around mine and closed his eyes. "It's just as well. This is fine just like this."

"Well, I'm not going to stay here for the night if that was an invitation you just gave me."

"Afraid to be seen coming out of the woods?"

"No," I said. "Just afraid." It was so quiet right then that I could hear little dog-panting sounds all around me in every direction. I waited, thinking he had passed out, but then I felt his thumb rubbing up and down the back of my hand.

"I know what you mean." He turned his head to look at me then, our noses no more than a few inches apart. I apologized just in case I smelled like the garlic toast I had eaten for supper, but he just laughed and said he loved garlic. I thought he was going to try and kiss me again, and I was thinking I was ready for him, but instead he looked back up at the moon and started talking about how he had felt scared a lot of times. He talked about his father killing himself, which Quee had already mentioned a couple of times in passing, and he talked about the woman he went with in high school. He started to tell something but then stopped all of a sudden, like he suddenly remembered I was there. He said, "You know, just this very summer . . ."

"What?" I asked and leaned up so I could see his face but he just shook his head and closed his eyes. I had my nerve up by then, and so I leaned close and kissed him, just a little one, lips barely brushing. If he had given me the green light, there we would have gone, but he only responded with a squeeze of my hand. In no time at all, he was sound asleep, and I could have easily stayed right there where I was.

I *wanted* to stay where I was, but for some reason I felt like I *had* to get back to Quee's. For all of her big talk, I can't imagine that she'd ever just go off and stay out all night.

I shook his shoulder to get him to at least see me to my car but he just rolled over and tried to pull me closer. By then there was this huge hairy dog in bed with us, the one who always sits in his truck, and it had licked one leg of my jeans until it was saturated with dog spit or foam, whatever it is they have in their mouths. It was just fifty feet from his door to my car but it felt like it took forever, like my feet were made of lead. The whole time I kept thinking I heard something like Hookarm or the Maco Man. I kept picturing the body of Jones Jameson and the way it had been described to me off and on all day long, it seemed. I got in and slammed and locked all the doors. I reached in the backseat quickly to make sure nothing was waiting there. Ever since I read how Charles Manson was hiding in a tiny little kitchen cabinet, I check everything. It drove Gerald crazy; I checked every closet and under the beds at night. I checked inside the dryer. I scared myself in the rearview mirror, and then I backed out so fast, I left smoke and now, as I say, here I am. I wish I smoked or drank or something right now. It's one of those times. Instead I'm just sitting here talking my head off and wondering why I didn't just lie back and shut up when he was in the mood and see what happened. Could it be as simple as not wanting to be rejected again? Or maybe me not wanting to be seen coming out of his makeshift trailer park the next morning? I just can't figure it out, because now that it's all behind me I wish so bad that I had kissed him back, taken off his clothes. All I know is that tomorrow has got to be better than today, and of course the amazing thing is that I didn't sneeze or wheeze once. It could be that what I was allergic to was Gerald; I was allergic to boredom, and I'll tell you something, there's a lot you can say about this establishment but boring is *not* one of them. Right now I hear the hum of Quee's sewing machine as she tries to get Fatass's clothes so they'll fit him come tomorrow when he goes on the outpatient plan, which means I don't have to talk to him nearly as often. And now I guess even if I *did* make a pass earlier, I can consider us even. We're like one of those cars that can go from zero to eighty in something like two seconds. Of course we can also go from eighty to zero in about two seconds. Our timing is way off. Now Quee's machine has cut off, and I can angle myself and look down to see that all the lights are out below. I look out into that dark yard and I keep thinking of *Songs to Stalk By* and that scarecrow all dressed up like he's going to play golf. Now you can call me strange, but that's the kind of image—the scarecrow—that I find the scariest of all. Don't ask me why. Maybe it's because it's the middle of the night and I'm too tired to sleep. I have searched my purse three times and there is not a Tylenol PM or Benadryl to be found. I'm sure Quee has something that would knock me out down below, but now I'm afraid to leave my room. Something just doesn't feel quite right tonight. There is bad karma all over creation, in spite of the fact that I haven't felt so hopeful of a possible love affair in my whole life.

When Mack's phone rings the next morning, it seems like it's ringing for the second time. Then he realizes all in one sweep of a moment that he slept through his alarm, that he's running an hour late, that the sitter will be at the door ready to begin her day with Sarah any minute now. He looks at Sarah as he always does to see if there has been any change at all in her body; he writes down the amount of urine in the plastic bag by their bed—400 cc. Then June's voice is on the machine. He reaches to pick up and then stops.

"Mack? I waited until I knew you weren't there to call. You have so much going on." Her voice drops and he thinks for a minute that she might really talk, that she might now be able to tell him what is going on with her. But of course she can't do that, she wouldn't do it with Sarah right here. "I just wanted to see if I can help you out today. You know, like can I bring dinner *tonight?* Call me."

The sitter was ringing the bell, but he had to sit for a minute and replay the message in his thoughts. The way she said *tonight* did mean something. It meant we got interrupted last night and so let's try it again, take it from the top. He pulls his robe around him and goes to the front door. The sunlight is blinding, and he steps back as the sitter pushes herself through the door. She glances at him and then at her watch. "Am I early?" she asks, and he shakes his head, tells her he's late. He's going to put on a pot of coffee and take a quick shower.

He can hear the sitter going through the house and raising every shade, pulling the drapery cords in the living room so that with one big swish daylight invades his home. He feels like shit, mouth dry and thick, head pounding; he stands for as long as he can just breathing steam and wondering why June didn't call him at work. Didn't she know that he wouldn't even get the message until five? Were their lives so predictable? Yes, absolutely. Her life is as predictable as his.

When he steps back in the bedroom, the sitter leaves, so he can get dressed, and already there is evidence that her day has begun. There is the smell of baby powder hanging in the air like a cloud, Sarah's legs and back made silky white. She has changed the pillowcase and the bag to the catheter. He dresses quickly, the smell of his aftershave temporarily masking the odor of this room, this house that has become his life. Bottle it and sell it to those who have no idea what sickness can do to the air, and when those people are moaning and groaning about this or that bullshit something at work, or what so and so said about so and so, have them inhale deeply, taking the filthy smell of illness into their lungs.

"Have a good day, dear," the sitter whispers. She has asked him to call her Barbara instead of Mrs. Wilcox, but he hasn't been able to find the heart or energy to give her a name. Then it all is too personal, too close to reality. This way she's like the IV drip, the oxygen they have used in the past, the catheter. She's just part of the equipment, part of the treatment.

"Thanks." In the kitchen he gets a cup of coffee and dials June's number. Even though she's probably in her classroom by now, twenty-odd kids waving their arms for one second of her attention, he pictures her there by the phone, screening his words, listening.

"Dinner sounds great. Tonight. I will see you tonight." He hesitates after putting the phone back down. What is he hoping for after all?

On the refrigerator there is a picture of his in-laws with Sarah hugged between them. It is a small picture taken at her high school graduation, a time when she doesn't even know he exists.

This is Gwendolyn," Quee says, once again giving her "ghost wall" tour. She points to a black-and-white photo of a young woman with long wavy hair, perched on a cutout crescent moon. The legs of her swimsuit fit down on her thighs like short shorts, and her head is tossed back to reveal an ample bosom and slightly rounded tummy. Above her head a sign says: Carolina Moon. "She's on a vacation at the beach and she has spent the whole day just stretched out on the beach frying her skin with a bunch of girlfriends who have done the same. Her stepfather works as one of the assistant managers at the Ocean Forest, and as a result, Gwendolyn has been allowed to have several girls spend the night. Her stepfather is a son of a bitch; he likes to cup his hands under those warm fannies when the girls greet him and pass through his door. He points to his cheek for someone to kiss him and then turns his face and gets them on the mouth, slips his tongue between their lips if he can. But now, Gwendolyn is happy because just beyond this photo is a young man who has caught her eye. He's winking at her, and it makes her toss her head back and cross her ankles tightly. There's a rush of excitement. There's the promise that this may very well be her ticket out of her present life and into another. That's Gwendolyn."

Quee steps back and moves on down the hall, Denny and Alicia right on her heels. "And?" Denny asks. "So did she go away with him? Do we know his name?"

"See? I told you." Alicia reaches out and pats Denny's arm. "Doesn't she tell a story? I swear I find myself believing all of these stories she makes up."

"She did go away with him," Quee says. "But this is the sad part of the story. She didn't go away with him until years later. She went away with him after she was married and after he was married."

"Where?" Denny asks, and she realizes that she has lowered her voice the way you would do if you were interrupting a ghost story. "Where did they go?"

Quee shrugs. "I'm not sure. I would suspect a city. Yes, a big city, maybe New York or Boston, someplace so big they could walk around arm in arm without anybody taking notice. They could stop underneath a bridge and kiss and nobody would care. The man bought Gwendolyn something real nice, a gift, a silver pillbox, and he told her that later, when they were apart, she should open the box and read the little note. They did bump into someone she knew, though. She said, Small world! She offered no explanation. It was her best friend in the world, so there was no need. Besides, her friend was there, locked in that apartment, with a child about Taylor's age." She paused and looked at Alicia, who rolled her eyes and gave a knowing nod. "The friend was desperate for company. I mean it was one of those old apartments that only had windows that opened out onto ventilation shafts. The child would spend hours standing on a little chair and staring down into that dirty alley."

"How tragic." Alicia shakes her head. "Do you think sometime you could tell a funny story?"

"Like about these folks?" Quee points to a little dwarf couple dressed up like Napoleon and Josephine. They are both plump and laughing with their mouths wide open. "I call them Mickey Rooney's cousins. If you look closely, he has got his hand up her skirt."

"He does! He really does!" Now Ruthie Crow has joined the tour, a Bic pen sticking out of her mouth like a cigarette. "What a hoot!"

"What was on the note?" Denny asks.

"What note?"

"In the pillbox."

"Oh." Quee points to a photo way up high, a woman standing at the far edge of the photo, her hand up and shielding the sun from her eyes. Behind her is the ocean. "It was something he had copied from a book."

"A poem?" Ruthie asks. "If it's a poem, I bet I will have heard of it."

"She was more beautiful than thy first love, this lady by the trees," Quee says, to which Ruthie shrugs and smirks.

"Nope, doesn't ring any bells."

"What an odd thing to put," Alicia says. "Does that mean that he thought Gwendolyn was prettier than his wife?"

"Who knows?" Quee laughs. "I'm making it up as I go, right?" She turns to Ruthie and whispers, "Have you ever heard of a man named Yeats?"

"Did he have asthma?" Denny asks. "If he did, I'm sure I've heard everything he ever did."

"I think I've heard the name," Ruthie says, still studying the dwarf couple. "Yeah, I'm sure I have. He's from somewhere near Taborville, right?"

"The line is from something called 'A Dream of Death,' now don't ask me why I thought of it." Quee points to the woman up top, her head wrapped in a scarf the ends of which are blowing out behind her. "I bought this photo because as you all know I'm rather partial to scarves myself. Besides, when I first glimpsed her, I thought somehow she might be the older Gwendolyn."

Now Ruthie is coming down the hall with the photo of the masquerading dwarfs clutched to her chest. "May I take this back to my room?" she asks. "I am really feeling inspired."

"By all means," Quee says. "I wish you would."

"Thanks!" When Ruthie closes her door, Quee turns back to the wall. "Things couldn't last with him. How could they? She knew that, always had, and was always prepared for the day when they would agree that it was all over. What she wasn't prepared for was that he would die." She turns to Alicia. "Oh dear, sweetheart, how thoughtless of me."

"Was it murder?" Alicia asks in an almost trancelike voice.

"Oh, no, honey, no." Quee pats her on the shoulder. "This man took his own life. He was a burdened sad man, and he felt torn between lives."

"You know, Tom Lowe's father killed himself," Denny offers. At this, Quee looks at Alicia and nods. "Yes, that's right."

"He told me all about it," Denny says, eyebrows raised in anticipation of a response. "Do you think that means, you know, that he likes me or something? You know, since he is kind of the independent type?"

"I hear discussions of death are always a good sign." Alicia remains deadpan until Quee laughs and gives her the reaction she had expected. The girl is finally starting to relax, the life slowly creeping back into her now that Jones Jameson isn't all set up like a siphon to drain her soul. "So finish the story, and then let's go give Ruthie and Mr. Radio Jr. a rubdown."

"Well, when she got word that he was dead, she suddenly thought that there might have been something there for her. There might have been a note, something. And she went to the Ocean Forest expecting to find him there, but no, so she ran down the beach to where he was staying in a small house, one of those perched way up on pillars like a big spider. And she stood under the coolness of that house, complete silence over her head. The smell of pitch was in her nose and the wind had left her hair damp and tangled. Her heart was pounding so loud she could feel it in her neck and ears and as she stood there trying not to cry, trying to understand, she saw a scrap of paper over in front of the trash cans. It was damp and sticky but she recognized his handwriting. It said: 'I loved you. I love you. Only now do I know how much. Only now do I . . .' but the rest was torn away so she held on to this and she slipped it into her little pillbox and walked up to the top of the dunes, her scarf blowing while a passerby with no knowledge whatsoever of her loss clicked the shutter."

"That's beautiful," Alicia says. "If only you could make a naked man in a pile of topsoil sound good."

"There's no way to do that, sweetheart." Quee goes now and hugs Alicia into her, her big arms wrapping and squeezing. "I wish so much that I could. If I could, then you know that I would."

"If you could, you'd be a magician."

"If I could, I'd be God."

*T*om Lowe has spent the whole day sitting on the beach. Once his property lines surfaced, he picked up an old soggy stick and drew his dream house. Now he and Blackbeard are stretched out in the master bedroom, dozing in and out with the sound of the surf and the whine of gulls overhead. He imagines glass everywhere in this house, a view from every angle. Today he has even drawn another bedroom—two other bedrooms—as if for a family. It's hard to imagine, though not impossible.

Whenever he's here, drifting and dozing, it's like he's a receiver of sorts, all kinds of images and words floating in and out of his mind. The grand staircase of the *Titanic*, ladies in ball gowns coming and going, the men working out in the gymnasium below, the seagulls circling above, or Atlantis, the underwater world. He imagines swimming in the deep, down at such a pitch-black depth that evolution has robbed some fish of their unnecessary eyes, swimming down and down, feeling over coral and rock and the debris of wreck after wreck, whale bone and rusty anchor, and then there is a door no bigger than a porthole that leads to a small chamber and then another and then another until finally he pushes free and swims out into a pure blue bay, a whole world encapsulated there at the bottom of the sea. He has gotten this far, swimming close to the shore with its fine white sand and shade just beyond. "I'm home," he calls out, and Sarah is there looking just as she did in high school with cutoff jeans and a big embroidered peasant shirt that covers her shorts. Her hair is pulled back and tied with a big piece of yarn like the first time he saw her. But as he travels the fantasy, he gets interrupted, he hears people talking in the distance, people walking the beach in search of sand dollars and conchs, kids screaming and throwing Frisbees, and with all the distraction, all the noise, it's hard to focus on Sarah's face and instead he sees his father, how he must have looked when found by an old fisherman who heard the shot. Did his father think of him at all in those minutes? How could he, and with the image comes panic, the need to get back. There is an urgency—a need for light and for air.

"Hey." The voice stuns him. He opens his eyes to black dots and brightness. Denny is standing over him, hands on her hips, hair falling forward. "Quee said I might find you here."

He sits up and Blackbeard does the same. "So, what's up?"

"I don't know." She sits down right beside him and studies the lines around them. "So am I in a box or what?"

"No."

"I hope it's okay that I'm here."

"Sure." His eyes have adjusted now, and he turns to look at her. "I hope I didn't scare you last night."

"Scare me?" She laughs and scoops up sand in a tiny scallop shell. "Why'd you think that?"

"Because you said you were. Because you talked a thousand miles an hour when you thought something might happen."

"It just surprised me is all. I mean I'm not used to celibate people acting that way."

"Just other people."

"Yeah, right." She breathed out as if she was about to say more, but instead closed her eyes and tilted her face up to the sun.

"Well, I'm thinking maybe I'm tired of being celibate."

"Yeah?"

"Yeah. What about you?"

"Is this a trick?"

"No trick."

"Do you absolutely promise?" She puts her hand on top of his. "You're not going to make fun of my underwear? or me? or how I do things?"

"No." He shakes his head and laughs.

"Okay then." She stands up and brushes the sand from the back of her white shorts. "I can do that."

"*Do that?*"

"Yeah, you know, what you were just saying."

"So say it." He gets up and follows her down to the water. "Tell me."

She wades out knee deep, her arms stretched out to the sides to balance as the undercurrent pulls and swirls. "It's rough today."

"That's what you want? Rough?" He stands behind her, his hands on her hips as they sway with the waves.

"No!" She turns into him. "I don't know what I want."

"Me? Do you want me?" He hears Blackbeard splashing and barking behind him but he doesn't turn to look. She looks down and then out at the ocean, her hair all tangled as the wind whips it back from her face. "I swear it's not a joke." He has to yell over the waves. "Denny?"

"Yes, yes, I guess I do."

$\mathcal{M}$ack left work early, and now he is standing in the Winn-Dixie looking over the produce. It's been ages since he prepared a real meal complete with flowers and dessert and gourmet coffee. He even grabs a bottle of burgundy on the way out, though tonight he will only nurse a glass or two.

The last time he was in charge of such a meal was when he surprised Sarah after she and June had gone on an all-day shopping trip at Myrtle Beach. The two of them came into the house with squeals and laughs and more baskets than he could imagine anybody ever needing or wanting, and there he was with candles lit and music playing, clam chowder, shrimp scampi, and key lime pie (all of which he bought at a local restaurant).

"Look!" Sarah said and pulled June into the dining room where everything was all set up. "I can't believe it."

"Now when am I going to find me somebody who cooks and cleans?" June asked.

"I'm not cheap," Mack had said, and Sarah gave him that look, that slight smirk and lift of an eyebrow that said *just you wait until later.*

And now the mouth and the brow never move at all, and now he and June are just trying to make something happen so that they can stop thinking, can somehow if only for a second forget what is happening. He puts down the artichokes he's been holding and turns, abandoning his cart. As he leaves the store, he sees a woman he recognizes from one of Sarah's parents' parties when they first moved to town. She nods and gives him a slight smile, the one other people give him, the one he's used to, the one that says, *Oh you poor, poor boy. You must feel as if your life is over.*

All the way home he tries to think of what to say to June, how he has, with great guilt, imagined every scenario. He tells the sitter he's on a *date?* Sarah, oh miracle of miracles, gets up and walks through the house, down the long hall to his office, and finds them there on the old futon he had in college. He tells her parents that they can come get her, that he is young and deserves to have a life. "I am not an old man," he would yell. "I don't *deserve* this." He can go on and on, but the truth is that he can't think of anything that would excuse him when it was all over. There is no way that he and June could ever untangle the lines—what was love for Sarah and what was love for each other? Maybe they needed to possess each other because they were Sarah's most valuable possessions, her loved ones, her heart.

What to say to June, how to apologize, how to suggest that they try to forget whatever has been passing between them and go back to being friends. As he parks his car, the children next door are playing a game of freeze tag; three are standing like statues while the oldest child chases the last free one. They run circles around the Mother Mary statuette until finally the big kid reaches over Mary's head and slaps the little one on the arm.

By the time Mack is on his porch, they are all unfrozen and screaming again. He has watched them do this every afternoon this week, their voices loud and then dwindling to silence, only to flare up and start all over again. He has decided that he will order pizza, nothing special, nothing fancy, and that he will sit June down at the kitchen table and tell her in slow simple sentences that the two of them are making a mistake. That what each of them truly wants is Sarah.

He sees the note before he gets to the door and with the first line knows that he won't have to say everything he's planned after all. She is so sorry not to have let him know sooner but she has a date—no, not Ted—there really is someone from work who has been asking her out and she finally decided to go. *Please let me know whenever there's anything I can do. I'll check in with you or Sarah's mom soon. And again, I'm sorry.*

Mack is met at the door by the sitter and in a flurry of cheerful chatter, which he is sure she musters for his benefit, she is gone until tomorrow. He stands in the doorway looking at Sarah, hoping for something, a blink, a sigh. She's too young for this. He sits on the foot of the bed and pulls the covers to the side. Her leg is thin and cool as he lifts it, up and down and up and down. He massages her ankles and feet, rubs lotion into her skin. And outside the voices continue to rise and fall, screams and laughs from children he has not met. *Freeze. You're it.*

$\mathcal{Q}$uee's picture tours have become a regular pastime, and now somebody is forever asking her to tell about this one or that one. Just yesterday, Alicia and Taylor and that Bobbin man were over and asking about the one where there's an old man wearing nothing but a barrel. Quee doesn't mind telling old silly stories. It's rare for people to point to the ones that actually mean something to her. When she got Alicia alone in the kitchen to see how she was getting along, Alicia told her fine, but that she was afraid Robert was getting too interested in her, that all she wanted right then was a friend. "I don't want to use him," Alicia said, and Quee told her she had every right to go ahead and do as she pleased.

"He's a grown-up," Quee said. "Let him take care of himself."

"He has been getting calls from Ruthie," Alicia whispered, and they both fell out laughing. Quee said, More power to him then; bless him. "Ruthie told him that her aunt *told* her to call him."

"That Carter woman is insane," Quee said. "She convinced herself years ago that I slept with that old husband of hers." Bobbin and Taylor came in about then, so Quee gave them all a piece of pound cake as a nice send-off on their drive to a little local zoo. That cop actually looked right good; amazing what having yourself a full dance card will do for the soul. Taylor had only asked after his daddy a couple of times and now had pretty much stopped, or so Alicia said. Jones was never around much anyway, she said. But Jones. The talk is still going on but there are no leads, not a single clue, nothing.

"Tell me about this one." Jason, who has kicked smoking but still drops in every day to talk to Quee, points to a picture of a little infant in a woman's lap, and she tells him that's a photo of a baby who was left behind and how as a result he was one of the strongest, sweetest boys in the whole town of Fulton, a boy who ought not to smoke and surely shouldn't drink and get himself all messed up with drugs when he could have a job right here at a successful business for addicts.

"Me?" His hand goes up to his own skinny chest, and then twists the silver cross dangling from his ear. "You mean I can work here?"

"And live if you like." She turns away, so he won't be embarrassed if he wants to say no; but then he is gone like a rocket through the screen door and across the yard. He is going as fast as he can to get his few possessions and move in. So there'll be one less smoke-out room, that's okay. She can build more if Tommy Lowe can keep his mind on work and off of Denny for an hour or two. Those two smile and wink and pat like they are the first to ever have sex.

$\mathcal{M}$yra Carter is dreaming of compost and topsoil and fat red earthworms eating their way through it all. She is dreaming of Howard and Ruthie and Geraldo Rivera. Sometimes at night she can't sleep for thinking of Jones Jameson; she will never ever garden in quite the same way.

For over a week now, at least one member of her Sunday school class has been by to check on her, and she is sure that Connie Briley must have spread around that she said the Lord talked to her all about Jones Jameson. Connie has probably told that Myra said Jesus said that Myra was good-looking. She can just hear Connie: "Now you know, ladies, if the Lord *was* to speak to Myra that he wouldn't say *that!*"

She was so mad at Howard when he died and left her, but he couldn't help it. She finally sees that now. You'd think since he took care of everybody else's health problems that somebody, like Jesus for example, might step in and take care of his. He really was a good man, and if he fell under that old Purdy whore's spell, well what can you say? A man will do that. A man just has no control over those parts when tampered with, and she's a tamperer that Queen Mary

Stutts Purdy. Oh, yes. He couldn't have done anything with that Jezebel, and if Myra had had her wits about her that day in the Winn-Dixie when the old floozy was waving around her avocados like she might be Angie Dickinson, who also looks cheap, then she would have said, "Why would my Howard ever even think about the likes of *you* and your tawdry tarty self?" Still, as much as Myra can't stand that old harlot, she thinks she'd rather have dinner with her than Connie if given a choice in life. But life doesn't always give you a choice. Life might just say: Here's your old gummed-up hand, now play it! Life might say: Here's your topsoil, and we threw a dead man in for good measure. It might say: Here's your husband you love so dearly, and now he's gone.

*T*esting . . . testing. Sorry I haven't talked in over a week but I mean how could I? I've been so busy. Busier than I have ever been in my life. First of all the business is going great, and Quee has agreed to have a little day clinic of sorts for people who can't afford to leave their families for so long. There was a horde of people at the impotency clinic yesterday, and just as many taking the samples of cinnamon dental floss and Close-Up toothpaste.

But all of that is beside the point. The truth is that I have been with Tom Lowe practically nonstop ever since I drove out to the beach to find him. I don't know, but it kind of seems like we were just kind of waiting for somebody to come along at the right place and at the right time and then there we were. I mean of course it all started out kind of sexual, but doesn't everything, when you get right down to it? Especially if you are more the oral, free-giving type, which it seems to me that both of us are. And just look at the foliage in his yard— ramblers and weeds gone wild!

We left the beach and went straight to his little camper, and I swear to you we both shed our clothes so fast that I lost a sock; I'm sure it fell out that little half door and one of those dogs ran off with it. And all that time I was telling him about how it had been a long time since I'd thought of anybody like I'd been thinking of him, and then that made me think of how I used to think for long periods of time as a child about the daddy that my mother had told me all about, and then it came to me that *I* had stood up on a little kitchen step stool and stared out into a ventilation shaft when I was a tiny thing and living in that apartment in New York. I thought *What a coincidence*, how odd that Quee seems to know so much. I asked Tom did he think that Quee had some kind of special powers, and he asked me did I want to do this or not. I said, Yes, I told you yes all the way home, and then he asked me well then, could I please shut up and pay attention for just a minute because it had been so long for him that he was certain it was only going to take a second or two. I started to ask if he always liked it quiet when he was *doing things* but I decided not to because I didn't want to end up like last time I talked him right out of it. So I shut my mouth, and I am so damn glad that I did.

Ever since then it's like we can't wait to get to that trailer or the car or even up here in my room, though we have to be a little careful here because we have to pass in front of a line of people waiting for their feet to be massaged. Tom says, "So who cares?" and I tell him that I do. I don't want anybody listening to what I might have to say.

Just the other night we went to the Maco Light and parked. Of course, Tom wanted to get out of the car to sit like he has done many many times before, but I just couldn't do it. Even sitting right there I was all over him, scared to death that I might really *see* that old engineer swing by with a lantern and no head. He said in high school kids used to go out there on dates; he said it was a guarantee that your date would press all up against you and that if it was a good hazy night with lots of lantern potential, that you could probably touch something you weren't supposed to touch and get away with it, which of course he *did*. I suspect he has touched about everything I've got by now, and there is a nice comfortable feeling to come from that.

He has taken me all over this town, past where his mama lives (she was out watering her lawn and didn't even see us—she is a little tiny woman with white hair), up in the bank building where Quee's husband used to work (he told me that this was where he came the last time that he ever saw his dad), the high school football field (we *did* things under the bleachers because I felt left out that I never did anything like that while in high school, at least not that I could actually remember).

And it was there at the high school that he acted a little bit strange. He was trying hard, to be sure. I mean we had a blanket spread and a little transistor radio that he still *has* from high school. It was like he was having to try hard. He said, So what do you want to do? I said, You *know* what I want to do.

"So say it," he said and laughed though his eyes and heart weren't quite in it.

"Let's do it," I said, because I had already explained to him that I hated all the ways people referred to *it*. I mean I'm not going to say "make love" because that sounds so posed and old somehow and I'm not going to say the *word* because it makes me feel cheap and dirty, which he said was fine with him. So he said the words, every word he could think of, and then asked me which I wanted to do. I asked if I could have a sampling of each and then get back to him. We laughed and all, but there still wasn't something right, and afterward when we were lying there half-dressed, I said what I'd been thinking the whole time. I didn't plan to, but I said, "You're in love with a ghost." I got up and finished dressing and then knelt there right beside him and waited.

"No, no, I'm not." He whispered and his jaw clenched with each word as if to hold him all together. "I guess maybe I'm afraid that you are, though."

"Me? In love with a ghost?" I waved my hands through the air like they were floating, and then I let them fall, solid and firm, on his stomach. "I'm not in love with a ghost. Just you." Can you believe that I said that? I mean, I can't. My heart nearly stopped because he could so easily break the whole spell; he could laugh at me, say something like *fat chance* which I would never in my life get over. But he didn't do that.

"But maybe I'm a ghost" is what he said and then he paused and took a deep breath. "I mean, you probably have some ideas about who I am or who I can be, but this is it. I'm it." He sat up and patted his chest. "I mean, for years now I've been waiting for that famous ship to come in, for the ocean to cough up my land, for somebody to find out my old man left me something after all. But now I know that this is it. I'm it. There is no ship. No treasure."

"So maybe the ship did come in," I told him. "Maybe being nice and smart and handsome are part of having a ship come in. Come to think of it, maybe *you* are *my* ship."

He thought that part was funny. He didn't say anything back to me like that maybe I was his ship or that maybe he loved me, and I was glad really. I don't want somebody just to spout back at me like a mynah bird might do. I could tell by the way that he looked at me that I shouldn't be as nervous as I had been.

I tell you all of this because I need to tell somebody. Quee is taking it all in, but I've almost felt like she was jealous somehow or feeling left out. Believe it or not, I've actually been a little discreet with her. But the truth is that I have never been so happy in my whole life, and if that big old meteor or whatever it was to hit Jupiter *did* hit me about now, I wouldn't care, except that I'd miss all the time that would have been ahead of me. Even if it doesn't work out. At least now I know that such a thing is possible.

uee is in need of a little breather herself and has pro-
claimed a day off for Smoke-Out. Ruthie is off somewhere quoting, and Mr. Radio is boasting about being a smoke-free
person, and Quee is just damn glad to get a little peace and quiet, a
little time to catch up with Denny and find out exactly what *is* going
on with Tom Lowe. A day of rest; every great creation calls for one.
Then tomorrow at noon a brand-new group of addicts will come calling, and it'll be business as usual.

"Now, this is a picture I want you to see." Quee leads Denny and
Tom down to the very end of the hall. It's dark and she has to turn on
a light for them to be able to see the little frame that she pulls from
the wall. It's a picture of the river, vines dangling into the water. She
bought the picture long ago because it made her think of Rapunzel,
the vines like long braids reaching to pull somebody out. Off to the
side is half of a person, someone who was never even supposed to be
in the picture.

"This looks like the Braveman Bridge," Tom says and leans down to
study the photo. "Good fishing there." He shakes his head. "You might
even catch a body these days."

"That is the Braveman Bridge," Quee says. "It says so on the back, though I didn't know it when I bought it."

"So, is there a story to it?" Denny asks and steps right up close to Tom. If she got any closer she would *be* Tom.

"Oh, my, yes," Quee says and places the frame back on its rusty nail. "You see, something has just happened here."

"Yeah, we know." Tom laughs again, and she waits until they are quiet. "I'm sorry, we'll listen." Tom reaches for Denny's hand and she wiggles right up to him.

"Well, you see, the story is about a man and a woman meeting down here at the Braveman Bridge but the story doesn't start there, Lord, no." She leans closer to the wall, thick nubby bedroom shoes spread apart and turned out like she might be getting frisked. "The story starts, oh, maybe a year before that, when this same young man appeared at the woman's door to say that he was in need of her services." She turns and grins a fake grin. "You see, he thought she was in the business of prostitution."

"One of the oldest professions," Tom Lowe adds, and Quee has to sigh again. He has gotten to be a regular chatterbox.

"Well, anyway, he wanted her services and she said, *You git from my door you old dog*, because the truth was that he had a very nice sweet wife at home who didn't even know what a horrible monster she had married." She pauses to make sure that she has Tom and Denny's full attention. She does. My, yes. You could hear a feather. "You see, the wife was a *friend* of this older woman, too. The fool man just had no sense about what loyalty means and about what a good friend will do for you.

"So he goes off in a great big huff, needing to pay city prices, you see. Go ahead and sit down there on the floor if you're getting fidgety."

"I'm not fidgety," Denny says, consciously making herself like stone.

"And I'm petite," Quee says. "Go on, take a load off. This is a long story. You guys can play footsie or whatever a lot better sitting than standing, too." She waits for them to sit, both wide-eyed like the children she never had.

"So about a year later this same fella comes back with the very same request. He needs her services, and he is prepared to pay whatever it takes. Well, she has no intentions of giving him what he wants, but still she says, *All right then, meet me at the river, Braveman Bridge*, and he says he will. He drives a car, she goes on foot. He parks his car, oh round about here," she rubs her finger along the wall beyond the frame. "And there they are on the bridge. Now in her pocket she has a little old pistol that doesn't even work but she has brought it along for effect.

" 'I'm not in the business you think I'm in,' she says. 'Just what is it you *want?*' He laughs and shakes his head from side to side. He pulls out his wallet and fans some money, takes out a credit card, and presses it into her hand, cool plastic in her palm.

" 'You name your price,' he says. So she tells him first off that she is very thirsty and does he have some liquor. Well, it just so happens that if they walk up to his car, he has a flask in his glove compartment. When she gets to the car, she takes a big slug of that liquor herself and then, when he isn't looking, she drops some little sleep pills in and then watches his Adam's apple chug back and forth while he drains it. She knows it won't hit him right off, him being such a big fella, but it won't be too long. So to kill time, she suggests that he take off his clothes. Now he resists and laughs and tries to get her to take off *her* clothes. They go on a bit and then, by the time that she pulls out her little gun and *orders* that he take his clothes off, he listens. She makes him fold every article neatly like he might work in the laundromat and then she has him put the clothes on the backseat, all but the shoes, of course; he needs those shoes to walk back down to the river."

"This is it," Denny says. "The murder. You've figured it out?"

"Oh, yes, indeed," Quee says. "I've spent hours thinking on it. You see, he was threatening her, he knew something about her."

"So keep going," Tom says. "I can't wait for the scarecrow part." They giggle like children, and so she waits for them to finish up *again*.

"By the time they get to the bridge, he's real groggy, slips and hits his head which pretty much does him in. Then all she has to do is roll his old naked body down onto the bank and not more than eight to ten feet, where an old farmer does his composting of autumn leaves and such. He is face down in the mud and she leaves him that way, pushes dirt all up around him so that it might be hard to move around. More and more dirt and limbs and such and then he fits right into nature."

"And she takes his sweater and puts it on the scarecrow," Denny says and laughs, but the look in her eyes is saying something else.

"But there's evidence," Tom says. "There's a wallet, credit card."

"Gun," Denny adds.

"The gun isn't important," Quee says. "It was never used."

"Wallet?"

"Oh, the wallet. Well, the card goes back in the wallet and then this woman, let's call her, oh, Eunice; Eunice goes on home, and who is there but a good friend of hers, who has a little boy who has grown, my, yes, but he has grown, but he does still wear diapers and, oh, my goodness, he is in need of a change as soon as Eunice gets in the door.

"Well, Eunice's friend has been having some problems in her life, marital problems I guess, and while she's making some calls, Eunice tells her to go on and relax, take care of her business, that she, Eunice, will change the boy's diaper. And she does and as she's about to wrap it up in plastic she slips the wallet in, bags it, carries it to the street and tells the trashman he better drive as fast as he can with that load."

"And that's it?" Tom asks. "What about the flask?"

"That's it," Quee says. "She pulled her sleeves down long enough to grab the flask with fabric. She never touched the flask."

"Pretty good," Tom says.

"Yeah." Denny stands now and pulls him with her. "You ought to do something with all these stories you tell."

"Oh, I do," Quee says. "I sure do." They are both looking at her now, as if wondering exactly what she does do. "Your father made up some wild stories, didn't he, Tommy?"

"Yeah, I guess. Or so people say." He turns to Denny. "My dad was a writer when he wasn't drinking and screwing around."

"Oh, I always thought he was a nice man," Quee says. "I always heard such wonderful things about him being kind-hearted and about how much he loved you."

"Yeah, right." Tom steps up to look at the bridge picture again. "He left me a piece of underwater property, and he left my mom a shredded-up letter."

"Really?" Quee moves and starts walking back down the hall in front of them. "I always heard there was no note."

"He meant for there *not* to be, but there was. My mom found it in the trash, and she put it back in the trash, and then I pulled it out again."

"You have it?" Denny asks. Now they are back in the parlor, and Quee sits on the edge of the velvet ottoman and toys with the ball fringe.

"It's in my wallet," he says and reaches into his back pocket. "Now don't put *my* wallet in a diaper." He waits for Quee to glance back at him and he laughs. She watches from across the room. She watches him spread out the crumpled paper, pieces held by yellowed tape; she hears him read: "'Dear Betty, Here at the end I beg your forgiveness. I know that you will probably never give it to me but I beg nonetheless. Here I finally tell the truth for once. Don't you see that . . .' And that's where it stops and then it says, 'wish I'd seen sooner. We have a nice boy. I wish we had had a nice life.'" Tom folds up the paper and puts it back into his wallet; he takes a deep mocking bow and then nods to first Denny and then Quee. "And that, ladies, is my legacy."

"At least there's something," Denny says. "I don't have anything from my father." She puts her arm around Tom and kisses his cheek. "He said you're a nice boy."

"Wow." He put one finger in his mouth and pulled with a loud pop. "Whoopee-gee, as we used to say in about the eighth grade, which is how old I was when I read this the first time."

"Did you show your mother?" Quee asks as she goes around filling each candy dish with M&Ms.

"Tried to. She said that she didn't want to see it. If he loved her or if he hated her, she didn't give a damn."

"How sad," Denny says. "I'd want to know, wouldn't you?"

"No, I don't think I would," Quee says and turns just in time to see the two of them kiss.

Quee stands in the darkness of her hallway and watches Denny and Tom slip up the stairs to the garage apartment, Denny's ponytail all straggly, his hand on her hip as she climbs. Quee can hear their whispers but can't make out the words, just a rising and falling like waves. She will never forget the day that Tom Lowe appeared at her door, right around at the back of this very house. He was in high school, and she gasped to see him there, expecting a confrontation of some kind. He was his father's son, physically at any rate, the deep blue eyes, the dark straight hair that had always put her in mind of an Indian brave—lean body in a leather thong skimming the forest floor without a sound. But there he was, a boy in blue jeans and Converse sneakers, a plain white T-shirt that looked like it had been bleached and pressed. She thought that maybe he had found the other part of the letter, the part with her name written. Maybe his mother had sent him, to blame her, to charge her, and she was preparing herself as she reached for the door handle. She would go outside where Lonnie wouldn't hear them.

"Yes?" She opened the door and stepped onto the porch. It was hard to look him in the eye, and she caught herself focusing on the car on the street, Cecil's old car, the dirty white Chevrolet that he had left with his wife. There was a girl sitting there where she herself had sat on so many different occasions.

"Yes?" she repeated, and now she looked him in the eye. He glanced over at the girl in the car, and then she understood. He knew nothing of her except that she was the witch doctor, the magician, the eraser, and a host of other names that filtered through the safe reign of the parents and into the ears of their children.

"I'm Tom Lowe," he said. "I think I need your help." He reached in his back pocket. "All I've got is fifty dollars right now, but I swear I'm good for the rest. I get paid Friday. I bag groceries."

"What do you want?" Quee lowered her voice, looked behind her to make sure that Lonnie hadn't come into the room.

"Please." He looked up at her, and for a split second she would have grabbed and pulled him to her. "She's a nice girl. A nice, nice girl. You've got to help me."

"Bring her in," she said, wishing so much that his father had said those very words.

"She's scared."

"Tell her it's okay. I don't bite." Quee waited while he opened the car door and took the young woman's hand. She was wearing what looked like a band uniform, short black satin shorts with a gold sash and tassel. Her face was pale, tear-streaked, and she watched Quee the whole time they approached.

"Young man, why don't you go out there in the TV room."

"No!" The girl reached for Tommy but Quee put her arm out to separate them.

"Really, honey." Quee patted her hand. "It's okay. You are okay." She nodded toward the next room where they could hear the music of *The Big Valley*. Every day Lonnie watched *The Big Valley* and *Bonanza*.

"I'll be sewing a bit, honey," she said and led Tom Lowe in there to the couch. "This is . . .?" She paused while Tom introduced himself. "Another little girl, Tom's friend, needing a prom gown pinched in a little. Gonna close this door." When she turned back, the girl was crouched there at the edge of the table, her body all curling into itself like she was trying to disappear.

"Lie down, honey." Quee went and put the kettle on. "It's real, real simple what I do. My husband doesn't even know what I do. It's called digital irritation. There's no coat hanger or shish kebab stick. Just a *digit*, one little finger; you could do it yourself, but I don't think you're able. Here, I'll get you some tea, special tea. There are all sorts of herbs that have some ways of working on the body." She stopped by her sewing machine and pressed the pedal into a frenzied whirr. Lonnie knew that she did *alterations* for the kids around town. She washed her hands with alcohol right there so that the girl could see and then put on some rubber gloves on top of that.

"How do you know all this?" the girl whispered, her voice suddenly much stronger than before.

"I was once a desperate young woman." She paused and smoothed back her hair. "Hard to believe, huh?" She went and peeked out the door, glimpsed Tommy; he could have been hers, some version of her, as he sat there straight as a stick, his eyes focused on the TV. She latched the door and then pulled down all the shades.

THE LATE AFTERNOON sun was strong enough that she didn't even need a lamp and chose not to use one. It would be easier for the girl in low light, more like a little nap, a bad dream. Quee draped a sheet around her and then felt to unsnap and unzip her shorts. There were gunshots and horse whinneys in the next room. She watched the girl stare at the ceiling, biting her lower lip, pretending that she was anywhere except here. Not once did the girl look at her but continued to stare upward as if she was praying or having to answer to somebody. "This is as natural as can be," Quee whispered. "It's as natural as what got you this way." The girl nodded. "There are no guarantees with this way. Sometimes it takes several tries. Sometimes it never works at all. A good friend of mine who is a doctor taught me, and if this doesn't help you, dear, then you come on back, and I'll get hold of him."

"What will happen?"

"Cramps. Just like normal."

"Okay." The girl sighed and closed her eyes.

"What's your name?" Quee asked.

"Do I have to tell?"

"Not at all, honey. Not at all." Now she knew who the girl was. She had seen her picture in the paper for good grades, for pep rallies. She held her left palm firmly on the abdomen while her right finger stretched and moved, the girls eyes clenched in discomfort. "Cottonroot, mistletoe, tansy." She whispered the words like a jump-rope rhyme. "These are things that can help, too, but you can't rush, can't take in too much because they can also kill you, okay?" She paused with her work and waited for the girl to look at her. "I mean it now, honey. And what's more there are folks you can go to with the same promise, and *they* will kill you. You go to a doctor or you go to somebody who knows what she's doing. Somebody like me."

"This never should have happened," the girl whispered. "It's my fault."

"It's nobody's *fault*," Quee said. "It's called life. It's called biology. Here now, get dressed, and I'm going to fix you a little tea. We can join the gentlemen." She stepped on the sewing pedal again and then opened the door. In the next room the boy was sitting forward in his chair, hands clasped while Lonnie explained what he'd read about the horses falling down in Westerns; a lot of the horses *did* get hurt, and this was concerning him greatly. Lonnie Purdy did not believe in pain of any kind, even if it was applied to bring about good.

Four days later, Tommy Lowe was at her door with more money and a quiet thank-you. It had worked. They would be okay.

"You know there's a chance," she said and pushed the money back in his hand, "that she was never pregnant at all."

"There is?"

"Oh, yes." She gently pushed his hand away, watched as he put the money back into his pocket. "Just try not to let it happen again. If Cleopatra knew about birth control, ain't no reason why smart kids in the nineteen-seventies shouldn't."

"Thanks." He backed out, easing the screen door to before turning and running back to his car. She could see his breath as he got in and she wanted to call out to him, to say, "You're Cecil's son aren't you?" but what purpose would that serve, except to get Lonnie's attention?

When the engine turned over and his car had disappeared around the corner, she went to her glass table and lifted out a little antique pillbox. She had found the scrap of paper on the very day that he died, a scrap trapped in the dampness of the garbage bin beneath his house. It was dusk and she was surprised to find that people were no longer circling the house, it was no longer closed off. She had parked at the pier and walked the distance, climbed up through the dunes, past the outdoor shower. There the smell of creosote and ocean air was like a heady elixir she could breathe, the mildewed dampness of the earth conjured every indiscretion, sandy sheets and soured sweat, the lingering yeasty residue. She wanted to go in, to see the spot, to touch his things, but she was left with what had been tossed out, garbage and old papers. They said he had gone into a frenzy, shredding papers all over the house, out the windows, into the toilet. And she had come looking. "I loved you. I *love* you. Only now do I know how much. Only now do I . . ."

Did he what? She had spent years wondering what the end of the sentence could be. Years making up stories to help it turn out as well as it could. But now she knows. Now Quee watches as just the pale glow of the nightlight shines from Denny's apartment. And, *Denny* was never supposed to have come into the world. Denny's mother had come for help, just like anyone else, and that time Quee had made a choice. She said, Let there be life. She thought it would do the girl good to have to be responsible, and if she didn't want the responsibility, then Quee would be there to take the baby, she *wanted* that baby.

No, Howard Carter had taught her just enough that was safe to do, and when all else failed, he'd come around and help her out. She'd ring his house or office and speak a secret language. She might say: "Is this Mr. Howard?" and his wife would say: "No, this is Dr. Carter's house, and who is *this?*" Within a half hour of such a call he would appear, weathered and tired-looking. She had known him since they were children. He had once tried to get her to love him, but it just didn't work. There are some people, try as you might, you will never feel anything beyond friendship.

"You know what people say about me, now don't you?" she asked him one night when he had come around. There was a scared fourteen-year-old perched up on the table, and they were over at her stove where he was having her boil up a soap mixture. "They say I'm a whore."

"And just let them keep right on thinking it," he said. "It's a hell of a lot better that they think that."

"And think what of you, Howard? That you visit the whore?"

"Right now, yes."

"I know that's why that old school principal is always flirting with me so." She went over and helped the girl lie back, smoothed a cool cloth over her dark forehead. "He thinks he's gonna get something out of it."

"Do you flirt back?" Howard asked and raised his eyebrows. He had some of the best teeth that the town of Fulton ever produced; he was a fine man ahead of his time, and how he came to marry such a stiff Quee never understood.

"Yes, I do, and every year I get a schoolbus whenever I want one." She turned to the girl. "Did you go to the beach in the first grade?" The girl nodded, looked at her as if with recognition, though she was too scared to speak or smile.

"I drove the bus," she said and squeezed the girl's hand while Howard filled a turkey baster with suds. Lonnie was upstairs asleep and had been for hours. "That was me. Quee Purdy. A woman with a cause. A woman with a mission." Howard grinned at her, said like he always said, what a fine team they made working together. By the eighties there were enough good doctors in the bigger cities, Wilmington and Raleigh and Charlotte, that there was no reason for Quee to do what she did, and she gladly handed out phone numbers to the young people who appeared at her door. *Good luck*, she might call out. *Protect yourselves.* Some said she sold drugs, and some said she sold herself, so she decided, well, she would sell something. What about wedding cakes? How about ceramic meats?

Dear Cecil,

I wish you could see your son. Your son! *and my goddaughter. You may remember her. That time we went to Boston, we stopped off in New York, and we saw them there. Her mama was still mad at me. She was having a hard time making ends meet, and there she had little Mary Denise, who was standing on a stool in the kitchen when we got there. She told me she was looking for birds and I thought then, my what an optimistic child, to look out on an old garbage chute where at best she might see some mangy pigeon and she was looking for* birds. *She hasn't changed a whole lot and I've come to truly love her. I see the two of them standing side by side and I think of me and you. I think* we gave them life. *We were the creators, the gods of the universe. So why then couldn't we save each other, Cecil? Why didn't you ever say how you really felt?*

What's really amazing is that I don't feel as bad as I might think I should. I had a whole life with Lonnie that nobody can even touch. I do have nine lives, Cecil, and I plan to milk mine for all they are worth. I mean sure I've done some things. I sure have got some secrets. Just like earlier today as I was telling Tom and Denny the story of Jones Jameson.

Well, he did come around here last year, just as I said. He had knocked up a woman out in the county and came crawling up my walk to see if I could fix his problem, like he heard I would do back in high school. Ha! I sent him on his way, though I did give him a reputable name just because I don't wish death on any woman and especially not one who already has the misfortune to have gotten tangled up with him. You know, it's getting harder and harder to find a doctor doing what put me out of my little business way back. Anyway, Jones calls me up again, just a month ago for the same reason, needed my assistance, seems the latest was quite young, a high school girl. He said he was ready to go on the radio and tell all about me and the alterations I have done for folks in the past. Somehow he had found out about the time Tommy came around here with the girl who now might as well not even be in this world. Imagine her husband and parents hearing such right about now. I thought of Tommy and how he's probably spent all these years working it all out for himself. And of course I thought of Alicia. I told Jones to meet me down at Braveman Bridge by himself to discuss it and he did and that's that. What is worrying me is wondering who is the poor little girl out there with such a bad seed taking root. I tried to get him to tell me. He just ground out a cigarette butt under his heel and tossed that sweater of his over on a bush, where I guess it stayed until some passerby decided to dress up the scarecrow. He said, "Do you think I'm stupid?" and I said, "Why no, Jones, I hear you are Phi Beta Kappa. Here, pull up a tree stump, have yourself a drink while we talk."

My new business is good, Cecil. I'm curing the smokers right and left; there are some new weight problems out there but that's no big deal—I can fix that in the future. If this world keeps swinging the way it's swinging, then I suspect I'll always have some kind of business to do. Not too much new, though I do feel my heart drifting. You see, even before I found out about your letter, I was starting to confuse you a lit-

tle with Lonnie. I'd think of something sweet you had said, and then I'd say, "No wait. That was Lonnie."And so now I'm going to write to Lonnie, or maybe I'll just talk to him in my head. And if you can know what I'm saying, Cecil, well then I have to say that I guess there are no hard feelings. You did what you had to do and I do what I have to do and now we're left to live and die with whatever consequences may come. And I will live, Cecil. I will live until I die as that old song goes.

With love,
Queen Mary Purdy

The letter tumbles from the crate with all the others when the new guy sits down in the morning darkness with a cup of black coffee and begins his shift. It gives him the creeps, the quiet, the ticking of the big Seth Thomas clock out front, the wanted flyers—felons who escaped years ago. The man who retired told him that it would get easier, that he would come to appreciate this quiet time, this feeling of living and existing without regard to the rest of the town. The man had shown him a special drawer . . . letters without stamps, letters to Sandy Claws and God and whoever else might be scratched in illegibly. The letter is sorted with the others in rapid speed, no special treatment, no hesitation about what goes where. After all, he wants to finish his shift and get home where his wife and daughters will be coming in from church. He will find them all stripped down to nylon slips, patent leather shoes left by the door. The house will smell of chicken and potatoes, and he won't have to fear Monday, having already worked Sunday.

And in this same hour just minutes away, Wallace Johnson rises and dresses. He tiptoes quietly from the bedroom, his wife still sleeping. He fills his metal thermos with coffee and sets out for his drive to the beach, quiet miles through the Green Swamp, past Lamb's Folly. The blues are running, and he'll spend the day sitting there in the sand, taking in the salt, the breeze, the whole ocean, and if there is a God in heaven who is merciful and just, he will spend the next twenty years doing just this, casting and reeling, casting and reeling, casting and reeling with the very movement of the earth.